A Line Made by Walking

Sara Baume was born in Lancashire and grew up in County Cork, Ireland. She studied fine art and creative writing, and her fiction and criticism have been published in anthologies, newspapers and journals such as the Irish Times, the Guardian, the Stinging Fly and Granta magazine. She has won the Davy Byrnes Short Story Award, the Hennessy New Irish Writing Award, the Rooney Prize for Irish Literature, an Irish Book Award for Best Newcomer and the Kate O'Brien Award. Her debut novel, Spill Simmer Falter Wither, was shortlisted for the Costa First Novel Award and longlisted for the Guardian First Book Award, the Warwick Prize for Writing and the Desmond Elliott Prize, and won the Geoffrey Faber Memorial Prize. A Line Made by Walking is her second novel and was shortlisted for the Goldsmiths Prize.

She lives in West Cork.

Praise for A Line Made by Walking

'A novel of uniqueness, wonder, recognition, poignancy, truth-speaking, quiet power, strange beauty and luminous bedazzlement. Once again, I've been Baumed.'

Joseph O'Connor

'Baume is a writer of outstanding grace and style. She writes beyond the time we live in.'

Colum McCann

'A novel which picks apart strands of loneliness, art, misery and fa￼ ￼and what s￼

LANC

D0993847

￼orn

'Utterly compelling ... among the best accounts of grief, loneliness and depression that I have ever read. Every word of it rings true, the truth of hard-won knowledge wrested from the abyss. Shot through with a wild, yearning melancholy, it is nevertheless mordantly witty.'

Lucy Caldwell

'A fascinating portrait of an artist's breakdown in rural Ireland ... And along the way there are crucial questions raised about how we perceive reality ... [and] a reminder of the beauty that can be found when you allow yourself to look slowly and sadly at the world.'

Guardian

'Baume's writing is near faultless: instinctively balanced, precise and often surprising ... An insightful exploration of the psychological processes and potential emotional toll of a life whose goal is to turn experience into art ... The acuity of Baume's observations and the exacting lyricism of her writing are just as strong as in her debut; it will be fascinating to see what she tackles next.'

Melissa Harrison, *Financial Times*

'An immensely sensitive balancing act of a book, one that declines to resolve its tensions ... Carefully calibrated ... An original and affecting novel.'

Stephanie Cross, *Observer*

'A masterclass in the power of prose that will resonate with anyone who's ever felt lost.'

i *paper*

'Baume is a master at breathing the past into domestic spaces, of showing the presence of goneness ... It is evidence of Baume's true adeptness as a writer that there is no sense of merely posited meaning in her portrayal of this young woman's predicament, the nature of depression and the key to its lifting ... The imaginative richness and limberness of Baume's descriptions, their power to immerse the reader in Frankie's senses, emotions, and places on earth, is where this novel truly excels.'

Katherine A. Powers, *Irish Times*

'Baume treads a graceful line between mesmerising and infuriating. Her descriptions and characterisations are exacting ... This is a startlingly fresh work from a talented new voice.'

Violet Hudson, *Sunday Telegraph*

'Baume has once again proven that even the smallest lives can unveil the biggest truths.'

Ruth Gilligan, *Irish Independent*

'Baume's conceit is imaginative and well organised, her writing pellucid and open.'

Sally Bayley, *The Times*

'A profound, ruminative study of a young woman who takes photographs of dead animals ... *A Line Made by Walking* is self-interrogating autofiction plus art criticism in a distinctly Irish mode: Sara Baume has as much in common with, say, Maggie Nelson as she does with Edna O'Brien ... Brilliantly understated reflections on art and life.'

Ian Sansom, *Times Literary Supplement*

'It is clear from Baume's writing how her vivid apprehension of the natural world connects to her appreciation of artworks and her mapping of the psyche, a sensibility that puts her in company with writers such as Melissa Harrison, Helen Macdonald and Olivia Laing . . . [*A Line Made by Walking* is] a piece of raw invention.'

Alex Clark, *Guardian*

'[Baume's] prose begins to crackle with the textures and scents of rural Ireland . . . This is difficult material for fiction . . . [Baume] handles it skilfully . . . Elegant.'

Sunday Times

'The second novel by the award winning author of *Spill Simmer Falter Wither* is as tender and luminous as her debut.'

Mail on Sunday

'An extraordinarily compelling novel . . . What makes it so gripping is that the reader is trapped in Frankie's mind as much as she is . . . Almost every page has a sentence or an observation that made me wish I had a commonplace book to transcribe Frankie's – or Baume's – precisely opaque and fleeting thoughts.'

Stuart Kelly, *Spectator*

'Baume's mixing of the visual arts and fiction is as satisfying as Ali Smith's . . . Baume's evocation of depression is so precise and so powerful that, roughly two-thirds of the way through the book, Frankie's illness began to feel as if it were my own . . . [*A Line Made by Walking*] is, beautifully, about finding accommodation with the ordinary . . . [Sara Baume] deserves to feel wholly satisfied with this raw-nerved and wonderful novel.'

Sarah Ditum, *New Statesman*

'Baume achieves the feat of making a book about depression, alienation and other cheerful subjects deeply absorbing and, ultimately, uplifting. She does so through the elegant lucidity of her prose, the sharp truth of her insights and the wry humour that arises from her character's associative mind.'

Melanie White, *Literary Review*

'Baume's beautifully drawn portrait of the inside of Frankie's head will ring uncomfortably true. Baume's writing is lyrical and immensely readable ... Baume's portrait of a conflicted young woman is heart-wrenchingly real on every page, as are Frankie's observations on the futility of everyday existence ... I felt I knew Frankie. And with that, I was drawn into her world.'

Scotland on Sunday

'A beautiful meditation on universal frailty ... Baume is an astoundingly talented writer and her way with words is glorious ... Another thrillingly original novel.'

Stylist

'[Baume's] precise observations of nature and fresh, original images are compelling, full of lilting musicality and searing sadness. Open any page and you will be dazzled by the stunning language and insight.'

Justine Carbery, *Irish Independent on Sunday*

'A celebration of the extraordinary in the everyday, and Baume's prose elevates the ordinary and finds inspiration in the strange.'

Irish Times

A Line Made by Walking

Walking

SARA BAUME

WINDMILL BOOKS

1 3 5 7 9 10 8 6 4 2

Windmill Books
20 Vauxhall Bridge Road
London SW1V 2SA

Windmill Books is part of the Penguin Random House group of companies whose
addresses can be found at global.penguinrandomhouse.com.

Penguin
Random House
UK

First published by William Heinemann in 2017
First published in paperback by Windmill Books in 2018

www.penguin.co.uk

A CIP catalogue record for this book is available from the British Library.

ISBN 9780099592754

Typeset in 12.69/14.7 pt Perpetua Std by Jouve (UK), Milton Keynes
Printed and bound in Great Britain by Clays Ltd, St Ives Plc

For M, Em & Mum

The worst that being an artist could do to you would be that it would make you slightly unhappy constantly.

— J. D. Salinger, from *De Daumier-Smith's Blue Period*

1

ROBIN

Today, in the newspaper, a photograph of tribesmen in the Amazon rainforest. The picture taken from a low-flying aircraft. The men naked but for painted faces, lobbing spears into the air as high as they can lob them, trying to attack the largest and most horrifying sky-beast they've ever encountered, ever imagined. The caption says they are believed to be from the last 'uncontacted' tribe.

What a thing, I think, that there are still. People. Out there. And almost immediately, I forget.

A smudged-sky morning, mid-spring. And to mark it, a new dead thing, a robin.

Somehow, they always find me. Crouching in the cavern-ous ditches and hurling themselves under the wheels of my Fiesta. Toppling from the sky to land at my feet. And because my small world is coming apart in increments, it seems fitting that the creatures should be dying too. They are being killed with me; they are being killed for me.

I decide I will take a photograph of this robin. The first in a series, perhaps.

A series about how everything is being slowly killed.

Only it isn't. The white strata are bunching into clouds. The bunches are competing with each other to imitate animals. A sheep, a platypus, a sheep, a tortoise. A sheep, a sheep, a sheep. The leaves are breaking out, obscuring the white strata, the sky animals, the irregular spaces of cerulean between everything. The fields of the daffodil farm on the other side of the valley are speckling yellow and yellower as I watch. Why do I feel as if I'm being killed when it's the season of renewal? Cars don't crash when the days are long. Rapists don't prey in the sunshine and old folk don't catch pneumonia and expire in their rocking chairs. Houses don't burn down in spring.

But these things aren't true; Walt Disney lied to me. The weather doesn't match my mood; the script never supplies itself, nor is the score composed to instruct my feelings, and there isn't an audience. Most days I make it to dark without anybody seeing me at all. Or at least, anybody human.

I've been here in my grandmother's bungalow a full three weeks now. All on my own. Except for the creatures.

My grandmother died during a gloomy October, as one ought, three Octobers ago.

On the night she died the tail of a hurricane made landfall. It was called Antonio and had travelled all the way from Bermuda. It felled a tree which dragged down a wire and put out the lights across half the parish. Then the tree lay wretched on the ground, strangled by electric cable and blocking the road which led up the hill to her bungalow. My mother and aunts were trapped inside, but I wasn't there and Mum didn't phone until a couple of hours later. I was at work in a contemporary art gallery in Dublin. Painting over the previous day's scuff marks as I did every morning. Transforming the tarnished white into brilliant again.

Even though I had been expecting the call, I didn't pick up immediately.

Even though I had been expecting my grandmother to die, I couldn't believe it might happen in the morning.

For several rings my polyphonic 'Radetzky March' echoed irreverently around the exhibition space. When at last I answered, my mother confessed she hadn't called me straight away. And so my grandmother died in the night after all, as one should.

No change in the light. A temporary sleep becomes permanent.

Antonio passed on and men from the County Council came in their dump truck to clear the road. By the time my Fiesta climbed her hill there were only broken bits of tree left scattered and a great wiggly hole in the earth where it had stood. I stole a branch from amongst the mess; I stole a branch because I loved that tree; I loved that tree because it had acknowledged the ending of my grandmother's radiant yet under-celebrated life by momentously uprooting itself.

'When exactly did it fall?' I asked my mother. 'When she died or while she was dying, or after?'

'I don't know,' she said.

'But didn't you hear?'

The sound of the only tree I've ever heard falling began with a thunderous crack, the snapping of a monolith. The fall itself was unspectacular in comparison; it sounded like a thousand softer cracks in tuneless concord. There was no rustle and brush of leaves because it was winter and there

4

were no leaves, because trees know in their heartwood that if they don't surrender their foliage in autumn, high winds will sail them to the ground. They know they must expose their timber bones to increase their chance of remaining upstanding through to another spring.

The only tree I ever heard falling I also saw falling. It was in the Phoenix Park beyond the place where elephants and tigers and oryxes are enclosed, before the place where deer rove, and I was roving too. It was an ash and it had dieback. It was felled not by high wind but by men in helmets and luminescent overalls.

'No,' my mother said, 'I didn't hear a thing.' And when I asked my aunts the same question, they also said no.

Works about Falling, I test myself: Bas Jan Ader, 1970. The artist rolls off the roof of his house and lands in the shrubbery, a filmed performance. His house is so American: clapboard, with a veranda. It doesn't look like the sort of place a Dutch conceptual artist would live, but perhaps this is the point he was trying to make by climbing onto his roof to fall. I am not sure at what instant the film ends. The way I remember it: the screen blacks out at the moment of impact. The way I remember it: Jan Ader chose not to show himself getting up again.

Why must I test myself? Because no one else will, not any more. Now that I am no longer a student of any kind, I must take responsibility for the furniture inside my head. I must slide new drawers into chests and attach new rollers to armchairs. I must maintain the old highboys and side-boards and whatnots. Polish, patch, dust, buff. And, from scratch, I must build new frames and appendages; I must fill the drawers and roll along.

When I was five, I had the flu. Sitting up in bed, watching my bedroom wall. I must have had a soaring temperature which was causing me to hallucinate, but I didn't know this at the time. I believed that what I could see was as true as the wall itself. What I could see was the whole of the world rolled flat. Each of the continents, every island. And they were swelling, stuffing up the sea, and I was screaming, because I believed I would be squeezed away, that there would be no space left for me to perch on the grossly over-extended earth. Back there and then, this made certain, chilling sense, so I yelled until my mother came, and when she came, I couldn't explain why I was yelling. For twenty years I couldn't decipher what it was that had frightened me; it's only now I understand.

I understand how it can be that I am being killed when it is spring. I am being killed very slowly; now is only the outset. My small world is coming apart because it is swelling and there's no place for me any longer, and I still want to cry out but there's no point because I am a grown individual, responsible for myself.

My mother will not come.

Anyway, what's the point in perching on an earth without sea?

Once I saw a jackdaw flying amongst a flock of gulls. I was on the top deck of a bus, level with the flock. I witnessed the member of the family *Corvidae* who wanted to be – who maybe even trusted that he was – a seabird. I thought: I am that jackdaw. At home with the sea even though the sea is not my home, and never has been.

Works about Sea, I test myself: Bernard Moitessier, 1969. In promising position to win the first ever single-handed round-the-world yacht race, he chose to abandon the competition, veering off course for the finishing line, continuing on around the world again, going home to the sea.

But he was a sailor, and not a conceptual artist. I always forget about that.

DO NOT BE AFRAID, the angel Gabriel told the frightened people.

At midnight mass on Christmas Eve last year, the priest told us that DO NOT BE AFRAID is the phrase which appears most frequently in the scriptures. 'It appears three hundred and sixty-five times,' he said, 'once for every day of the year.' He was a man in his late sixties or early seventies and I cannot think of a single word to describe his manner and appearance other than 'priestly'. He was so priestly it was hard to think of him as a person made from hair and limb and skin. All I could picture beneath his cassock was another slightly smaller cassock and another, and another. It was easier to believe the priestly priest was a matryoshka doll of cassocks rather than a man. I pictured him trawling through his bible, carefully shaping this vaguely radical message, appointing an occasion for its delivery. Christmas Eve is his busiest mass of the year, his sell-out gig. At quarter past midnight, in a pool of candlelight, the priestly priest delicately suggested that for too long the Catholic Church has instilled fear – that now it needs to spread a message which is old but was there all along: DO NOT BE AFRAID.

How laudable, I thought. But then, at the end of the service, he sent an altar boy down into the congregation carrying a wicker dish, collecting money from pew to pew, and I was so angry about this intrusion that his laudable message, his small concession, didn't matter any more.

But mass hadn't changed; I had. There was always a wicker dish. I even used to be the server who carried it down. And on all the Sundays I went to church as a child, the collection of money was as meaningless as everything else that occurred between the hardwood pews and fibreglass saints.

Objects don't seem incongruous if they've been there forever; doings don't seem ridiculous if they've always been done that way.

Why is it only now that I can see how many ordinary things are actually grotesque?

This robin is the first of the dead creatures I'll record, but there were others before it; if there hadn't been I'd never have thought to begin. Beaked and scaled and furred. Struck and squashed and slaughtered. Shape-shifting into plastic bags, sugar beet, knolls of caked mud. Blending into the tinctures and textures of the countryside. The tree which falls without any human hearing still falls, as the creatures who die without being found by a human still die. But it's too late for them now. It begins today, with this robin.

There used to be a dainty woodland at the far end of my parents' garden. No more than a copse of straggled pines, their topmost branches so densely laden by rookeries that the red bricks of the garden path vanished from sight beneath splattered shit during nesting season. There was also a skinny hawthorn and an alder, but no tree was sturdy enough to hold a structure, and so my father built a Walden-esque hut on the ground between trunks instead. The hut had tin walls, a tin roof and timber pallets on the floor. It was too cold in winter and too dark in summer, then one day an enormous spider dropped from the door lintel into my sister's hair. She screamed and screamed and refused to play in Walden again after that.

But I'd still go and sit there alone, to sulk. In the hut-which-should-have-been-a-treehouse, I listened to the sound of twigs falling from the rookery and striking my tin roof. A great rippled drum being played by tens of different drumsticks. Sometimes I'd hear a duller sort of strike and find an eggshell and baby bird with a busted neck. Eyes the size of its feet, as yet unopened, never to open. I'd bury the baby and steal its broken shell for the classroom nature table.

Almost every time I sulked alone in the hut, a robin came to me. It would hop between the spindly trees and sing like a battered xylophone. It would speak to me in its language and I would speak back in mine. I'd tell it the unedited version of what I told the priest in confession, profess my pathetic sins. As a child, I used to believe that robin was my guardian angel. I didn't like the idea of yellow-haired girls in mini wedding dresses with wings, but I wanted there to be some inhuman thing which was looking out for me, and it made sense that my guardian might be a bird.

Most of the time, it was too high up, too far behind, too obscured by surroundings to distinguish, but in the boughs of our dainty woodland, my guardian would always reveal itself.

Today's robin has been thumped by a speeding windscreen, launched into artificial flight, crash-landed. I'm only a hundred yards from my grandmother's gateposts; this is why I decide to go back and fetch my camera.

I drop to my knees in the undergrowth. Old rain seeps through the shins of my trousers, smears across the screen. I point my lens at its motionless plumage. Click.

My mother says that robins are resolutely territorial; no more than one is likely to occupy an average-sized garden. If you want to summon a robin, my mother says, you should dig, and one will soon arrive to inspect your freshly turned earth for worms. Back in my grandmother's garden, I take a trowel from the greenhouse and hunker down in the strawberry patch. I dig and dig, but no robin comes. I pick the earthworms out myself and lay them on the surface.

'Here,' I say aloud. But still, no robin.

So now I know for sure that the dead one was my guardian. I place my trowel down.

You're on your own now, I am thinking.

Works about Flight, I test myself: Yves Klein, 1960. A black-and-white photograph which shows the artist lying in the air several feet above a Parisian street. Deserted save for the flying man and a bicyclist in the distance. At the time, people couldn't figure out how Klein had made the image without being seriously injured. Now, in this era when any illusion is possible, tedious even, nobody cares about the photograph any more, which was, of course, a photo-montage, and the artist was, in fact, hurt, despite being trained in judo and landing on a tightly drawn sheet. *Leap into the Void* it was called, and so maybe it wasn't a work about flying after all, but a work about falling. About how flying and falling are almost exactly the same.

As a toddler on a toddler leash, I used to grasp onto my mother's skirt, a fistful of pleated corduroy in either paw and holler: MUMMY I LOVE YOU AND I'LL NEVER LEAVE YOU, and she would laugh kindly in the face of my ferocious devotion and reply: 'Of course you will, once you are old enough. That's just the proper order of things.' Now that my sister and I are both older than old enough and gone, we joke about how we had such a quintessential child-hood that nothing since has ever quite lived up to it. We agree we'd both surrender everything we have now in an instant if it meant we could return to being kids.

It's a joke. Just a joke.

I am twenty-five, still young, I know. And yet, I am already so improper, so disordered.

There is a sentence I chant, compulsorily, inside my head. *I want to go home*, it goes, and has been going, at intervals, since as far back as I am capable of remembering. As a child,

I chanted it mostly during bad days at school, but also during trips and holidays and sleepovers at friends' houses: places I went in order to enjoy myself; places where I ought to have been content. Later on, I chanted it during college lectures, job interviews, and in every room I've rented since I was nineteen years old.

For a week before I came here, I stayed beneath my parents' roof, and even then, I continued to chant it. *I want to go home, I want to go home, I want to go home*, even though I was there. But that house doesn't feel like the place I grew up any more. Last year my mother replaced all the curtains, tore the old wallpaper away and painted every stripped surface a different shade of white. The dainty woodland is also gone. After my sister and I left for college, my father started buying clapped-out vintage cars. He razed the garden and erected a compound of haphazard sheds in which to shelter his steel children. He ploughed away the flower beds, chopped down the pines, sawed up the swing-set for scrap, sealed the rootlets and bulbs beneath concrete foundations. Whenever I visit, there is always some new structure flattening what used to be a patch of pleasant green.

Hunkering in the strawberry patch, I poke my worms back into the earth where they belong. I close my holes, return my grandmother's trowel to the greenhouse.

I find my grandmother in the greenhouse. The shape of her kneecaps in the old foam board, the mud-print of her right palm around the handle of the rusted secateurs. The compost in the flowerpots has turned hard and sprouted green crud. No one has emptied them since they were filled by her and so I wonder what my grandmother planted, three years ago, and why it never grew.

I knock the mud from my boots against the doorstep, lever them off with the mahogany shoehorn. I never used a shoehorn before I came here; I never needed one. But nowadays I deliberately leave my boots half-laced so I have no choice but to ram the tiny paddle down to shovel up my heel. It's a way of nodding to her customs, of recreating the rituals of her day. I find my grandmother in the shoehorn, and again, as I wash my hands, I find her in the kitchen windowsill curios. In a row above the draining board, there's a weathered wood St Joseph, a plastic flamenco dancer, a three-legged camel, a panda-bear-shaped pencil sharpener, an oblong pebble painted with the features of a mouse and each one of these silently onlooking objects are immeasurably precious to me, because my grandmother can be found in them.

When the house finally went on the market, Annika the auctioneer told my mother and her sisters that it would stand a better chance of selling if it wasn't so cluttered with the belongings of the former inhabitant. 'It ought to look as much as possible like a show house,' Annika said. The dead woman's worn furniture and weird trinkets will only freak out potentially interested parties, she didn't say, though this is what she meant. Because people don't want homes; they want show houses – only by means of a show house can they be distracted from the generalised going-nowhereness of their perfectly pointless lives.

Piece by piece, my mother and her sisters catalogued the bungalow's contents according to value, necessity and sentiment. Six months after my grandmother died, Mum emailed me an inventory of the objects that still remained. *Let me know if there's anything you want*, it read, and I got so angry about that message. Because I wanted everything, from the chaise longue to the velvet curtains, but my life wasn't large enough. At the time, I didn't have a car or a bedsit. I was renting a box-room in a shared house in the city with barely enough space for the things I already owned. By the time I arrived to stay, the bungalow was a neatly looted version of its former self. All that was left of the inventory were the things that everybody else in the family had unanimously rejected.

My aunts didn't want the windowsill curios; nor did my mother. She dug a shallow hole beneath the garden hedge and buried them. In spite of my substantial capacity for strangeness, this still strikes me as bizarre. My mother couldn't explain it. 'I just didn't want to throw them away,' she said, and yet, instead of keeping St Joseph and his flamenco wife and their personal menagerie, she treated them as if they were the dead creatures my sister and I used to come upon when playing in the garden. As children, we buried ladybirds and bees and beetles. The shrews our cats laid out on the doormat, the birds that plunged from their nests or dashed themselves against the windowpanes. Only the wasps which drowned in our jam traps were deprived of a dignified disposal.

I asked my mother what part of the hedge she'd buried the curios under, then I dug them up and rinsed the mud off and stood them one by one back along the sill above the draining board, and they leaked tiny brown pools which have since dried into tiny brown rings of sediment.

I cannot stand the thought of prospectively interested parties coming here and picturing a new life for themselves. Here is where my grandmother's life ended, and mine is ending still. I will not allow Annika the auctioneer to exorcise us.

But it's been almost a year now, and she hasn't scheduled a single viewing since the FOR SALE sign was nailed to its post and planted in the rose bed beside the cattle grid.

'It's because of the turbine,' my mother said: 'people don't like the idea of living so close to one.'

This bungalow sits on the brow of a yawning valley. To the rear there stands a solitary wind turbine. Sleek, white, monumental. It has always seemed to me more like a thing that had been shot down from space than raised up from the earth.

'I've heard about that,' I said, 'Wind Turbine Syndrome. People think the noise and shadow-flicker keep them up at night, make them sick. But they're only suffering from it because they believe they are.' And then my mother laughed. 'Sure how many days of the year do we have enough sun to make shadows anyway?'

My grandmother got on just fine with her two-hundred-foot neighbour; she admired its immensity.

*

With or without the turbine, it's no surprise the bungalow is unappealing to house hunters. The view of mountains comes and goes depending on the weather, the view of valley is filled with melancholy cows. The garden is terrifically overgrown, and everything indoors has fallen into disrepair. The avocado-coloured bathroom has a soggy carpet where lino ought to be. The water comes out of the taps in a series of tiny explosions. Each electric hob takes a full ten minutes to heat up and glows disconcertingly orange as soon as it has. One in three plug sockets are defunct and all the TV channels are tinged green no matter how many times I tweak the aerial. 'The whole house reeks of dog,' my father says, and though I cannot smell it, I suspect it smells like dog to people who do not like dogs.

So little happens, here in the bungalow on turbine hill, that however little the thing that happens, it throws me off kilter. Even though it's evening now and I'm usually at my best in the evenings, because of the robin I know it will be hard to realign what remains of the day. I go to the sun room where my laptop is. I press the power button and wait for the screen to ignite. My laptop has spongy plastic stars stuck to the lid. As it boots up, it makes a sound like the keyboard is chewing cotton wool.

Works about Wind, I test myself: Erik Wesselo, *Düffels Möll*, 1997. The artist is strapped to the blade of a traditional windmill and spun for several minutes, a performance. I look it up on YouTube. The camera follows Wesselo's rise and drop and rise and drop and rise and drop. Yet again, I think, flight and fall.

*

The sun room is at the rear of the bungalow, facing south. I spend most of my time in between its slimy panes, and I find more of my grandmother here in the sun room where she lived than in the bedroom where she died. I find her in the mould-speckled sofa, the Formica tabletop, the red geranium, the barometer, the owl-shaped paperweight, the upholstered chair. Some people call these rooms 'conservatories', but this one isn't a conservatory, it's a sun room, definitely.

I keep the branch pressed into the soil of the red geranium's pot. The branch broken from the unidentified tree which uprooted itself on the day she died. It looms over my keyboard, casts its shadow across my screen. What sort of tree was it? Because the branch will never come into leaf again, I cannot tell.

I plug my camera into my laptop and download the photos I took today. My robin looks angry, much angrier in reproduction than it appeared in life. Perhaps the Native Americans are right; perhaps the camera stole its spirit. I open my robin in Photoshop. I select Brightness/Contrast. I restore the vibrancy lost along with its spirit.

I check my emails: no emails. I knock a knuckle against the barometer beside me on the table. The needle doesn't move. I shut my laptop down and stand up. My phone doesn't ring and the doorbell doesn't either and I begin to wonder whether I am still alive.

I go to the back step and see the mud I knocked off my boots a little while ago. It's wet and soft and fresh, and so I know that I must exist after all — that I must still be here.

Works about Being, I test myself: On Kawara, beginning 1966. A series of paintings showing nothing but the date upon which they were made. He also sent missives to acquaintances and friends which simply read: I AM STILL ALIVE, followed by his signature.

For two months after my grandmother died, her morbidly obese and chronically arthritic golden retriever continued to live in the bungalow alone; this is the reason for the dog smell. He was called Joe, and my grandmother had owned him since he was a puppy. She was all he knew and he worshipped her and refused to be removed from the house in which they'd lived together for twelve years. During the wake, he lay in the corridor outside her bedroom, and once it was over and the door opened again, he lay on the floor in the exact spot where he'd last seen my grandmother.

My mother wanted, and tried, to bring Joe home with her. She managed to drag him as far as the driveway but then he cowered and whimpered and wouldn't climb into the car. He was too fat and arthritic to lift; my mother conceded defeat. Joe remained in the bungalow alone and the old man who lives halfway down the hill called in every day to check on him. Joe would take his medication and eat his meals and amble around the garden to cock and squat, then he'd return to his spot on the floor in her bedroom.

One day, he didn't get up when the old man came. His

heart had stopped. A soft, pink clock nobody remembered to wind. I go to my grandmother's bedroom and lie down in the place where her hospice bed used to be, on the patch where the dog died. I lay my cheek against the floor. I smell the carpet.

I remember: this is how it started.

It started with the smelling of carpet.

The carpet it started with covered the floor of my bedsit in the city, the place where I lived before I stayed in my parents' house for a week, before I came here. For my first several months in that bedsit, I barely noticed the floor. Then one evening, I lay down on it, and in the weeks that followed, barely an evening went by that I didn't resort to the same position at some stage or another. I became intimately acquainted with that faded pile, the scent of mouldy timber rising up from the boards, the particular shade of amber it had faded to, the colour of watery cider. I'd dig my fingernails down and scratch the lining, as if it was a short-coated pet.

My mother says that a male dust-mite lives for an average of ten days. If he is exceptionally robust, he could make it as far as nineteen. But this has as much to do with luck as with strength. The male mite might fall victim to a vacuum cleaner or an allergen-blocking bedcover and all his hard won good health will come to naught. There are people who think that they can see dust-mites or that they've been bitten by a dust-mite, my mother says, but these things aren't true. Dust-mites aren't able to eat skin scales unless they're already dead, dropped, partially broken down by fungi.

Because they are extremely small and transparent, dust-mites aren't visible to the human eye.

They are everywhere, yet they are nothing.

The last full day that I lived in my city bedsit, I went out only once, to return a DVD to the rental store. Nothing of significance happened while I was out. It wasn't raining and I didn't see anyone I knew or find that I'd forgotten to clip the disc back in its box. It was for no reason at all that as soon as I returned to the bedsit, my legs buckled and I lowered my cheek to its resting position against the carpet.

I don't know how long I'd been lying there when my mobile phone began to quake against the page of a sketch-book I'd left open on the table, a blank page. It started chirping out its cheerful 'Radetzky March' and I forced my face up until I could see the screen. JESS it said, and so I lay back down again. Jess was just a friend and she would only have been calling to see if I was okay, and seeing as I wasn't, I decided not to answer. I pressed my right ear into the carpet as hard as I could and suctioned the palm of my left hand around the up-facing one.

My eardrums sounded like the inside of a conch shell. Like what my mother told me, as a child, was supposed to be the sea, but was actually the wind.

Through the floorboards, I could hear the man who lived directly below me moving purposefully around his bedsit. I heard a cupboard door bang, a saucepan clank against a hob, the screech of curtain hooks against rail. I heard the soles of his boots stepping from the kitchen-zone lino, tap tap

tap. To the carpet, scuff scuff scuff. And back again. I wondered if his carpet was redder than mine; I wondered what it smelled like. Then I heard a saucepan tinkling and I knew that the man who lived directly below me was having hailstones for dinner again.

He was Russian, though I can't remember whether this is something the landlady told me when I moved in or something I decided for myself and remember as if it were a fact. He looked like a tin soldier: black leather boots and a jacket with symmetrical buttons and gold-trimmed epaulettes. I thought he was marvellous, far too marvellous to speak to, and because he had never spoken to me either, his mystique endured, uncontaminated by hallway chit-chat. On the last full day I spent in the bedsit, I listened to him taking cutlery from a drawer and clearing his throat in a Russian sort of way and I longed, how I longed, to have such purpose.

At six o'clock on the last full day, through my suction-cupped hand, I heard church bells and knew what time it was against my will. I heard somebody else from the building arrive home and climb the first flight of stairs to my door, and then pass my door and continue to climb. My bedsit was sandwiched between the ground and top floors. Because its sole, small window faced backwards into the communal yard, even after several months I wasn't able to recognise most of my housemates on the street. They came and went invisible to me. In the yard, there was no grass, just a couple of bicycles, a gargantuan wheelie bin and the low roof of the shed where the washing machine slumbered.

There wasn't a dryer and there wasn't a washing line and oftentimes I'd see clothes slung over my neighbour's curtain rails, trouser legs dangling, like a footless person hanged.

I never kept a bicycle there. The only time I ever cycled in the city was at the very beginning of my first year in college. One morning my front tyre bounced off the side of the footpath at too great a speed. My wheels skidded out in front of a taxi and I fell face first against the concrete, splitting my chin and fracturing my jawbone. The taxi driver drove me to hospital. He didn't charge a fare but he didn't wait around either and I had to get the bus back to my bicycle. I remember the other passengers staring at my swollen face and fresh stitches, the splashes of blood down the front of my coat. An old woman asked me if I was okay and when I replied my voice sounded wrong – weak and crumpled – as if my distended cheek had squeezed it away to practically nothing.

By the time I got back to the place where I'd left my bicycle, it was gone. Of course it was gone.

When I was a child, I used to believe that everyone experienced childhood in the countryside and simply chose or didn't choose to abandon their rural beginnings later on; that there was nobody under eighteen in the city at all.

I wasn't very good at living in Dublin. Every day I walked an unnecessarily circuitous route from my bedsit into the gallery simply because this was the way I walked the first day. I knew there were any number of shortcuts, but I refused to find them.

My sandwiched bedsit with its backward-facing window and faded carpet seems now like a good place – a fitting place – to have lost my mind. The walls were smudged in places by the greasy fingerprints of people who lived there before me. A spooky draught intermittently rattled the air duct, spindly spiders nested in the folds of the curtain and made a scuffling sound in the dead of night. There were three switches, one for the immersion, one for the cooker, one for the heater, and every time I set out anywhere, I used to recite: *watercookerheater watercookerheater watercookerheater* because I was so afraid I might have neglected to turn one off and the whole building would burn down in the time it took me to walk into the city centre and home again. Too often I turned around and went back. I added a half hour to my circuitous, unnecessary journey just to check a switch I knew was off, but couldn't trust myself.

And I never once used the communal washing machine. I don't know how to work a washing machine and I was too shy, when I first arrived, to ask anyone, and almost a year later I was too shy to admit that I'd never used it and still needed to ask. Instead I washed everything in my kitchen sink. Even the bedsheets, even the towels.

It started slowly, with the switches and the rattle and the spiders.

I spent most of the last full day with my cheek against the carpet. Just after six o'clock, I made a disconsolate attempt at snapping myself out of it. I heaved my head up, sat with my spine against the side of the bed and started whispering, earnestly, angrily:

23

There are women and children in a central African country nobody's ever heard of and they are being raped and slaughtered by their countrymen, I whispered, *YOU have NOTHING to cry about. There are people behind these closed doors and net curtains and they're old or blind or cancer-bald, they've been brain damaged by a car accident or tenderised by one of those horrible degenerative muscle-wasting illnesses. They're confined to wheelchairs or reduced to sippy cups or they have to re-bandage their entire bodies every other day just to stop their skin from falling off,* I whispered, *YOU have NOTHING to cry about. And then there are the people who love the people who are old or blind or cancer-bald or brain damaged, the people who look after them, who push their wheel-chairs and replenish their sippy cups, who bear the brunt of their perfectly justifiable rage* – I had raised my voice a little by then, from a whisper to a mutter – *YOU have NOTHING to cry about. You have NOTHING.*

Then I thought about Kylie.

Kylie was the only kid in my primary school who could not walk. Her arms and hands and fingers were twisted up. Her legs were manipulated into the most untwisted position possible and strapped to the special supports of her wheel-chair. Her head was permanently crooked to one shoulder; her mouth hung open. She could not speak or write or participate in PE but Kylie still came to school every day. She still understood everything in her books and on the blackboard. And then, one rainy playtime, when the super-vising teacher had stepped out of the classroom to attend to something, a couple of the bigger boys started to mess about. Gallivanting between desks, over chairs, knocking Kylie's wheelchair sideways onto the ground.

She fell against the carpet and then she cried, and because she could not move her face or speak like the other children, her crying was a terrible sight, a terrible sound. Distressed, despondent. The bigger boys righted her wheelchair immediately, lifted Kylie back up again. She was uninjured, but still she continued to keen and wail and bay until the teacher came back, until her mother was summoned to fetch her. She couldn't be consoled. It became as if Kylie was no longer crying over the fall, but over the cumulative indignity of every compromised schoolday gone by and yet to come, by the week after week after week of unspeakable unfairness which would not stop, not ever.

For a while, those thoughts succeeded in making me grateful for my youth, my sight, my mind, my family, my mobility. But gratitude was soon pressed down by the fear that I might contract a disease, or lose someone, or be involved in a horrible accident and then that fear was pressed down in turn by disgust at myself for being so selfish, so petty, so inadvertently ungrateful.

I am not supposed to be one of those people who cry easily; I was not one of those little kids who snuffled and gasped and blubbed at nothing. I was grubby and scab-kneed with a bedroom full of caged animals, and in college I learned to use all the big electric drills and wood-saws in the sculpture department and to weld. I've never been a crier and I've always prided myself on this.

Until then. Until there. Lying on the amber carpet.

What was it about the sound of a DVD case striking the bottom of a DVD deposit box on a drizzly day in spring that made me feel so abruptly and inexplicably bad?

Encounters at the End of the World. This was the DVD inside the case. I watched it the night before the last day I lay down on my bedsit carpet; I watched it alone and in the dark. *Encounters at the End of the World* is a Werner Herzog documentary about the South Pole. The setting is vast and white and barren. The cast are people who feel compelled to travel to the extreme edge of human existence, who believe that, for whatever reason, everywhere else on the entire planet has squeezed them away. It was a piece of art made expressly for me; which I had made myself in a previous existence.

And then, close to the end, there came the penguins.

The film is almost over when Herzog conducts an interview with an ornithologist alongside footage of a colony migrating towards their feeding grounds. The camera zooms in on a single penguin that has broken away from the group and set off in the opposite direction, towards the mountains. The ornithologist explains how it often happens that there is one member of the colony who becomes deranged. How, even if he fetched the misdirected penguin back, reunited it with its fellows and pointed it the right way, as soon as he let go it would immediately turn around again and resume its own course towards the hostile, boundless mountains which mark the southern limits of the Earth. 'The deranged ones couldn't possibly survive,' the ornithologist says, and in all his years of study, he still doesn't understand why they do it.

Was it from the deranged penguin that the huge and crushing sadness came? His pointed tail dragging the snow. His useless wings thrashing. Falling on his front. Pushing himself on again. Waddling, stumbling, waddling.

'But why?' Herzog asked. But why.

The world is wrong. It took me twenty-five years to realise and now I don't think I can bear it any more.

The world is wrong, and I am too small to fix it, too self-absorbed.

Cheek against the faded pile of my bedsit carpet, I stared and stared into the darkness beneath my bed. After a while, my eyes adjusted and I could see boxes outlined against the pale wall, a miniature horizon. It made me remember how I used to draw pictures at Halloween. Of buildings silhouetted against skylines with a big white moon in the middle and a witch on a broomstick, tilting her hooked nose back and into space. I remembered how most of those boxes contained rolls and sheaves and pads of paper either with drawings on or waiting to be drawn upon, and I wondered when – I wondered if – I would ever feel like making another picture.

I raised myself up again. I took a deep and cathartic sniff. I lifted my phone from the table. Cradled it in my lap. Then I called my mother.

Works about Carpet, I test myself: Mona Hatoum, 1995. An expanse of silicone rubber entrails fitted impeccably around one another to form a flawless floor. Our intestines are several metres long; a fact which has always astonished me. So maybe Hatoum's piece is about the astonishing capacity of the human body. Or maybe it's about how extravagantly attached we are to the things we own, as if they were the insides of our bodies and not just the insides of our houses. Furnishings, ornaments, even the upholstery. Such that we end up devoting more effort to preserving the carpet than we do to preserving our intestines.

On my grandmother's bedroom carpet, there is a chest of drawers, a fitted wardrobe, a tattered beanbag which belonged to the dog. High up on the wall, there are a few timber shelves and empty hooks where picture frames used to hang. Stacked beneath the windowsill, there are four cardboard boxes neatly duct-taped shut. When I first arrived my mother told me not to open the boxes and that she'd be over in a couple of weeks to collect them. I didn't ask what she had taped inside. At the beginning, I didn't care. My mind was so bunged up by all the sudden changes. But in the three weeks I've been here alone, my mother has yet to come, and now I am beginning to wonder.

Every morning my grandmother used to open every window in every room. Her houses were always cold, and even in her eighties, she didn't appear to notice. She valued fresh air above all forms of comfort.

And so this carpet is surprisingly luxurious for the bedroom of a woman so averse to luxury. It is intensely green; I cannot imagine a factory that would manufacture such a hue in such deep pile. I backcomb it with my fingers. It's almost fluffy. All the other carpets of the bungalow are flat-weave, though now I come to think of it, they are also green. Lime, pine, emerald, moss. As if my grandmother needed the illusion of flora as surely as she needed the outside air.

Every year during the summer holidays, she would take my sister and me on trips to peculiar places. An old gunpowder mill, a former women's prison, a deserted beach house gutted by a storm, an allegedly haunted graveyard and – over and over again – some coastal outcrop which got cut off at high tide. She could never resist straying from the designated path, racing against the rising sea. In her company my sister and I always ended up briar-scratched, muddied, wading, lost.

We thought my grandmother was glorious. We looked forward to those trips all year.

There are more of her weird trinkets here in the bedroom. A miniature Eiffel Tower, a wobble-legged beetle in a wooden nutshell, a foot-shaped beach stone. What was it about these that persuaded my mother to spare them from the hedge-burial? Was it because these were the ones which kept my grandmother company in her final weeks? And so they are full up with her gazes, infused by her dying thoughts. Out the window, there's a short expanse of gravel, a short expanse of grass, the garden hedge. Over the hedge, there's the valley. Tiny cows in the distance and normal-sized cows up close and the closest one of all is stretching his neck across the electric fence to munch on my grandmother's cotoneaster.

In her fitted wardrobe, there are fourteen naked hangers. In the bottom drawer of her chest of drawers, there are two tattered handkerchiefs, and on the top there's a coaster and a solitary picture frame squashed full of black-and-white photos of my mother and aunts as children in bell-bottoms and bare feet. There is just the one of me; I am chasing the dog who preceded Joe across the lawn of her old house. These are my inaugural steps; the very first time I chased something.

Without her teacup on top, the coaster looks abandoned, as does the chest of drawers, without her bed beside it. On each of the timber shelves, there's a row of books. There are books in the living room as well, books in the dining room she used as a study, books on the coffee table in the entry hall. My mother and aunts have long since divided between them and taken away the ones they want and yet there's still a whole bus load left behind, a whole library bus load. I get up from the floor. Stand in front of the shelves. Place my finger on a spine and draw its cover out. *A Concise History of Modern Sculpture: 339 Plates; 49 in colour.*

I pick a plate at random. Helen Phillips, the caption reads, 1960, *Moon.* But it isn't a moon. It's a great lump of bronze. Brown and hard and twisted like the moon never was.

I tuck the book under my arm, pull the bedroom curtains.

Is the valley full up with my grandmother's gazes too? The hedge, the cows.

I catch the reflection of a figure in the wardrobe mirror, turn my head to face it. A person too old to be a child but too young to be an adult. Hair falling limply yet somehow wild, short yet somehow knotted. Baggy eyes, blotchy skin. I notice for the first time all day what I'm wearing: a woolly winter cardigan that hangs down to my knees, even though it is warm, even though it is spring.

I picture my grandmother in the mirror instead. A hazy effigy in tweed skirt and tracksuit jumper, levitating above the fluffy carpet, shimmering. How glorious that would be. I summon and summon my grandmother's ghost. But nothing happens.

Even the cows she gazed at are dead now too, of course.

I step out into the corridor, close the bedroom door, and, almost at once, open it again.

If my grandmother is in there, I don't want to trap her. I want her to waft free, and find me.

For the last few weeks I occupied my city bedsit, I didn't cook an awful lot of meals. It wasn't that I didn't want to eat; I just couldn't face all the rinsing and chopping and stirring and tossing that cooking entails. It seemed to me only the same sort of a waste of time as lying on the carpet.

Just a few feet beyond my bedsit, the streets were lined with cafés, grocers, takeaway joints. Most evenings I'd stop by the posh supermarket on my walk home. I always shopped there even though I could only barely afford it. There was a Lidl a few streets away but I hated Lidl; it reminded me of the dole queue, only with vegetables. I'd pick up a basket from the doorway of the posh one and drift the aisles. I'd stand perfectly still and stare at an item for an uncomfortable length of time. Several other customers would come and go in the minutes it took me to remember whether I had any honey left, whether I prefer my tuna in oil or brine, whether or not I am able to tolerate wheat. Eventually I'd make it to the checkouts with a few random products sliding from side to side in my basket, and then at home again I'd lie on my floor for a couple of hours before going to bed on a bar of chocolate – something slightly revolting like a Double Decker or a Toffee Crisp – because only the slightly revolting chocolate bars were suitably evocative of childhood.

Every night I did this, I'd be woken by the angry burbling and sloshing of my almost entirely empty stomach. I'd get up and sit at my breakfast bar and eat bowlfuls of muesli and curse myself for having forgotten the one thing I always needed and always forgot. The milk, the milk, the fucking milk.

The point of being here, alone in the bungalow on turbine hill, is to recover. This is what I told my mother before she agreed to let me care take, and the only thing I can do to stop her from worrying is to try and look well when she comes to visit. Because she cannot see inside my head, out-side my head I must be nourished and calm and bright. The straightforwardness of this comforts me: body over brain.

With only a poorly stocked village shop, the absence of choice is liberating. I buy whatever they have and challenge myself to cobble it into something. They always have milk and I always remember. Here on turbine hill, meals are the only thing that structure my days and so I force myself to maintain their pattern. Because structure and maintenance and pattern, and broccoli, are what sanity consists of.

In my grandmother's kitchen I measure three handfuls of brown rice into a pot. I heat oil in the only frying pan. It has a great dint in the base and I have to push my irregularly chopped vegetables to and fro across the hot part to ensure they, irregularly, fry. I place a tray of peanuts to roast beneath the grill. They are red and pointy and I suspect the shop woman had intended them for bird feeders.

When I arrived here, there were two bags of flour in the cupboard. One wholemeal, one cream. The flour had set into bag-shaped blocks and a posse of weevils were gnawing the paper. The flour and the weevils were kept company by a few leftover jars. Bovril, mustard, pickled beetroot and maple syrup, none of which I remember my grandmother eating. I dumped everything into the standard waste wheelie bin without emptying the bags or rinsing the jars. Because right at that moment, I did not – could not – care a shit about recycling.

I carry my dinner plate through to the living room. On the coffee table there's an open bottle of wine and I pour a generous glug down on the burgundy stain at the bottom of last night's unrinsed tumbler. In the village shop the wine bottles are positioned on the highest shelf behind the counter. The only choice is red or white and then the shop woman brushes the dust off before squirrelling it away in a brown paper bag. She does the same with toilet roll and paracetamol. By means of her brown paper bags, the shop woman shows me which purchases I ought to be ashamed of.

Now that it's evening, I push the power button on the tiny television set. I don't really care what programme I'm watching; I just like how it chatters softly from the corner, requiring no particular response. When I was growing up, my parents didn't allow the set to be switched on during the hours of light. Daytime television was for incapacitated or lazy people, not for us, not for our family. Even now that I'm free to watch it whenever I want, I don't. I wouldn't dare.

Nowadays most people on the telly seem to have recently recovered from either cancer or depression and feel compelled to talk about it, to add their personal nuggets of wisdom to the broken taboo. First it was only ambiguously famous people: Gaelic sportsmen, celebrity chefs, traditional musicians. Then the spouses of ambiguously famous people began to pipe up, and now any civilian who can spin a decent line about their horrifying struggle is deemed worthy of airtime. Away they yammer all week on the talk radio programmes – and then at the weekend I get to see them in the unremarkable flesh on *The Late Late Show* – until it seems to me it would be more taboo not to talk about it at all, but to hold back and suffer in decorous silence.

If each one perceived their respective illness in a unique and interesting way, it wouldn't bother me so much. But they each say the same slim range of things and end on the same slim range of messages: 'Be Sure To Get Your Balls And

Boobs Checked,' they say. 'It's Okay Not To Feel Okay And Ask For Help.'

As soon as my dinner plate is empty, I pick up *A Concise History of Modern Sculpture* and drink another generous glass of wine. It must be Friday because here it comes now: *The Late Late Show*, and the first guest is a millionaire who suffers from depression. The angle, I presume, is that even people with obscene amounts of money are not immune to bouts of tremendous sadness; that tremendous sadness does not necessarily target the poor. To be fair to the depressed million-aire, he describes the nature of his bouts with a lucidity I haven't heard before; with poetry, almost.

He describes how, when he feels bad, every colour drains from his surroundings.

He describes how, when he feels bad, he can't taste food – even garlic, even spice.

He describes how, when he feels bad, all of the things that usually animate him suddenly don't. He describes the whole dead world and how he feels as if it has died for no one but him.

'Now I can spot the signs it's coming,' he says, meaning the cartoon cloud of desolation which appears from nowhere and remains for an unspecified spell, hovering above his head, following him everywhere he goes. A coffee cup left unwashed is a sign, a misplaced set of keys, an unmade bed. When the depressed millionaire walks past an expanse of fresh-cut grass and forgets to inhale, this is the most irrefutable of signs, the point at which he knows it's time to start extending the metaphorical stretchers of his metaphorical umbrella of defence. 'I run,' he says, and for just a moment everybody in the audience and everybody watching at home thinks that he is speaking figuratively, but now he starts to espouse the healing power of exercise and we realise he means it literally. The depressed millionaire literally runs until the forward thrust has caused his cartoon cloud to disperse back into ordinary life again, into ordinary feeling.

Works about Running, I test myself: every winter, a Dutch performance artist and musician called Guido van der Werve runs thirty-two miles from an art gallery in Chelsea to Kensico Cemetery in Valhalla, upstate New York. Where he lays a bouquet of chamomile flowers at the tombstone of Sergei Rachmaninoff, the Russian maestro composer who died in 1943. *Running to Rachmaninoff*, the piece is called, and van der Werve runs because Rachmaninoff suffered debilitating depression for three significant years of his life. And running. Ah yes. Is supposed to make depression go away.

He brings chamomile because chamomile is Russia's national flower, but also because it is supposed to alleviate the symptoms of hysteria. From which Rachmaninoff, apparently, also suffered.

It's half past ten and would be entirely dark if it wasn't for this clear sky, this perfectly completed moon. In the hall I kick off my slipper-boots and pull on my sneakers. Throw the front door open. Hurdle over the gate.

I run.

And for approximately the first three minutes of running, I feel spectacular.

Through the dark, the grey road stands out faintly against the black ditches and guides me. I run like I ran when I was a child, without realising I am running, without considering that I might at any moment twist an unsuspecting ankle or be stopped dead in my tracks by an undetected heart defect or trip over and fall flat on my face and smash my nose away.

I run.

Like my sister is racing after me. Like she is only a few strides behind and I am in with a viable chance of winning a perfectly pointless round of Chase.

But after another minute I'm losing puff. The weariness of adulthood nips at my heels. I notice how the sole of my right sneaker is flapping loose, how my hair is batting my eye-balls, how my cardigan has slipped from my shoulders to dangle annoyingly off my elbows, to sail in my wake as if it is a cape and I am trying to be a superhero.

I never beat my sister at Chase. She was always taller than me, faster than me.

Because my grandmother's bungalow sits on the hill's brow, every outing is always down on the outward journey, up on the way home. I turn around and begin to plod up the hill, limping slightly in order to accommodate my flapping sole. I remember that I hate running, that I can't stand any form of exercise unless it has some purpose other than exercising, unless I have arrived somewhere by the time it is over.

I remember that going back is always the hardest part.

2

RABBIT

I see them. At the very bottom of my grandmother's garden. The rabbits.

In the grass beside the hedge between the redcurrant bushes, I see them sometimes during the day but most often when it is either early or late and the light is lustreless, on the brink of either coming or going. It surprises me to learn that rabbits are crepuscular. Flopsy, Mopsy, Cotton-tail. Peter and Roger and Thumper and Bugs. I realise I know very little about how actual rabbits actually live. Do they hibernate? Mate for life? Eat insects in addition to greenery? And what is it about dusk and dawn? Are they able to tell when it's light enough to see their way, yet dark enough that it's difficult for others to see them?

Whatever the rabbity logic, out they come from the hedge, nibbling, hopping. A family of brown splodges between the overlong grass and ragged shrubs. All except one, who is completely black. How does a wild rabbit in a cohort of brown rabbits come to be black? I think at once of *Watership Down*; I wonder is the black rabbit Death.

'Bright eyes . . .' Blah blah, something something.

After the first time I saw it, I mentioned the extraordinary rabbit to my mother on the phone, and she told me it was not so extraordinary.

'It will have escaped from a hutch,' she said, 'or it'll be the descendant of a rabbit who escaped from a hutch, still carrying the old black gene.'

My mother knows everything. I used to think all mothers did but in recent years I've come to realise it's just mine. My mother alone knows that, in point of fact, nothing is extraordinary.

When I was little I had a friend called Georgina who lived a quarter mile up the road. For her sixth birthday, she got a white rabbit and named it Snowball. For roughly a fortnight, Snowball lived in a pretty timber hutch on the back lawn, fortressed by a wire mesh run. Then one morning, Georgina went out to find a jagged hole in the mesh and the rabbit gone. Her mother told her this wasn't the horrific tragedy it appeared; Snowball had simply made the decision to go and live in the fields with her wild friends instead.

Georgina passed this story on to me in the playground, and I passed it on to my sister, and she laughed and declared it a load of crap.

Now it seems she was wrong to be so cynical so young.

I didn't sleep in any of my grandmother's beds last night. I returned to the living room sofa to see out *The Late Late Show*. Then I nodded off and when I woke again it was *The Afternoon Show* and I had to get up and peek out the curtain to check if it was actually afternoon. But outside the sky was still sable, the cows still huddled against the hedge, the turbine's eyes still glowing. And it came as a revelation to me that daytime television is repeated at night; that you can live your whole waking life over again in the dark.

Works about Bed, I test myself: Tracey Emin, 1998. *My Bed*, she called it, but Emin's artwork was not simply the disarranged item of furniture upon which she slept, and it wasn't simply about furniture or sleeping or even disarrangement. There were cigarette butts and besmirched knickers. Bunched-up tights and empty bottles of vodka. Moccasins and newspapers and a white toy poodle sitting obediently back on his haunches, regarding everything. It was about feeling shit first thing in the morning. About tossing beneath the covers, not wanting to get up and yet making everything worse by not getting up. It was about workaday despair.

And yet people were so angry over that bed; they did not realise it was the easiest piece of art in the world with which to identify.

*

The last night I spent in my city bedsit, I didn't sleep on my colonised mattress with the parasite dust-mites. I didn't sleep anywhere; I didn't sleep.

By the time I'd completed negotiations with my mother, the yearning to cry had passed. Having arrived at a starting decision, I felt calmed, encouraged. And so, I phoned my landlady and told her that an unforeseen emergency was forcing me to renege on my lease.

I didn't take any care in packing; I didn't care. I wrenched my postcards and photos and clippings from the walls, wrapped my cacti in aluminium foil, bundled my clothes into a bin liner, boxed my books with the contents of my sock drawer, my shoes with the contents of my fridge. And once every garment and ornament and utensil had been wrapped and bundled and boxed from sight, I lugged it all out into the hallway.

It was late when my phone rang. I don't know how late but the street-lamp sensors had long since sensed it was time to light, my neighbouring bedsits long since fallen silent. It was Jess again, and because I still contained some calm and courage, I answered. I told her I did not feel so good, that my mum was coming for me in the morning, and in less than half an hour, Jess arrived on her bicycle with, in a red leather satchel strapped to her back carrier, two bottles of red wine and a box of Black Magic.

Jess is my tall, blonde friend. Stylish and buxom with a crop of marvellously fine yellow hair. Outgoing and popular such that I never understood why she bothered hanging around with plain and shy and solitary, unpopular me. But

Jess was only bright and boisterous in a crowd. Once it was just us, she'd contract and release her inner bleakness. She was on a low dose of antidepressant medication and wasn't supposed to mix the pills with alcohol, though she often did. 'If I can't have a few drinks I'm only going to be depressed anyway,' she'd say. It didn't stop them from working; it only made her get drunk faster. And this was always fine by me because I get drunk fast on alcohol alone.

'The pills are just a new sort of sadness,' she'd say. 'Softer, slyer.'

On the last night I spent in my bedsit in the city, Jess and I did what we'd done many nights before in similar but less symbolic circumstances. We washed a box of Black Magic down with two bottles of Cabernet Sauvignon. We confusedly attempted to put our chaotic world to rights. Raspberry parfait, orange sensation, caramel caress, and then at some godawful early hour, Jess remembered to ask me: 'Have you told Ben you're leaving?' And with the last almond crunch and my ambling thumb I sent him a maudlin text message which I have long since deleted from my phone in disgust.

Ben, Jess and I had worked together in the gallery, but because it was gallery policy never to extend more than a twelve-month contract to part-time staff, none of us did any more, and there was no reason for us to be friends, and I can't remember exactly why it was that we were still trying to be.

Ben replied fast. A casual message asking if I'd need a hand loading my mother's car. I accepted. We arranged a time for the morning and bid one another a polite goodnight. I reported this back to Jess, but she only nodded and sipped. She only looked drunk and drugged and tired.

After the wine and chocolate and rectification was all done, off she wobbled. My tall, blonde friend, home through the deserted streets on her retro bicycle. I stood in my gateway and watched her wheeling from pool of street-lamp light to pool of street-lamp light until she reached the corner and threw me a bockety wave.

My last night in the city, I didn't sleep.

I vomited up a bucket of burgundy sick. Rolled listlessly on the carpet for an hour. Got up to clean.

Swept and scrubbed. Scraped blue spores from the window-sill and black ones from the wall behind the bedstead, combed a soft mountain of moulted hair from the amber carpet, knocked the cobwebs down and scratched my Blu-Tack from the peach paint with a blunt bread knife.

At last the bedsit was as empty and clean as I found it. As characterless, as cold. And out in the hallway, the swaddled trappings of my independent life lay like dead bodies in the wake of a murderous typhoon.

I see him now, the black one. This morning, I don't bother showering or changing my clothes. I don't even brush my teeth. People are too clean nowadays, I think. We are all too clean and take too many antibiotics and when the bird flu and swine flu and fruit bat flu arrive, it'll serve us right. But not me, not any more. I tidy last night's dinner plate and wine glass away. I make a coffee, carry it down to the sun room. And here he is at the end of the garden. The Death Rabbit all surrounded by his paler brethren.

Works about Bed, I thought of another one: Felix Gonzalez-Torres, *Untitled*, 1991. In 1992, the same gigantic image appeared on twenty-four different billboards around the city of New York. A photograph of a double bed. Sheets dishevelled, pillows indented by an absent pair of heads. There was no accompanying text, no title, but I know from secondary sources that the absent heads were those of the artist and his partner who, in 1991 and 1996 respectively, died of AIDS.

This is the best of conceptual art: by means of nominal material, vast feeling is evoked. A message enduring long after the posters have been replaced by car ads and clothes ads and Coke ads at Christmas.

Its message: appreciate the people around you. Don't re-plump their pillows until they return safely in the evening.

My father comes to mow my grandmother's lawn. It is Sunday. Only on a Sunday could he allow himself to fritter away the afternoon on somebody else's overgrown grass.

For my father, mowing is a leisure pursuit, as is axing up a week's worth of kindling, rotavating the potato patch, replenishing the oil and wiper water in everybody's car, and he saves all such leisurely jobs concerning gardens and family for Sundays. On Monday through Friday, my father works in a sand and gravel quarry. Operating heavy machinery, handling industrial explosives, transforming escarpments into rubble; that sort of thing.

When I was a kid, I used to try and make his job sound more sophisticated in front of my friends, one little girl called Caitriona in particular, whose father had some sort of high-flying office-based occupation which required a tie and an arduous daily commute. 'My dad works in the min-er-al-ex-tract-ion-in-dust-ree,' I'd say, which was a far cry from his own explanation. 'I make big rocks into small rocks,' he'd say, and chuckle.

I watch my father from the window.

A man of sixty in a lumberjack shirt jouncing about atop a miniaturised tractor. Feet hitched up and perched on a narrow platform either side, moving unsettlingly fast for a front garden so small, so obstructed by flower beds. He draws perfectly parallel trails of new green as he goes, kicking up the cut blades in a grass-storm behind him. From here, it almost looks as if his hair is still brown. From here, even his bald patch is too small to notice. 'Your father was blond when I first met him,' my mother often says, 'and you and your sister were both blonde too when you were little.' My mother signed up for a family of angel-heads and look at us now: mine dyed black and my sister's sienna, our father's thin in places, grey in places, gone.

He sees me at the window and I wave.

He's almost finished the front now and he said that once he's finished the front he'll come in for a cup of tea. I've bought a box of teabags in preparation, white sugar and full-fat milk. A packet of cream crackers I dress up in Marmite and grated Cheddar, a packet of chocolate fancies I arrange on a cake plate. Now I totter it all down to the sun room on one of my grandmother's tin tea trays. The mower engine has ceased its whingeing, and so I return again to the kitchen, set the whistling kettle to boil.

By the time I get back to the sun room, my father's already on the sofa with a smattering of cracker crumbs across the chest of his shirt. He dusts them off and begins to give out about my grandmother's overabundance of flower beds.

'Remember the cosy?' I interrupt as I pour, indicating the knitted cottage which covers the pot. 'And the fancies?' Sponge disc foundations topped by truffly brown blobs, coated with sprinkles. It's years since I had a fancy. I used to nibble the sponge away first, save the blob until last. All my life I've eaten things in order of preference; whole dinner plates item by item, and individual items component by component.

My father looks baffled so I prompt him. 'It's the old Sunday tea cosy,' I say, 'and Grannie always used to buy fancies, or sometimes baby Battenbergs or sometimes Viennese swirls.' Dad harrumphs his agreement, grabs a cake with a grubby fist and devours it in a single bite, making them seem not so fancy after all.

I should know that my father doesn't pay attention to details such as these; I should know because for decades my mother and sister and I have played sneaky little games of let's-see-how-long-it-takes-Dad-to-notice, and he never noticed, not once. The tongue piercing, the nose piercing, the lip.

*

In the space of a sunnyish, warmish fortnight, the grass has blasted up and broken out in daisies. There are daisies around the redcurrant bushes, daisies in the strawberry patch, daisies beneath the hedge where my mother buried the curios. I've never seen so many white specks since the lawn of the last house my grandmother lived in, as if she brought them with her – the soles of her shoes stuffed with seeds which shook free with every stamp.

It's strange to have an afternoon tea I prepared myself with only my father for company. Usually it's my mother who stacks the tray with coasters, saucers, shortbread, crustless sandwiches trickling bits of mashed, boiled egg, and my sister who steers the flow of cheerful chatter for the time it takes to empty two teapots, from obligatory savoury through to obligatory sweet. Now that it's just Dad and I, the curmudgeonly ones, we don't really know what to say to each other.

'Well,' he says. 'How are you, then? Your mother's woeful fucking worried.'

My father doesn't really want to talk about my feelings. That would be excruciating for both of us. He only wants me to tell him that I am okay, so he can return to my mother and tell her there's no need to worry.

'I'm okay,' I say. 'There's no need to worry.'

My parents did not want me to come here to stay. They are, like everybody, fearful of being completely alone and sus-picious of people who choose to be. They hesitate, like everybody, to understand how it could heal me, as I believe it can. I believe: I am less fearful of being alone than I am of not being able to be alone.

But I say none of this. My father is not susceptible to philosophy.

Instead I ask him about the salt flats in Australia.

Because there was a time when he used to harvest salt in a place called Dampier. Now, in the sun room, my father talks about the piles he drove in the ocean, the cargo-ship jetty he raised. He talks about the aerodromes in Lincoln between which he laid underground pipes for refuelling Vulcan bombers during the Falklands War. 'You were born then, during that war,' he says and even though that was my sister, I don't correct him, and I wonder whether all fathers do this: tell their children stories of the wide open life they led before we came along to confine it. My father owned a Land Rover and a caravan. He travelled from place to place, laying pipelines behind him as he went, frying rashers on the heat of his engine. My mother and sister travelled in the caravan with him until I was born. Then he bought a house, got a job as a quarry foreman. He put down roots. Tortuous, unyielding, necessary roots.

And so my father has every right in the world to be disappointed by the dog's dinner I am making of the last life he gave up his own for.

But, of course, we don't talk about this either.

Now I see he's drained the mug, the time has come to ask him the thing I want to ask him: I've always longed to have a patch of personal wilderness. Of waist-high grass entwined with wild flowers through which I can prance; within which

I can lie down and disappear from sight. I suspect the long-ing can be traced back to the opening sequence of every episode of *Little House on the Prairie*.

'No way,' my father says, before I've even finished con-juring it. 'This bungalow is on the bloody market, you know.'

'But Dad! There's about a hundred reasons why it won't sell before you've even reached the back garden. Nobody's seriously going to be put off by having to give the grass a trim. They're going to have to trim it at some point anyway . . . and then there's the turbine, and then there's the dog smell . . .'

'It does reek of dog,' my father says.

Jackpot.

He finishes up in under an hour. He loads the tractor lawn-mower back into the car trailer and ambles around the shrubbery for a while, carrying my grandmother's shears and wheeling her barrow. Finally he knocks on the glass of the sun room to rouse my attention, bids me an abrupt farewell, and is gone.

I go out to lock the gate. I can still hear the revving and rattling of his departure.

I realise I no longer care whether or not my father is sophisticated. He has more effervescence – more sturdy grace – than any man who ever wore a tie to an office.

Whenever I get very drunk at night, I always wake in the morning with a sonorous headache and a heightened sense of despair.

On the last night I spent in my city bedsit, in the early

hours of the morning, after everything was cleared and cleaned, I unpacked my stove-top coffee pot, stuffed it full of Authentic Italian Espresso Blend and began to brew. I decided that if I didn't allow myself to fall asleep, then I wouldn't have to wake up again and despair.

I sat at the desk where I'd drawn barely anything in several weeks, and where anything I did draw had turned out badly. I looked out the window as I drank my coffee, down to the roof of the washing machine shed. I saw how it was littered with short twigs and I remembered the tree-house which was actually a hut, and I wondered where they came from, the twigs, when there weren't even any trees.

I listened to the birdsong, the grumble of trams, the click of my electricity meter. The shuffle and bump of the early-rising residents. I heard the girl who worked in Statoil slam the front door and then the gate behind her, and I heard the tin soldier scuff and tap, push down his toast and pause, then the ker-ching as it popped itself back up again.

I was waiting for my mother, for the landlady, and for Ben, but I had no idea what order they'd arrive in or what I was going to say to any of them when they did. At nine o'clock I left first my chair and then the bedsit, and went outside. The front garden was brown but the dew on the part of the lawn which the sun hadn't yet reached was sharp to the touch, and sparkling.

Ben came first, as I was crouching, touching the sharp and sparkling lawn. I saw him round the corner, the collar of his army coat raised and his fists pushed down to the seams of his pockets. I waved up at him from my crouch. I wanted to thank him for putting up with me these past weeks; I wanted to apologise for my inconsistency. But I only waved when he was a short distance away and only said good morning once he had reached the gate, and then we only went inside.

Ben was disappointed that I'd already moved everything into the hall. He swept his arm through the air above my plastic necropolis.

'You don't need me at all,' he said.

In my empty bedsit, we perched side by side on the tiny stools at the tiny breakfast bar. Normally I'd offer him a coffee, but I'd already packed the pot for a second time. The mugs, even the mug tree. And so we just perched there and tried to think of things to say.

'Look, um, I just wanted to thank you,' I said.

'I haven't done anything yet,' he said, smiling. But this wasn't what I meant and I assumed it was his way of swatting away a potentially serious conversation, and so I dropped it.

The meter clicked. The trams grumbled. A blackbird sang irreverently.

Hurdygurdy hurdygurdy hurdygurdy hurdygurdy hurdygurdy, it sang.

Then the intercom above the light switch buzzed. Downstairs and outside on the doorstep, the landlady and my mother had arrived in unison.

The landlady was called Loretta Nagle. She was uncommonly old and small but always made a point of informing me of how capable she was. During the months I lived beneath her roof, she claimed to be able to plunge out a blocked drain with a single hand, to work an electric drill to fix a shelf, to climb onto the roof and tweak a satellite dish gone awry. Yet I'd never seen her perform any such tasks; I can't imagine a tenant had dared ask her to for fifteen years, at least. And so because she had never actually failed, I suppose Loretta continued to believe that she was still able.

The landlady was also uncommonly rich; Jess and I had worked it out once. She owned two houses in the same street, both divided into several bedsits each costing a minimum of one hundred euro a week. And once you have enough money, it doesn't matter if you are old or small.

Once you have enough money, you can buy yourself youth and you can buy yourself magnitude.

On the morning I reneged on my lease, Loretta held both banisters and took two unsteady steps for every stair and I followed behind, pretending this was a normal pace, pretending I was equally slow. At last she closed the door of the empty bedsit behind us, to talk money and assess my cleaning job. Before the edge of the door hit the frame, I saw Ben and my mother below us in the hallway. Meeting each other for the first time. Together lifting and carrying my belongings away.

Loretta's fingertips were white and puckered as though she was in a permanent state of having emerged from the bath. That morning she ran them across the countertop and squinted into the smelly darkness of my oven. Even though I could clearly see pocks in the paint where my pictures had come down, even though I was not legally entitled to my deposit back, still she counted five hundred euro in fifties out onto the breakfast bar and I thanked her, repeatedly. I simpered and fawned.

By the time Loretta and I had baby-stepped back down to the front door, my mother's car was packed. Out on the footpath, Mum was making some final adjustments and there was a stranger lingering between the gateposts and speaking to Ben. A black man, no more than thirty, with close-cropped hair and pale blue jeans. Ben must have told him that the landlady had gone inside and would soon come back again, because he seemed to be waiting for her. When Loretta emerged he stopped speaking to Ben and stepped forward and held his hand out.

'I'm Daniel,' he said, 'I'm here to see the studio apartment.'

Loretta held her arms firmly against her sides. Her eyes were blank.

'There must be some mistake,' she said: 'there are no vacancies here.'

'Mrs Nagle?' Daniel said. 'Number 26? You phoned me late last night. You told me to come and view it this morning . . .'

I caught my mother's eye and nodded to let her know I was ready to leave. She turned to Ben and told him it was good to meet him and thanked him for his help. She climbed into the driver's seat.

'I can see these people are moving out,' Daniel said, but Loretta would not budge.

'There must be some mistake,' she repeated: 'there are no vacancies.'

I climbed into the passenger seat and rolled the window down and Ben leaned in.

'Thanks again for . . .' I said. He nodded.

'Let me know, okay . . .' he said. I nodded.

'I'll be alright now . . .' I said, as if it were actually that simple, as if my mother was a magic potion which I could drink.

Behind us on the footpath, Daniel's voice had dropped and hardened. I rolled the passenger window up and we pulled away. I twisted around in my seat and peered through the over-packed rear windscreen to wave to Ben. But he'd already raised his collar and shoved his fists into his pockets and turned around. He was already walking away.

I remember the first black person I saw in Lisduff; the first black person I ever saw anywhere. A woman with intricately braided hair, a dress printed in blazing tangerine and teal. She was beautiful and dazzling. We were in the old grocery store, so it must still have been the eighties, before the supermarket arrived. As soon as I saw her, I yanked Mum's sleeve and started to yammer, and she swung down and hissed at me through gritted teeth, telling me to shut up and not make a show.

I have always suffered from this misconception: that my mother is a magic potion.

My sister and I went to a primary school small enough to domicile three different classes inside a single room and the single teacher would take turns to attend to each group, leaving the other groups with an exercise to complete. The school's three teachers were all women of middle age, and back then I believed that it was only women of middle age who were authorised to be teachers. I was a smart child, or maybe just impatient. I always finished my exercises too fast. Then I'd lay my pencil down and glower out the window and contemplate how much I wanted to go home. I understood that the only circumstance which might permit a pupil to leave before the end-of-day bell was if they fell sick and their mother came to collect them. And so, each day as I glowered and contemplated, I longed to be sick.

The view out of every classroom window was the same. A grassy bank tasselled by pine trees. All year round, the trees blocked out the sky and barely changed. In deepest winter the grass would sallow and in late spring it would break out in dandelions. But for most of each season, there wasn't much to look out at. My contemplations would slide into darker places. I knew that I could fake sick if I really wanted to, but as soon as we got home Mum would take my temperature and know. It seemed unlikely I'd get a chance to press the thermometer against a radiator like the boy in *ET*. And even without the betrayal of a thermometer, if I faked it, she'd know. The only solution was to actually feel sick and be telling the truth. And so, I'd hide my hands under the desk and poke myself hard in the stomach, over and over until it actually hurt, until I had a legitimate stomach ache. Then I'd release a hand and raise it high above my head.

My mother did not go out to work in those days and so was nearly always free to come and fetch me when the teacher phoned. In the car on the way home, I'd experience a feeling somewhere between triumph and guilt. I was not lying. I did feel sick. But I had also wanted to be; I had made myself.

*

I drop the latch and stand inside my grandmother's front gate absentmindedly retying the string for ensuring nobody lets the dog out, forgetting there's no dog to let out any more anyway.

I inhale my father's cut grass. It makes me remember the depressed millionaire. I throw my head back and drink it through my nostrils, this most utopian of smells. I notice it unprompted, and so this means there are no signs of impending collapse – I must still be okay.

I set off around the side of the house in the direction of the plum trees. Dispersed across my grandmother's garden are a number of strange objects. Several slimy sculptures carved in soft stone, mostly male figures with multiple, elongated limbs. A ceramic hippo, a timber cross marking Joe's grave. A bench in the shape of a weird animal, buckled planks held in place by wrought-iron legs which taper into wrought-iron paws – too large for a cat and too small for a lion – and so my grandmother's bench must be a lynx. There are two bird tables. A proper one mounted on a pole with varnished walls and a slanted roof, and an improvised one made from a steel saucepan lid nailed to a tree stump. Then there's a basin full of rainwater in which I often see the small birds splashing in spite of both the baths.

I pass it all by: the lynx, the paddling birds, the stone men, the dog skeleton.

Dad has done a stellar job on my wilderness. At ground level it's a meadow in Minnesota but at eye level, with the plum trees about to fusillade into blossom, it's a Japanese wood-block. There's hardly any wind and so the turbine is only murmuring. The sun comes out and turns up the contrast on everything. It makes me want to paint even though I cannot paint. I have always been too inclined towards geometric shapes, precise lines and regimented pencil scratching. I have never been limp-wristed and free-spirited enough to paint.

I follow the path my father mowed for me, to the cowfield fence which marks the garden's end. Here between the nettle patch and compost heap where he dumped the clippings the smell of cut grass and psychological stability is at its strongest. I lean over to inhale again, and here I find a rabbit. Perfectly dead.

It's grey-brown and only a kit, neither bloody nor battered. I presume my father spotted it chewing the tulips and clouted its skull with the butt of his shears. A single, clean blow. Every year, rabbits raid his lettuce bed, nibble down his baby leeks, rummage up his daffodil bulbs. Peter and Roger and Thumper and Bugs are vermin to my father, as are the slugs he pellet-poisons, as are the pigeons he shoots and nails to a timber post alongside his vegetable patch as a warning to the other pigeons.

The baby rabbit, so frail and sweet, is slumped atop a pretty mess of onion skins, palm fronds, wilted laurel. I go back to the house to fetch my camera. Now to the greenhouse, to fetch the trowel. I have to bow down over the compost heap to get my shot. I can feel the nettles stinging my kneecaps through the threadbare part of my jeans. I remember refusing to believe my mother when she told me that it was more dangerous to lightly brush against a nettle than to grab on and tightly clutch. I remember rubbing a dock leaf against my sting, after I'd put my mother's information to the test, until it was worn down to its stem, my skin green and sticky.

I take the photograph. I trowel a parting in the pretty mess. I roll the kit in and cover it.

I rested my forehead against the passenger window as my mother drove me away from my bedsit.

I watched the city dwindle into suburbs and industrial estates.

My mother has owned the same cadmium-red Ford Estate since the late eighties. It always declines to start on cold mornings, chugs and splutters in wet weather. It fails the NCT every year – three times, at least – before it passes, yet whenever my mother mentions getting a new one, my sister and I protest, vigorously, as if the car's an old pet she wants to put down. Before the days of mandatory safety belts, we played all kinds of make-believe games in the seatless boot space. Around the time we were into *Jaws*, we'd pretend it was a pool of sea off Amity Island and take turns to be the shark; around the time we were into *The Diary of Anne Frank* we'd pretend it was a secret attic and take turns to be the SS. Once I even fell out of my mother's car. I was four or five. It was before the days of central locking and she'd forgotten to push my button down. The door swung free as we rounded a bend. It was just a few yards from home and the car wasn't travelling very fast. Out I tumbled into the ditch and suffered an almighty nosebleed.

'Ben seems nice,' Mum said, 'really nice.' Her voice was cautiously upbeat.

'It doesn't matter now anyway,' I said, and drew my feet up onto the seat and clutched my knees and tried to vanquish the sobs with thoughts of things which were not Ben. I considered the dust-mites raised up on my dead skin and whether or not they would survive until a new tenant arrived.

We filtered onto the motorway and left the concrete behind. We passed cabbage fields and mud-caked sheep, trees so bare they seemed to consist of more negative space than timber. After several miles, my mother spoke again. The cheer had dropped out of her voice.

'I don't know,' she said, 'if you're hubbubing because of something, or because there's something wrong with you.'

My limbs mangled about the passenger seat. My leaking nostrils pressed into my sleeve. My leaking eyes fixed on the windscreen, flicking between the paper discs and the stalled wipers. It was then that the heightened sense of unfounded despair I thought I'd managed to stave off came clattering down. I pressed my eyelids together and pictured the windscreen I'd just closed out; pictured the swirling, white oblong of sky brilliant, petrol blue instead.

When I was a child, I used to believe there was a sky roof. Perhaps every child does, but I had a very particular panorama in my head, replete with all the floated-away stuff which had snagged there. Balloons, kites, bubbles, plastic bags.

Now I wonder if flying birds become deranged in the same way as penguins? And if this is what ultimately halts them? The sky roof.

Works about Sky, I test myself: Cai Guo-Qiang. Well known for his work involving pyrotechnics. Beginning in the early nineties, using lengthy trails of gunpowder, he made a series of ambitious environmental works. One beneath the ocean spanning a thirty-thousand-metre stretch of the coastline of Japan. Another along ten thousand metres of the Gobi Desert, beginning where the Great Wall finishes. The series is called *Project for Extraterrestrials*, and so, of course – it's actually about communication.

I despise my mother's use of words that are not words. Like 'hubbub'. As if she is the child.

'Because of nothing,' I said. 'Because there's nothing right with me. Because I cannot fucking help it.'

I knew it was unnecessary to swear, that I would not have sworn at Ben or Jess, nor would I have cried in front of them, but the rules are different with my mother. With my mother, there are no rules. When I opened my eyes again, the cloud had solidified. Mum was staring out the oblong. Her eyeballs had turned twinkly. She took a CD from the stack between us and pushed it gently into the slot. It was the *Easy Rider* soundtrack I gave her for her birthday last year. From somewhere deep inside a box on the back seat behind us, there came the sigh of an unknown object being slowly crushed beneath the pressure of its fellow objects, and all the while, the Holy Modal Rounders snarled from the dashboard, something about wanting to be a bird.

3

RAT

The last of the tree buds bust out. The grass clippings shrink down as surely as the living grass grows up again. The daffodil farm across the valley yellows and yellows until a truckload of huddled figures arrive very early one morning and spread out in a row and begin an uneven procession uphill. Even though I am too far away to discern their individual hands or the individual flowers, I know the figures must be picking. Slowly, slowly, the field turns patchy in their wake. Green again, brown again.

They'll appear in the supermarket in Lisduff one of these days, the daffodils. Divided into bunches, elastic-banded, propped up in water buckets. But I won't buy them.

Daffodils only remind me of cancer, forget-me-nots of kidney disease, red poppies of the trenches.

I wonder are the huddlers the heavyset, hazel-skinned men who congregate in a corner of Lisduff square early every weekday morning. Loitering between the dry cleaner's and the discount store, offering their muscle to passing trucks. They arrived during the boom to work in the meat factories, my father says. But now there are too many Brazilians and not enough beef, or at least, not enough demand for it. I see the same faces every time I pass through town. Now I wonder is it the daffodil farmer to whom these mammoth, silent men must prostitute themselves.

My mother always buys flowers from the supermarket water bucket. She divvies them into vases and distributes the vases between low-sized tables, mantelpieces, window-sills. My parents' garden is overflowing with daffodils at this time of year, of every frill and petal-shape and shade of yellow imaginable. But it is against my mother's rituals to pick them. According to ritual, there are outdoor flowers and indoor flowers in the same way as there are wild animals and pet animals, free fish and farmed fish, garden vegetables and shop vegetables; they must not be muddled.

I stare out at the daffodil farm. I think how strange it is to imagine the indoor flowers un-bunched and outside, almost as strange as it is to picture all the mammoths daintily plucking them.

*

Works about Flowers, I test myself: Anya Gallaccio, *preserve 'beauty'*, 1991–2003. Two thousand red blooms pressed between glass panes, left to atrophy into brown pulp. They are gerbera–daisy hybrids; their heads are so classically floret-shaped. If somebody gave you a pencil and pad and asked you to draw a flower, you'd draw a gerbera–daisy hybrid without even knowing you had. I wouldn't know either if it wasn't for Anya Gallaccio; she chose them because they are biotechnologically mass-produced to meet the demands of the global market.

So many people covet their cut stems, the Earth can't keep up.

Most of Gallaccio's materials are perishable, her artworks concern mortality, inevitability, powerlessness. You can grow as many mutant flowers as you want, Gallaccio is saying. But you cannot stop a single one from dying.

The house where I grew up was built more than one hundred and fifty years ago, at the tail end of the Famine. The building was originally supposed to function as a hospital, my mother told us, but by the time it had been completed, the Great Famine was more or less over. Two million people had either died or deserted; a new hospital was no longer necessary. For many years, I doubted this story. The house, though reasonably large, seemed absurdly small in comparison to a hospital, and besides, I didn't really want it to be true. If it was, who knew what ghosts might be gliding down the corridor at night? As a child, I did not believe, as I do now, that ghosts are like God: things you can't see because they aren't there. Instead of like dust-mites: things you can't see even though they are there.

Mine is the pokiest of the bedrooms, only as long as a single bed and narrow bookcase. Side by side, the headboard and a lumpish armchair take up its entire width. On the wall, there are drawings I did in college, a corkboard pinned with old, irrelevant notices, and a photographic image of an X-rayed chest, a ghostly ribcage floating in softly focused darkness. The chair is positioned directly beneath the skylight in the ceiling and the bones on the wall, and it was there I took refuge on my arrival home. It was there I sat with my legs crossed in the patch of perfectly rectangular sunlight which falls through my slanted roof, and for the first four days read *Midnight's Children*.

It was during *Midnight's Children* that I became convinced my hair was falling out.

My hair was a statement. It hung down to my belly button, got caught in my fly, tried to strangle me during the night. Each strand was split, each split was split again, and yet I loved it so much I freaked out each time the brush filled up with lost hairs; I checked my pillow every morning to make sure it hadn't somehow severed itself and was left lying there. I'd believed my hair was falling out for some time, but it was only once I was alone with my Rushdie in the lumpish armchair that the idea gripped me. I was certain that a single strand had fallen onto every page, that every time I ran my fingers through my ponytail I pulled out four or five more. Every time I showered, the plughole got clogged, and every time I drew the clog out, it was big as a drowned rat, only more of a drowned mink; the same unforgiving shade of black. So I stopped washing it and plaited it instead, to tie it to my head somehow, and left it plaited for days on end, to prevent it from escaping.

The escaped hairs I tugged from the brush's bristles and rolled between my palms until they formed a tight ball. Then I squashed my hairballs inside a jam jar and placed the jar on the top shelf of my bookcase. I had carelessly selected, from my mother's marmalade-making stash, a jar which formerly contained baby onions. Almost immediately, the knitted fibres of each ball were impregnated by the scent of vinegar – of preservation and corrosion both at once.

Works about Hair, I test myself: I learned how to roll strands from Mona Hatoum, an installation entitled *Recollection*, 1995. Compressed balls of her own long, black, lost locks, collected over the course of years, arrayed across the gallery floor. I want to believe it was in reference to a period of her life in which she had been clutched by the fear that her hair was falling out and felt compelled to collect the fallen strands so that it might in some sense still belong to her. I want to believe this because I want to believe I have things in common with great artists, and that this must mean I might one day be a great artist too.

I kept a pocket mirror tucked beneath the lumpish cushion.

I'd take it out and check my hairline every ten minutes at least, to see if I could detect it retreating. I kept thinking about the cashier in the health food shop in the city where I used to buy my mung beans, my yellow split peas. She had a hideous bald patch right at the top of her face, and I always thought it was a poor advertisement for health food and tried not to look. She was only about my age, and she never made any attempt to hide the patch; she didn't even seem to be aware of it. How noble, I thought, as I checked my own hairline in the pocket mirror incessantly, and all the other mirrors in the house as well, intermittently. But mirrors are treacherous things. Each one revised my reflection according to its position on the wall, my position on the floor, the angle of the light. Because I could not manage to get a complete view, on the fourth day I asked my mother to check the back of my head for signs of impending baldness.

'It's fine,' she said, 'it looks just like it's always looked.'

We were in the bathroom and I was sitting backwards on the toilet bowl with the lid lowered. The last time I'd sat like that with my mother standing behind I was fifteen and she was helping me to bleach my dreadlocks.

'But it's coming out,' I said, 'it's coming out by the handful.'

Her fingers were warm against my scalp. Long before the bleach, she used to arrange my hair into pigtails every morning before school. I only requested the pigtails because I wanted her to touch my head. I thought it was the most relaxing sensation in the world.

'It's spring,' my mother said, 'you're moulting.'

'I'm not a fucking cat,' I said.

'Alright then. You're imagining it,' she said. 'Is that what you want me to tell you? That it's all in your head?'

She withdrew her warm fingers, and I stood up from the toilet bowl.

'But it isn't all in my fucking head,' I said. 'It's all in the fucking pickle jar. That's what I'm worried about.'

Ever since I learned to read, I've had a book on the go – one after another – an unbroken chain from Winnie-the-Pooh to Salman Rushdie. There are so many left behind here in my grandmother's bungalow; publication dates to span her entire life. Every evening after I've eaten, I make myself open one and read, for a while, and then lay the book down spine up on the sofa cushions at the page where I stopped.

The trick to keeping going is to break going into bursts: to stop, and otherwise occupy my brain for a spell, and then start going again. Nowadays I apply this to my whole day long. Each is a succession of shallow occupations, enforced intervals. Even my sleep is only ankle deep, interrupted.

By the time I reached the end of *Midnight's Children*, I could not name a single character nor recount a single chain of events.

Up again. Another day. A new one. The next.

Up late. To find the facing field of the daffodil farm full green and brown. My Brazilians have already crested the hilltop and disappeared.

An aeroplane has disappeared too.

I hear about it from the kitchen radio, as I wait for my coffee to ascend its spout. A behemoth of modern machinery vaporised in the space of a single sleep and 'gone missing' – the phrase the newsreader uses, as if it was a dog, a pair of glasses, a solitary glove, as if it might turn up down the back of the sofa or in a lost property box at the

train station. And it isn't just a great lump of riveted ti-
tanium or – whatever it is planes are made from – it's two
hundred and thirty-nine passengers, the newsreader says. In
this age of ear-splitting communicativeness, how can it be
that so many people can have gone so suddenly silent? I
don't understand. Perhaps the world is vaster, more
bottomless, less discovered than I've always believed.

I carry my coffee down the corridor to the sun room and
scrutinise my own small expanse of sky for missing aircraft.
If it could be anywhere, I think, then it could be here. Why
couldn't it be here?

Only clouds. Only pigeons. Only the green slime and brown
moss which grows between the panes. The world within my
sight span remains precisely as it was.

I've lived here long enough now to fall into a routine. I
finish my coffee and go back to the kitchen. I measure out
my breakfast things, select my implements. Tear a square of
tissue from the roll, pour milk from carton to jug, arrange it
all on a tin tea tray. People nowadays don't have jugs and trays
just like they don't have shoehorns, even though such things
become weirdly vital as soon as you fall accidentally into using
them. My grandmother has three trays. One with a picture
of rose bushes and one with a picture of a sailing ship and
one with a reproduction of a L. S. Lowry painting. The Lowry
is my favourite. In the living room, I found a book of his
industrial landscapes and flicked through the plates at the
back until I recognised *The Irwell at Salford*, 1947. It shows
chimneys, smoke, streets and warehouses; I can't imagine a
less appropriate scene for transference to a tea tray.

Whilst flicking I came upon a mess of dead petals. Real ones, I mean, and not a painting. They were pressed between factories and matchstick men. They had mostly turned a dirty mustard, and so I couldn't tell what colour or flower they had once been.

This morning, I retrieve the book I left behind on the living room sofa cushions last night and continue down the corridor to the sun room with my Lowry tray. The day is dull; the dullness makes it airless between the glass walls; the airlessness makes it almost warm.

I'm reading *The Siege of Krishnapur* by J. G. Farrell. I found it in the dining room and chose it because J. G. Farrell tripped off the Sheep's Head peninsula into the North Atlantic and, mysteriously, drowned. He was trying to fish. I knew this about the author before I chose his book. I liked this about him, or rather, I liked him for this, his elegiac death. *The Siege of Krishnapur* is strong enough to stave off reality. I plump up the foam of my chair and slip away to a garrison surrounded by sepoys, the advancing infantrymen of the East India Company.

When I look up, there is an old man standing on the path. Gawping in at me.

I don't recognise him at first. The last, and perhaps only, time we came face to face must have been my grandmother's funeral and he must have queued to shake my hand like all the others. I remember his name, Jink, though I don't remember what real name it is short for. He was her closest neighbour, and now he is mine. If the hedge was a little lower and less furry I'd be able to see the thatched roof of his cottage from my kitchen window. I get up from the table, slide the glass door and go to the place where he is standing.

'Jink,' he says when I get there, and I say 'Frankie', as if neither of us can speak or understand the other's language, and so have agreed – subliminally, mutually – to begin with a name.

The old man's surprise at seeing me has subsided now.

'Sure didn't I nearly take you for a robber,' he says.

Two and a half years have passed since the funeral queue. I can't say if I look different. People in their twenties tend to change a lot in two and a half years, whereas men, as soon as they summit fifty, remain perpetually the same. Jink looked old then and still looks old now. Hook-nosed and bent-backed, one eye slightly smaller than the other, a jersey displaying the insignia of a university I doubt he was ever a student of. Up close there's a pattern of tiny holes across the part where his belly pulls the cotton taut, as if he's been clawed by a cat, or splashed by hot oil, or stabbed in the gut with a toothpick.

'I'm staying here for a while,' I say. 'I'm sorry, I meant to come down and let you know.' Which I didn't, though now I see this would have been the polite thing to do.

'I've just been coming around every now and again, taking a turn of the place, keeping an eye on it, like,' Jink says.

I find it hard to believe he hasn't seen me before now and I wonder why he wouldn't say so instead of making an effort to appear startled.

'You're very good,' I say. 'We're all very grateful for what you did for the dog, after she died.'

'Ah sure 'twas no bother, no need to be thanking me. He

was a grand old dog. I'd a had him up the house with myself only he wouldn't come, wouldn't step beyond the gate there.'

I smile and hold his asymmetrical eyes and hope he'll speak on, unprompted. I remember the night we buried Joe, how Dad dug a great hole beside the greenhouse and it took the whole family to hoist the dog's flaxen body from the house and down the garden. By the time we got to the hole, our arms were tired. We fumbled him unceremoniously into the ground. It was dark by the time we'd covered it in again. The sun had gone down with the dog.

'He was happy enough just having a stroll on the grass.' Jink nods his head towards the compost heap and I wonder whether he has noted my wilderness.

'Do you've a dog yourself?' I ask.

'I'd a grand old sheepdog there for years but then it up and died like your nan's and 'twas desperate sad. 'Twould put you off getting another one, y'know? Only to see it go like that.' He chuckles again, dispelling the sombre note.

That's nonsense, I think. I want to tell him: you're an old man now, maybe you'll die first. I want to reason that one can't not do things because they might go wrong.

I remember something I heard on the radio.

'Did you know there's this place in London called the Death Café?' I say. 'It's for people to go and drink coffee and talk about their own death, or somebody else's, but the point is to get it off their chest, y'know? The point is that it will stop them from being frightened.'

Jink looks astounded, but after a moment, he seems to realise this is something which happens very far away, conducted by total strangers.

'And you couldn't even get a cup of tea?' he says. 'Fierce funny fellas, them Londoners.'

We gaze across the garden. I wish at least one of us had a dog upon which to focus our idling attention; upon which to pass meaningless comment.

'Your father done a great job on the grass there,' Jink says. 'He's a grand man, your father.'

I um-hum my agreement.

'Sure I'd better be getting on,' he says. 'If there's anything you need doing, call down to me.'

'Thanks for that, thanks a million.' Now his offer makes me remember something.

'JINK!' I say, wishing I had a proper name to call him. 'Actually if you have a minute? There is maybe just the one thing . . .'

The door of my grandmother's shed opens inward and the only unfilled space is that which was cleared by the opening door. Stacks of junk lean against the walls or free-stand on the concrete beyond the walls' reach. Old bedsheets are draped across almost everything. Each sheet is blobbed with different shades of pastel-coloured paint. I'm sure I could match each colour to one of my grandmother's rooms if I tried, that these are the ones she laid down to redecorate when she first moved in. I don't know exactly what manner of junk lies underneath. My father says that once the bunga-low has been sold he'll load up the car trailer with everything still here, drive it to the quarry where he works and dump it into his burning pit. The burning pit in the quarry is the place where our old possessions go to die, everything that can't be stamped down into a wheelie bin. Busted furniture, worn-out boots, electrical appliances, sweat-stained duvets. I've never understood how other people dispose of these things. As a child, I believed every family had their own personal burning pit.

The only things in the shed which haven't been draped by bedsheets are the shelves and their contents. Plant pots, white spirit, spanners, screwdrivers and a rusted handsaw. Beyond the space cleared by the opening door, there's a coal sack, a tower of peat briquettes, and a bicycle. I presume it was my grandmother's, from before she had dogs and had to walk or drive everywhere. The frame is black gloss and hefty. There are reflective cockerels fastened to the spokes. I suddenly remember that they came free inside a packet of Corn Flakes. Do things still come free inside cereal packets? I remember digging my fist down towards the plastic-wrapped toy, smashing an elbow's length of gold flakes in my wake. Or is it a health and safety issue now? Like everything else that used to be fun.

I've told Jink to wait outside because it's too cramped in the shed to admit more than one body at a time. Now I haul out the bicycle, push it over the gravel and present it to him.

Works about Sheds, I test myself: Cornelia Parker, *Cold Dark Matter: An Exploded View*. In 1991 the Banbury Army School of Ammunition agreed to blow up a perfectly ordinary garden shed at the artist's request in order that, after it had been reduced to kindling and splinters, Parker could pick up every piece and suspend them in a maelstrom from a gallery ceiling.

Backlit by a single bulb, this is what the best of art does: uncovers an unrecoverable view of the world.

Now I wonder did Parker reorder the pieces according to how they were originally ordered? I hope so. Because this is something else the best of art does: the seemingly impossible.

For those seven strange days I spent in the famine hospital, all but one of the boxes and bags which arrived back with me went into my father's largest shed and remained packed. For seven days, I used only essentials. I wore the same jeans and jumper, the same socks and vest. I wore pants I'd never worn before, which I found in a drawer in my bedroom I hadn't opened since my teens. I hadn't opened the packet of pants either. They were patterned with sailboats and starfish. They smelled of plastic and mildew.

I knew my bedroom wardrobe was full and I knew I'd never kept clothes inside, but I'd forgotten exactly what else it was I last filled it with and battened the door shut against. On the first day, I dared myself to open the wardrobe. It stuck at first, then jolted free. A gerbil ball fell out and biffed me in the chest. It was the size of a football, but hollow and hard. I remembered how I used to select a gerbil, pick it up by its tail, drop it inside the transparent plastic sphere. Then I'd lock the door and leave the selected gerbil to trundle itself around the playroom carpet, checking back every now and again to dislodge the ball from beneath an armchair. I could see a few bits of ancient poo in there, desiccated, rattling as it hit the floor and rolled across my bedroom.

Inside the wardrobe, I found cages, water bottles, food bowls, exercise wheels, gnaw blocks, baskets, balls with bells inside, tug toys and tiny tunnels, a squeaky lamb chop and a bundle of sawdust. So the last time I opened my wardrobe must have been after the final pet died. Patchie-the-black-and-white-tomcat was thirteen years old when he suffered an aneurysm and plunged from the kitchen window-sill, and then suffered a broken neck. It was during my first year in college and I was riding on the upper deck of a Dublin bus when my mother phoned. It was dark and raining. I was right at the front. Drops flung themselves out of the black and burst against the glass. A little boy across the aisle saw me crying and started to cry too. I caught a train home. By the time I arrived, my mother had laid Patchie out in the shed on a blanket in a cardboard box. KING Cheese & Onion, the box said. It had come from the local shop. I stroked Patchie's black-and-white patches for the final time and thought about how I'd been there to witness his litter being born, thirteen years ago in the same shed in a box just like the one he was about to be buried in. I remembered how that box had been a KING Cheese & Onion one as well.

How I worshipped that cat when I was a child. How cruelly I lost interest as I aged. Not just in the cat, but in all of the pets. As if they were toys, or haircuts.

I threw the ball back into the wardrobe and battened the door shut again.

I forgot about the goldfish. I always forget about the goldfish. Patchie wasn't the last pet because the goldfish is still there on my parents' kitchen countertop, drifting in her murky tank-water, wiggling to the rhythm of the filter's ripples.

She's big as a halibut now, and she carries an ocean's worth of sadness in her watery eyes. The halibut who refuses to die.

Works about Cats, I test myself: Cory Arcangel, *Drei Klavierstücke, op. 11.* 2009. One hundred years earlier, the Austrian composer, Arnold Schoenberg, wrote a significant piece of music by the same name. Significant, because it's considered to be the first atonal composition. Atonal, meaning that it was written in no particular key. I don't know a thing about classical music but my understanding is that this represented a total defection from the traditions of Western harmony; that the original *Drei Klavierstücke, op. 11.* sounded not so much like music as like plunder, like dereliction.

For *Drei Klavierstücke, op. 11.* 2009, Arcangel edited together videos of cats striking piano keys which he found on YouTube. Note by note, they play the piece, gradually, laboriously, in all its discordant glory. When I first learned of Arcangel's work, I immediately wanted to believe that he'd chosen cats for some appropriately profound reason and not just because cats happen to be the species most commonly filmed by their owners while striking piano keys. I read down through every section of Schoenberg's entry on Wikipedia, desperate to discover that he once owned a cat or had a cat-related experience. What I learned instead was that *Drei Klavierstücke, op. 11.* was written in the aftermath of his wife's desertion and subsequent elopement with a young painter and friend of Schoenberg. And so, I must assume: the sound that came out of the music was produced simply by the feeling that went in.

*

Works about Goldfish, I test myself; I think and think. I can't come up with a single one.

Dusk. The burgeoning sunset pink and grey like a weird marsh-mallow. Soon the slugs and bats and black rabbit will be out.

I have a car, what do I want a bicycle for? I'm guessing this is what Jink will think.

The sensation of freewheeling down steep hills, over-taking sparrowhawks, the buzz and bliss of speed. Even though I have a car, I shouldn't really be trusted with horse-power because I get so incredibly bored, forgetting I'm not meant to look at things that aren't the road. Pedestrians, central embankments, the houses of perfect strangers.

Outside the shed by the bench on the gravel, the old man beams at the sight of the knackered bicycle; his old lips crack with the unfamiliar pleasure of being required to be of use. I show him the rusted chain, the seized-up brakes.

'I'd love to get it going again,' I say. 'I found a pump in the house, though I guess the tyres might be punctured. I haven't checked yet because I couldn't get the chain back on anyway.'

Jink kneels down and runs his hands along the brake cable and over the chain-stays like a spiritual healer. As I watch I try to remember how well my grandmother knew him. Was he ever mentioned when she was alive, and why, and in what tone of voice?

I try to remember my grandmother's voice. I can't.

'You need a new chain put on alright, a bitta grease here and there.' He straightens up again, or at least back to as straight as he was in the first place. 'I've some stuff down below in the shed that might do for it. I'll have a look and call back up?'

'Of course,' I say. 'That'd be great.'

'Right so.'

'There's no rush, I can have a go at pumping the tyres up in the meanwhile.'

'Right so.'

I walk with him to the road and notice for the first time that he is terribly slow and drags one of his feet. At the gate I say thank you again and again he says right so. He starts away down the hill as I tie the dog string. He hasn't travelled very far when I call after him, again.

'Jink!' I say. 'Do you remember that tree?'

He is right beside it now. Or rather, right beside the place from where its fallen pieces were removed.

'Aye,' Jink says.

'Do you remember the day it fell?'

'Aye. It blocked the road the same day your nan passed.'

'Did you hear it? Can you remember hearing it fall?'

Jink answers faster and with more certainty than I'd expected.

'No,' he says. 'Didn't hear a thing.'

Now he turns around, and I go back in.

Works about Bicycles, I test myself: Bas Jan Ader, again. *Fall II, Amsterdam*, 1970. The artist cycles purposefully into a canal. A symbolic splash, and the film ends, scarcely twenty seconds long. It doesn't wait for the water to settle. It doesn't wait for the artist to surface.

Bas Jan Ader didn't do happy endings.

*

On day three in the lumpish armchair – somewhere in between balling up hair and failing to absorb Salman Rushdie – I noticed an ornament on one of my shelves, pushed into the corner. A ceramic dolphin cresting the ceramic froth of a ceramic wave. From tail fin through froth to nose-tip, standing no higher than a toothpick, pinned in by cobwebs and cassette tape cases. In a flash I remembered how I used to adjust the position of that dolphin last thing at night, every night, fraction by fraction, sometimes for hours on end. Last thing at night, every night, I adjusted that ornament until it was precisely aligned with an invisible point which I perceived to represent completion, and if I didn't get it absolutely right, then something monstrous would happen to me or someone close to me, or so I believed: some dolphin-induced calamity.

It wasn't just the dolphin. Every time I put on a pair of socks, I had to turn them inside-out and backwards, until the heels bulged around the bridge of each foot, and if the socks managed to twist themselves right again during the course of the day, this meant that my grandmother would be struck down with a kidney stone.

Because most of the calamities I foresaw were bizarrely specific.

I used to believe that if I didn't cross the hall from the bathroom and touch down on the kitchen tiles before the toilet stopped flushing, the cat – my Patchie – would get hit by a car. And every time I ate a banana, I had to ask it a question. It was a trick Mum showed my sister and me when we were kids. We'd ask the banana something with a straightforward yes/no answer, then she'd chop the very tip off with a sharp knife to reveal a black shape that was either a clear Y or an indistinguishable smudge which stood for no. Of course she couldn't possibly have predicted I'd become obsessed with the wisdom of banana skins. Over and over, I turned to them to settle arguments with my conscience; I obeyed the Y or smudge irrespective of sense, of consequence.

A part of me knew my rituals and the things they prophesied were insane, but a larger part of me was too wary to refute them. Doubt beat inside me like a metronome, setting the tempo of my days. *Just in case, just in case, just in case.*

When the ceramic cetacean crested out of the shadows, I realised that these small torments had each gone away, or rather, I had ceased to perform for them, as thoughtlessly as I invented them in the first place. The metronome had faded into a cat arbitrarily striking piano keys; faded away.

I got up from the armchair and approached the dolphin. I stroked the dust from its back and then I flicked it with my index finger, as hard as I could, and it hit the wall and fell down behind the bedstead.

More recently, I watched a TV documentary about people suffering from Obsessive Compulsive Disorder.

'People say "I'm a little bit OCD",' says a young man, an art student, who pushes the button for the pedestrian crossing with his foot, who keeps his credit card wrapped in special plastic, who believes everything – absolutely everything – is capable of contaminating him. 'They're not,' he says. 'They have no idea.'

And I felt like such a failure. I thought: I can't even do mental illness properly.

Works about Goldfish, I remembered one: Marco Evaristti, *Helena*, 2000. An installation in a gallery in Kolding, Denmark. It consisted of ten food blenders, each containing a measure of water and a single goldfish. It presented audience members with an opportunity to press the button and mince the goldfish, or not.

The director of the gallery was sued; on grounds of animal cruelty, I suppose. More than a decade later, Evaristti remade the work for a retrospective, but on this occasion he used already-dead goldfish preserved in clear jelly. Goldfish killed in a private place, by some other means.

I search around online. I want to find out whether anyone pressed the button. Or whether everybody did.

Around the same time I noticed the dolphin ornament, my parents suddenly started to annoy me.

My mother was forever reminding me of things I had not forgotten. 'You'll need a knife to open that,' she said when I reached for a vacuum-pack of coffee in the kitchen cupboard. 'You'll need to empty the strainer,' she said when she found me standing over a sink full of smoggy water doing nothing in particular, just waiting. It was as if I hadn't learned a single thing in the seven years I'd lived independently, as if my mother refused to acknowledge knowledge attained from any source which wasn't her.

I only saw Dad in the evenings. After dinner, he'd go back out to one of his sheds and not reappear until the nine o'clock news. Then he'd take up position in his indelible sofa dip and Mum would entreat me to 'let your father watch what he wants' because of the 'long day' he inflicted upon himself, every day. It didn't matter that he only ever watched the screen with half his concentration; the other half he split between loudly rustling a newspaper and making the occasional, sweeping statement. 'Them feckers up the North are off again,' he'd say, or 'all them Greens should be shot from a height.'

I've often stayed more than a week at home since I moved out, at Christmas and during the summer holidays, but on those occasions I'd always had an independent life to return to: a bedsit, a college course, a job. And for each new place and situation and set of people, I'd made up a new version of myself, a better version in accordance with my changing tastes and values and perspectives. In the famine hospital, there were no people but the people who made me, no option to be anything but my original self. For abridged periods, this was nice; this was reassuring. But faced with an undetermined length of stay and no independence to return to, my sadness lengthened, my temper shortened.

It wasn't my parents who annoyed me; it was the forsaken version of myself I helplessly revert to in their presence; it was the fact that my life was suddenly wide open. I had not yet, at that point, decided whether I wanted to get better or die altogether. I only knew that I couldn't go back to Dublin, and couldn't stay where I was either. That was the point at which I remembered my grandmother's bungalow.

There's a vox-pop item on the radio. The presenter is asking people in the street: what's the first thing you think about when you get up in the morning? They say approximately the things I expect them to say. 'I think how much I love my lovely hubby who is lying beside me,' an old woman says. I can tell she is old from the weak spot in her voice and I wonder what she'll do if her beloved lovely hubby kicks the bucket before she does, as the law of probability dictates. 'I think: oh shit, am I late?' says a man, and laughs. A different man wonders whether the dog has crapped on the kitchen floor again. Someone else thanks God he made it through another night without succumbing to 'the demon drink'. The item closes with a woman who confesses: 'I think about the gap, the huge gap between my life as it is and my life as I would like it to be . . .'

As I screw the compartments of my coffee pot together, I try to remember the first thought I had on waking this morning. As the water boils and begins its upward dispatch through the grounds, it comes to me: the penguin; I was thinking about Herzog's solitary penguin.

As if the radio can read my thoughts, the vox pop is followed by an interview with a keeper at Dingle Oceanworld. She tells the story of Missy and Penelope the penguins, who appear to have paired off and built a nest together in spite of the fact they are sisters. The keeper explains how females will often make 'special friends' but this is the first time she's experienced a same-sex twosome attempting to hump one another. 'They can lay eggs,' she says, 'but the eggs won't be fertilised.' Now the keeper pauses and considers how this might be construed. 'But of course I don't see any reason why it can't be arranged for them to foster a fertilised egg from one of the opposite-sex pairs . . .' she corrects herself.

Jink comes in the afternoon.

Carrying a can of Easy Oil and a bicycle chain which looks brand new. It embarrasses me to think he might have made a special trip to the hardware store in Lisduff and purchased it for me, but he doesn't say so and I don't ask; he'd probably be embarrassed too.

I bring out the bike and show him the pumped-up tyres. They seem to have held their air and must not be punctured after all. He gets down on the gravel and as he tinkers with his canister and chain, I make a pot of tea. Reload the Lowry tray.

Jink sits on the bench with his mug and watches as I ride the healed-and-risen-again bicycle in a loop around the house. I try to ring the bell. It only makes a wheezing sound. More cough than chirp, frog than bird.

My mother phones every other evening. Tonight I tell her about the old man and the bicycle. I try to find out if she knows anything about Jink I don't already, or that I've forgotten.

'Harmless,' she says, 'keeps to himself.'

'He didn't hear the tree either,' I say, 'the morning it fell.'

Now she starts talking about that morning, telling the story of how her mother died.

'Joe would always get up and look to be let out at 6 a.m.,' she says, 'on the button. This was the appointed hour of each day's inaugural piss. And on the morning we were keeping vigil around the bed, as it approached piss o'clock we started watching the dog, knowing that none of us could leave her bedside in order to let him out, not then, when she was so close.'

'But I thought she died earlier,' I interrupt. 'I thought she died in the dark, in the night.'

'No,' Mum says. 'I never told you that. She died just after seven. It was bright and the dog never got up for his piss. He just stayed there with his head rested on the bed-covers. He knew to not pee. He didn't budge.'

'I think I must have read this somewhere . . .' I say '. . . about a chimp who was raised in captivity, right? Well he was given a bundle of photographs, some of chimps and some of humans, and apparently sorted them perfectly into two piles, one human, one chimp, all except for a single one, right? He put the photograph of himself into the human pile.'

'Isn't that fascinating?' Mum says.

She doesn't ask me why I mentioned it. My mother is always able to follow my trail of rationalisation, no matter how weaving. I suppose it must be from her that I inherited the guidelines of my thoughts.

'Where did you hear it again?' she says.

'A book,' I say, 'but a novel. Which I guess means it probably isn't true.'

I get up an hour, two hours, three hours earlier than before. I freewheel down the hill and at the hill's foot, I meet the crossroads – as many alternatives as possible whilst remaining on a man-made path. I pick a path and cycle. Furiously, impetuously. Minuscule flies dash themselves against the bones of my cheeks, the back of my throat.

I find only living creatures; the birds and rabbits at their busiest. I bring my camera, strapped to the back carrier. I am waiting for a photograph. Hoping, without thinking, for something to die.

There came a point at which I understood about my hair: if it wasn't so long and I didn't like it so much then nor would I care whether it was falling out or not; no more would I harbour irrational fears for its safety.

The Navajo Indians believe hair is memory. When a member of the tribe dies, the mourning family cut off their hair and move away to a different settlement. Deserting their ghosts.

So I took my mother's tailor's shears: the largest and sharpest pair of scissors in the house. I stole them from her needlework box. I sat cross-legged on my bedroom carpet with the mirror propped against a cushion on the armchair. And I sawed my hair, lock by lock, from waist up to earlobes.

Then I gathered the sawn hair and carried it downstairs. Stretched out in my arms, at last it looked properly like a mink. Lying limp, cudgelled.

It was early afternoon and my mother was standing at the kitchen countertop preparing my father's lunch.

'Look,' I said, holding out my arms to show her. 'I'm free now.'

Mum was angry that I'd taken her shears without asking.

'It knackers them if you use them on anything that isn't fabric,' she said.

Then she asked me if I wanted to go to a professional to have it tidied up, and offered to pay.

'But I'm not supposed to care what it looks like,' I said: 'that's the point.'

I grew up in a house without beauty products. No lipstick, no lady razors, no aftershave, not even any conditioner. All my life my mother's fingernails have remained un-varnished, her skin un-powdered, her eyelashes un-painted. No varnish or powder or mascara crossed the threshold of the famine hospital until my sister carried it in. But our beatific mother never objected. Instead, countless times over the years, she's helped to bleach, or wrapped a tiny plait in coloured thread, or teased a bead onto a dreadlock. Over the years, my mother has come to think of me as a person who, unlike her, cares about appearances. And this is the only reason she mentioned the professional, and then mentioned it again and again in the following days.

But it was just as I'd hoped. I stopped looking in all the mirrors. I didn't care any more whether my hair fell out. And so every time she offered, I refused.

And my father, of course, he did not even notice.

A wet day. The potholes brimming. The clouds too thick to search the sky for planes, too low to see the fields on either side as I cycle. I hear a lamb cry through the thick white and a second later a fox drops from the hedge onto the road. I squeeze my brakes and the fox takes fright at the shrieking sound they make. He releases the thing he's holding in his jaws and nosedives into the opposite hedge.

Not a lamb: a rat. Already crunched so hard its tongue has been disconnected and pushed forward, out. Teeth hanging from bloody gums, raindrops collecting in its whiskers as I fumble for my camera. A drowned rat, I think. A phrase I've used a thousand flippant times and now here it is in the fur and flesh. I set the camera down on the tarmac in front of the rat's face and push the button. Click. And with the click, at the other end of its body, the rat tail lashes the road, a single, gentle lash. Its head is mangled, how can it possibly still be alive? The rat body's reaction to the rat soul's desertion? No, just a nerve ending, surely.

I turn my bike around, the morning's mission accomplished. Before reaching the next corner, I check to see if the fox has doubled back. But there is only a rook on the telegraph wire.

Watching the rat. Watching me. Watching for the fox.

In the newspaper: an article about a charity that is soliciting donations of real hair to make into wigs for people suffering from cancer.

I go to the drawer where my grandmother used to keep her stationery. I pull out a padded envelope, and in black felt-tip, I write the address provided at the end of the article. Now I fetch my severed locks, because I brought them with me to my grandmother's house, wrapped in kitchen roll. I prise open the sticky strip; it has already been sealed by damp. I slide the hair inside, seal it again.

How badly I want to post it.

Lying in my child-bed in the famine hospital at night, I started to hear the high-pitched screaming of hungry rodents; I started to believe my neglected pets were all in there amongst the junk of my cupboard. Risen from the dead, nibbling the bars of their cages, rolling around in their exercise balls. The uncanny red of their rodent eyes piercing the dark.

Finally I asked Mum if there was any chance I could go and stay in Grannie's bungalow, just for a little while. It was early evening and she was standing at the kitchen countertop where she mostly stands, preparing my father's dinner.

'I could look after it,' I said, 'caretake it, if you will, stop it from falling into disrepair.'

My mother laid down the tiny garlic clove she was

peeling. My mother grows enough tiny garlic bulbs in summer to keep her peeling their tiny cloves all year round. She listened as she peeled and then loaded several cloves into the crusher all at once and said:

'I'll have to ask the sisters, I suppose, but I don't see why they'd mind.'

'I think it will do me good,' I said. 'I think it will make me feel better.'

My mother squeezed the crusher's handle and garlic exploded into the pot. She thought for a moment. She said:

'I might have to set a condition.'

'Okay,' I said, cautiously. 'What?'

She picked up a small knife. A perfectly stab-shaped one.

'I want you to go and see Dr Clancy,' she said. 'I want you to tell her what you tell me. About the way you are feeling, about how often you have to try not to cry.'

And then she scraped the crusher with the knife. A sound like tooth pain. Clearing the vestiges away.

A week since the missing aeroplane went missing. I don't hear about it on the radio any more. Instead I hear that, in England, supermarkets are no longer allowed to display daffodils in the fruit and vegetable section, because there are immigrants who mistake them for something edible. Who chop and cook and eat the stalks, and make themselves terrifically sick.

I try to picture a country where daffodils don't exist. A raked landscape of cement and grout and stone. A place where no food crop but some kind of green stalks with closed buds grow.

*

I think up a pretext for calling down to Jink's cottage; I want to take my own measure of the man by means of the things he owns, the ways in which he chooses to arrange them.

Though I am naturally curious about people, I'm also naturally uneasy when they are right in front of me; when I am right in front of them. Especially with strangers I would like to impress, but even with those I know really well, who are already aware that I am not remotely impressive. I struggle to say aloud the sentences which form inside my head, either clamming up or feverishly rambling. Jess used to try and reassure me that I came across just fine in company: chatty and bright.

But I have never wanted to be perceived as chatty and bright. I have always wanted to be solemn and mysterious.

Walking up the crazy-paved garden path, I notice how the old half-door has been replaced by an alu-clad one-piece, the thatch by polycarbonate. I stop and behold: all the new surfaces pieced together into the old-fashioned shape of a cottage. I ring the electric bell and when Jink answers, I tell him how well his home looks. I rattle off false compliments, and though he feigns modesty, I can see how proud he is.

How strange, that he is old and admires modern, synthetic things. Whereas I am young and admire that which is antiquated, tumbledown, fusty.

Jink invites me in and I'm pleased to find that, beyond the door, it's desperately shabby. There's mould mottling the walls, dust balls on the carpet. There's a vase of plastic carnations on a hall table, a plastic holy water font attached to a crucifix nailed into the plaster. There's a smell of dog even though the dog is dead; or perhaps the smell of dog is Jink.

Now he says how well I'm looking, as though I am a cottage too. I tell him how my looking well must be because of all the bicycling and we laugh, spuriously. He tells me 'Come down to the living room' and, once we arrive, to 'have a sit down there for yourself now'. He clears a pile of magazines off a chair. It's high and hard and straight-backed as though it belongs to the kitchen table. It's impossible to sit comfortably on a straight-backed kitchen chair, feet together, shoulders pulled back and Jink looming over me, pleased but confused.

'I won't keep you,' I say. 'I only wanted to borrow something. I was wondering if you might have a hammer you could lend me, something hefty, like a lump hammer . . .'

The old man listens very closely, as though what I am saying is vastly important. I am about to explain the reason why I covet a small demolition tool, but Jink interrupts.

'I do, I do,' he says, rubbing his palms together. 'I'll just go out to the shed and fetch it now, you'll be alright for a minute?'

So here I am in Jink's living room, left in peace to snoop just like I'd hoped. I look first at the frames on the walls: they are holy pictures without exception. Here's Jesus carrying a lamb across his shoulders, Jesus extending a hand to a fallen woman, Jesus anointing a leper's feet. The ones that aren't holy pictures are quotes from the Bible, printed large. *BELIEVE IN THE LORD JESUS AND YOU WILL BE SAVED* says the closest. I have to get up in order to read the others.

YOUR INIQUITIES HAVE SEPARATED YOU FROM YOUR GOD; YOUR SINS HAVE HIDDEN HIS FACE FROM YOU, SO THAT HE WILL NOT HEAR. As though God listens with his face, like an owl.

When I was a child, I seemed to know rather a lot of old people; I seemed to have reasons to interact with them. Now I remember how most had a wooden crucifix or a water font or a picture of Christ with an electric bulb for a sacred heart stuck to a wall somewhere inside their house, and this was perfectly humdrum. But there's something different about the stuff inside Jink's cottage, something more intense. I reach down to the pile of magazines he moved onto the sofa. I lift the top copy and look. The banner-head is filled by a single word, followed by an exclamation mark: *SAVED!* I lift another and another. They are all the same.

Oh shit, I think. He's been born again.

It's taking Jink a long time to fetch his lump hammer. I'd forgotten how slow he is, how he limps. I should have asked for directions to its place in the shed and offered to fetch it myself. I consider leaving before he comes back. I get up, move towards the door, raise my hand to touch its knob. But suddenly I hear him. Step-drag, step-drag, step-drag, stop. Probably around about the kitchen, followed by silence as he attends to something there. Now the final few step-drags before reaching the living room.

Jink smiles when he sees I'm still on the straight-backed chair where he left me. His lump hammer has a pea-green handle. We talk about hammers for a couple of minutes.

Lumps are designed to shatter, I learn, and scatter the shattered debris like a miniature explosion. They have no claw, like smaller hammers. They don't do precision, only force.

At the first lull, I get up and thank Jink and begin to leave.

'I was just wanting to tell you . . .' He leaps up after me; his tone is urgent. 'I was just hoping it would be alright . . . to tell you about my accident . . . ?'

I stop and nod but don't sit down. I loiter between the dust balls and the mould-mottled walls as he tells me barely anything about the actual accident, only that he experienced an industrial one and spent a long time in hospital afterwards. What he really wants to tell me is that while he was recuperating he found Jesus, or rather, Jesus found him. What he really wants to tell me is that Jesus loves me and is there for me too.

'Have you ever thought about initiating a relationship with Jesus?' Jink says. His voice lowered to a husky whisper, as though the son of God is my secret admirer at the disco and this old man is one of his buddies who has been sent over to ascertain whether or not I reciprocate, to see if I'll agree to a slow dance.

That isn't his word: 'initiating'. That word belongs to some higher-ranking Born Again from whom Jink learned his spiel; one of the ones who must have gone to the hospital to prey upon those lost and bored and injured. Now he asks if it would be okay to give me a leaflet and I see he's been holding it in his hand all along. Small and yellow, stomach-bile yellow. Tightly folded.

*

Lump hammer in one hand, leaflet in the other, before I open the door I see something fixed to the wall above my head, almost as high as the ceiling. It's a cage with a budgie inside. Its feathers are terrifically pale; whiter than I believed a budgie could be. How odd that I haven't noticed it until now. Its talons are wrapped around a bar. It glowers into a tiny mirror. But as I pull the living room door open, the breeze upsets the budgie and he starts to hop. From ornament to ornament, to bar, to ornament again.

There is a bird market. On Peter Street. Every Sunday morning.

I visited it only once, in the earliest days of my years in Dublin. Before I grew accustomed to living in the city and stopped trying to do and find new things. The bird market was set up against the graffitied walls of a dingy alley between a warehouse and an office block in the city centre. It was a would-be artist's dream, but I didn't meet any of my fellow students there. Every stall belonged to a retired bloke from the Liberties and all of the people dawdling and browsing on Peter Street that morning were retired blokes from the Liberties too.

Most of the cages were mounted on the wall and each had bars at the front and a plyboard backdrop painted bright blue, cerulean, a small rectangle of surrogate sky. I can tell a finch from a tit from a sparrow, but that day, I couldn't identify a single bird, even though each was faintly familiar.

Of all the pets we had as children, my mother never allowed us to keep a bird. 'A caged gerbil can still run and jump and dig,' she explained, 'but a caged bird can't still fly.'

In the market I couldn't take my eyes off one cage in particular. It contained what looked like a cross between a blue tit and a canary. I pointed and asked the old man who owned the stall what species it was.

'That's a cross between a blue tit and a canary,' he said.

Then I realised what it was that made the birds seem familiar. Each one was a cross-breed, a mutant. I couldn't name what species they were because they were no species at all.

I can still hear it: the rhythm drummed by the mutant birds' delirious movement. From bar to bar, to floor to bar, to floor to bar to floor.

Works about Birds, I test myself: Jan Dibbets, *Robin Redbreast's Territory Sculpture*, 1969. I should have thought of this one first, after my guardian robin was struck down by a windscreen or wheel or whatever it was. Dibbets's piece wasn't a sculpture in any traditional sense but a series of studies which followed the movements of a robin around a park and were eventually collated, alongside other research, into a book. So where was the art? Dibbets manipulated the bird's movements by means of a number of wooden poles upon which it perched. A free bird, which could have flown anywhere it wished, perched upon anything it chose, and yet, it preferred to establish territory, to remain in that particular area of that particular park, hopping between man-made points.

The art was the manipulation.

*

In the sun room, I unfold the tightly folded leaflet. Smooth its stomach-bile yellow across the Formica. It's been in the pocket of my jeans since I visited Jink. And the lump hammer is still leaning against the kitchen wall on the floor beside the shoehorn. I was too annoyed, at first, to read his leaflet or employ his hardware. When my mother phoned in the evening, I didn't mention the old man or what happened between us. I ignored the bulge in my pocket, the dint in my frying pan, for the frying pan is the reason I needed the lump hammer in the first place, to belt its bottom flat. There is only one and it has come to bother me. The way half my vegetables are always charred, the other half raw. It just isn't the way a frying pan is supposed to work.

The first panel shows a cartoon man in a white robe standing outside a locked gate surrounded by clouds. *IF YOU WERE STANDING AT THE GATE OF HEAVEN AND GOD WERE TO ASK YOU WHY SHOULD HE LET YOU IN*, it says, *WHAT WOULD YOU TELL HIM?* Across the following panels, the cartoon man has a conversation with a speech bubble emanating from between the gate's bars, and in the end, sees the error of his seemingly typical but apparently sinful ways, wakes up to find it was all a dream and rushes off to join the Church of Jesus in God. At the very bottom, in red biro, Jink has written the address and phone number of the Church's closest branch. This must have been what he stopped to do in the kitchen.

I take the pan outside and lay it against the concrete. I fetch the lump hammer and strike it as hard as I can. As if it were a horizontal gong. Over and over, until it is flat again.

Now I feel a little better.

Still I wait until after sunset to go back to Jink's cottage. I lean the lump hammer against the front step. I leave without ringing the bell.

Works about Birds, again, I test myself: *Wheatfield with Crows*, 1890. Popularly believed to be the last painting Vincent van Gogh completed. An angry, churning sky, tall yellow stalks, a grass-green and mud-brown path cutting through the stalks, tapering into the distance; a line made by walking. And a murder of crows between the stalks and sky as though they are departing or arriving or have just been disturbed.

I know Van Gogh killed himself, but I can't remember how. He spent his last summer, Wikipedia says, staying in a single room in a hostel in Auvers-sur-Oise, a commune in the countryside beyond Paris. Near the end of July, he shot himself in a wheat field, Wikipedia says, but he angled the barrel incorrectly, and didn't die at once but struggled, wounded, back to the village. There he was attended by a doctor, and appeared quite well. It took twenty-nine hours for the infected bullet wound to kill Van Gogh, and I cannot help but wonder whether, during that time, he changed his mind.

The artist's last words to his brother, Wikipedia says, were: 'the sadness will last forever.'

It gets hot in between these glass panes when the sun shines. It makes me think it will be warm enough to sit with my book on the patio, to take a chance on my grandmother's rickety lounger.

But it turns freezing with each passing cloud, and the

freezing breeze turns the pages of my book for me, before I am ready.

I hear the drone of an aeroplane as I lounge in the cold. I see its contrails against the blue. The drone seems louder than it should be. Maybe just because I am outside, or maybe because it is lower than usual.

Now I remember the missing aeroplane. I remember it's still missing and could be anywhere, could be here.

I drop from the lounger and climb under the patio table. I lie down and pull my knees up to my chest and place my cheek against the ground.

I smell the grass. I wait for the plane to crash.

4

MOUSE

I always forget that crows have crow babies in the springtime.

In Junior Infants I learned that swallows have swallow babies and blackbirds have blackbird babies and song thrushes have song thrush babies, then we learned their names in Irish. On the classroom nature table there was a cup-sized nest. Encased in moss, lined with fur. And there was a single intact egg inside. Powder blue, no bigger than a boiled sweet. The teacher said it belonged to a *spideog*, a robin, or maybe a *druid*, a starling. But definitely not a crow.

I don't think I've ever known the word for crow in Irish or what colour a crow's egg is. I know they build their nests very high up and out of kindling. I see the odd one flapping low and carrying an ungainly stick in its beak as though the stick's a balance pole and the crow's flying a tightrope. I know they're smart, the family *Corvidae*. I've watched them solving puzzles on YouTube. Smart enough to open mussel shells and crisp packets, to lay their eggs in the safety of the treetops beyond the reach of badgers and foxes and little boys. Of course they must procreate at some point because they are everywhere, all year round. Every time I think I see a better sort of bird to sight – a kestrel, a buzzard, a glossy ibis – it turns out to be just another jackdaw, or magpie, or rook. So why wasn't I taught, in Junior Infants, that crows have crow babies in springtime too, just like the small and beautiful and stupid birds? The ones that insist on using the basin instead of the birdbaths.

When I cycle in the mornings, I make an effort to appreciate even the most ubiquitous bits of nature. Not just the exquisite infestations of white blossom, but the elegance of each black thorn. Not just the petal-packed dandelion buds, but the hollow stalks from which their yellow bursts. Not just the swallows and song thrushes, but every different kind of crow as well.

And I look out for the fox, the fox who dropped me a rat. I'd like him to drop me something I haven't photographed before, preferably exotic. A vole perhaps, a pine marten. I look and look, but there's only the same neighbours passing at the same time in the same cars and jeeps and vans on their way to the same jobs and schools and crèches.

*

When my grandmother first moved here, fifteen years ago, there wasn't any turbine on turbine hill. For miles around, nothing but pasture, pine forest and the occasional un-obtrusive cottage. But since then, vast plots have been levelled and poured with cement. Bizarre dormer bungalows have appeared, with white plaster wings and wide-as-a-wall windows, with turrets.

I watch the neighbours passing. I think: there are only two directions, really. Away from home, and back again, and you cannot, in all sincerity, say that you are going some-where when you return so soon, and play it over again the next day, without ever making any progress.

Works about Progress, I test myself: Vito Acconci, *Step Piece*, 1970. At 8 a.m. every day in Apartment 6B, 102 Christopher Street, New York City, Acconci stepped up and down off an eighteen-inch stool at a rate of thirty steps a minute for as long as was physically possible, and I know these particulars, because at the end of every month Acconci drew up a report delineating the negligible variation between days. Charting, exhaustively, his total lack of headway.

As well as the cars and jeeps and vans, there's a solitary minibus, and every day I seem to manage to meet it at a very narrow part of the road. Then I must stop, dismount, haul my bike into the ditch. As it passes, I see faces against the glass, peering tactlessly out at me. Sometimes a hand appears, waves. But I can never tell which face the hand belongs to, and then the minibus is gone.

*

On the phone I ask my mother about it.

'Do you remember William Shaughnessy who you were in school with?' Mum says. 'It picks him up every weekday morning and brings him to a place up in the city for the day, drops him back again in the evening. A centre for mentally handicapped people, or whatever it is you're supposed to say now. A centre for people with an intellectual disability . . . ?'

'I remember Willie,' I say. 'I didn't think he was that bad.'

'I don't really know,' she says. 'I don't think he'd be capable of holding down a job or anything, and this place just gives him somewhere to be every day.'

Willie and I started school together, but we weren't in the same class for more than a few terms. He repeated Junior Infants three times, at least. I can't remember how far behind he'd fallen by the time I moved on to secondary school. He always seemed to me more shy than stupid. He never played with any one or thing during lunch break, but loitered by the rubbish bin at the very edge of the school yard, wincing whenever anybody approached. I never saw him wear a coat in winter, and on one occasion, as I was depositing orange peel or maybe a chocolate wrapper or maybe a scrunched-up piece of aluminium foil, I noticed that he wasn't wearing a shirt beneath his jumper. The cheap, rough wool was scratching directly against his bare skin.

After the phone call is finished, long into the night, I think about William Shaughnessy; the many years we have been strangers, the essential things we have in common now.

*

I remember a conversation with Ben, during the installation of an exhibition of enormous textile paintings. He and I were both low down in the gallery hierarchy; we often partook of the most tedious tasks. We were refilling old screw holes, waiting for the filler to dry, sanding it impeccably smooth again, and, ultimately, painting the walls a newer, more brilliant shade of white. During one of these stages, we started to discuss how crazy a person is required to be in order to get committed.

The city psychiatric hospital is situated next door to the train station. I've passed it hundreds of times and often stopped to peek through its railings. A grandiose Victorian building surrounded by tall trees and sloping lawns. During the years I rented damp-smelling bedsits or the box rooms of draughty houses shared with people I didn't like, the psychiatric hospital seemed so peaceful and pleasant in comparison. If I lived there, I thought, I wouldn't have to fill out forms or pay bills or do my own washing. I'd be left alone, all day, to draw. As it turned out, Ben sometimes thought the same. 'No one would ever hassle you about getting a proper job and settling down and contributing to society,' he said.

Tedious though they may have been, there was something therapeutic about those gaps between exhibitions. The processes of erasing, repairing, re-whiting. I always liked working in the gallery. I never minded being low down. I didn't want to have to make decisions or shoulder blame.

Works about Fakery, I test myself: The Leeds 13, *Going Places*, 1998. A group of fine art students at the University of Leeds. For their end-of-year project, they presented documentation of a holiday they'd taken to Malaga. Funded, allegedly, by money provided by the university as a project grant. At first, it was the students' audacity that attracted media attention. Later on, the holiday was revealed to be a hoax. The Leeds 13 had faked everything from plane tickets to suntans. They had travelled no further than Scarborough. They had used photographic trickery to make the sun appear yellower, the sky and sea bluer.

More recently, I learned that the psychiatric hospital is located somewhere else in the city altogether. I tried to find out what the pretty building I'd always thought it was actually is, but nobody I asked was able to tell me.

Though I have not met Willie in years, now I know for certain he's a passenger on the minibus I recognise him immediately.

I am standing in the ditch at a narrow stretch of road, holding my bicycle up. Willie sits slightly apart from the others. He raises his head, just for a second, as if he knows. His pale hair is shaved close to the square shape of his skull; his features are chiselled, almost handsome. He looks older than he is, solemn and mysterious.

He does not wave; nobody waves at all.

I watch the rear doors shrink. It's an exceptionally straight stretch of road and so they shrink for a long time. I watch, and instinctively, I pity the passengers of the minibus.

But no. Perhaps witlessness is happiness, and pity an insult; perhaps I am the misfortunate one.

Before the minibus finally reaches the corner and disappears, I raise my right hand, a salute to simplicity.

My mother and I had struck a bargain, and so, after four days in the famine hospital, I made an appointment with the family doctor. But I cheated, telling Dr Clancy's secretary that I'd cut my hand on barbed wire and needed a tetanus shot. She said that Dr Clancy could slot me in early the following morning.

I woke as soon as the first crow croaked. I lay on my back in my child-bed, staring out the Velux, watching daylight grapple through the encrusted bird-crap. I felt deranged, penguin-like. I lay there for as long as I possibly could while still leaving myself enough minutes to rise and dress and drive to the surgery in time for my appointment. Eventually I heaved my legs out from beneath the duvet. I pulled on odd socks and a sweater with a prominent toothpaste blob on the front. Waddling, stumbling, waddling, I left the house, climbed into my car, swung onto the Lisduff road and spontaneously forgot which side to drive on. I coursed along in the middle until a tractor appeared in the distance, trundling towards me on the right. Ah yes, that's it, I thought. The left.

All the way to the surgery, I concentrated on not-crying. My eyes kept blurring, like tiny windscreens in heavy rain, and I blinked and blinked, wiping them clear again with my lids. Dr Clancy's surgery is a unit in a shopping centre. To one side, there's a traditional sweet shop; to the other, there's a dental hygienist. The woman herself is tall and fair and bulky. She has bricklayer's hands and a penchant for small acts of acceptable violence: the stabbing of syringes and the bleeding of fat veins. My father calls her 'Dr Blood'.

'Ah yes,' she said, when I repeated the barbed-wire story. 'Just pop yourself on the table there and roll up your sleeve.'

I tilted my head back and stared at another ceiling. This time, windowless and salmon. I tried to remember the sensation of the last injection I had, to prepare myself. The doctor was at her desk, rummaging loudly through my paperwork.

'I have it here,' she said, 'that you had a tetanus only three years ago.'

I dangled my feet off the edge of the examination table. Kicked them softly in the air, a baby in a highchair. I didn't know what to say.

'They cover you for ten,' she said, 'so there really isn't any need for you to be here today.'

I listened to the shuffle of a new patient in the waiting room. The hoarse squawk of yet another crow from a telephone wire outside the window. I started to sob.

Dr Clancy got up from her desk, gagged me with a man-sized tissue, manoeuvred me to the tableside chair. Then she waited as I sucked and blew, as I tried to explain that I had no explanation, that I just spent rather a lot of time trying not to cry; that trying-not-to-cry had become my normal state.

'Well, well. You're depressed,' she said, flatly. 'It's nothing to be ashamed of; a medical matter of imbalanced chemicals, depleted stores of serotonin, plain and simple. It requires a prescription, that's all.'

She turned back to her desk and took out her notepad and started to scribble. I made a small and stupid sound, some kind of honk-squeak of protest.

'If there was a blood test for it then I'd be able to show you,' she said, without looking up. 'It's a deficiency just the same as iron or thyroxin or whatever. It's basically a happiness deficiency.'

She shook the box of tissues at me. I took a new one and did not say anything. I stared past Dr Clancy at the eye chart and tried very hard to concentrate on singing the short-sighted person's deviant alphabet into the white noise of my head. F P T O Z L P E D U W Q. I wished that my tissue really was the size of a man, that I could cast it over my shoulders and hood my face, like a child in a ghost costume at Halloween. That I could cut two oval holes in front of my eyes and see the world without it seeing me back.

After a couple of minutes, the doctor handed me the prescription and an envelope with the address of the Mental Health Centre, Lisduff Hospital, on it.

'Look, let's get the antidepressants started and if you post this today you should have an appointment for an assessment in a couple of weeks, okay?' she said, and that was that.

I paid her the money my mother had given me, and left.

Works about Happiness, I test myself; but no.

How interesting that I cannot think of one.

For her money, my mother got the reassurance that my appointment had gone fine. I considered telling her that Dr Clancy had diagnosed me as emotionally well, but this would have been a deception too far. So I told her I was being referred to a counsellor in Lisduff Hospital, but withheld that I'd been prescribed antidepressants. I didn't feel good about lying, but I was afraid that if I told her what the doctor actually said, she'd insist I cash the prescription and remain in the famine hospital. So I chose this half-truth instead, and she was cautiously satisfied, as I had calculated, and okayed it with her sisters for me to go and stay in their mother's bungalow, as I had hoped.

I cleared the mess of boxed and bagged belongings from the floor of my father's shed into the boot of my Fiesta, and set off.

I've told my mother countless lies over the years. The past ten in particular. But I'm trying to be done with all that now. And I'm trying, diplomatically, to fix the lies I've already told.

I did not want to post the doctor's letter, but I knew I had to make amends. As for the prescription, my ticket to a softer, slyer sort of sadness, I left it folded inside a slot in my wallet and waited for Dr Clancy to somehow intuit that it was languishing there, and phone me.

But she didn't.

Works about Lying, I test myself: René Magritte, *The Treachery of Images*, 1929. The painting shows a pipe, and beneath it Magritte has painted the words: *Ceci n'est pas une pipe*. Because his image of a pipe is not a pipe, of course, it's a painting. Every painting is just a painting.

*

The last night I spent in my child-bed in the famine hospital, I lay awake, making ceiling studies.

A shadow, a dint, a scuff, a bump, and then, for the first time all week, I noticed the old sticky stars. Almost twenty years ago, I sketchily configured them to resemble the only two constellations I have ever been able to identify: Orion and the Plough. They had long since been painted over, which made them invisible during the day. But in the dark, they persisted in glowing weakly through the Dulux. Then I turned my head a fraction and looked out my skylight at the real stars. There were only two, and at first, I couldn't figure out why they appeared and disappeared as I watched, a jagged kind of twinkling. But after a while I realised, of course, that there must be clouds at night as well. That it must have been because of the night clouds.

Works about Stars, I test myself: William Anastasi, *Constellation Drawings*, a series from the 1960s. He made each by blindfolding himself and playing a specific fugue: Bach's *The Well-Tempered Clavier*. For the duration of the piece, he drew dots on a sheet of paper with black India ink, stopping when the music stopped. He made ninety-six in total, and named them as he named them because, I am guessing, he believed they resembled, more than anything else he could think of, star clusters as viewed from the Earth.

When I first saw some of these drawings in a book, I was struck by the limited amount of space they take up on each sheet of paper. Almost every one occupies just a tiny area. But then, isn't this as it should be? The ink in proportion to the whiteness a reasonably accurate replication of constellations in proportion to the galaxy.

After the minibus is lost from sight, I turn around and start back. At the bottom of the hill, I dismount and hold the handlebars and push. Although it doesn't seem like a windy day, I can see the blades of the turbine spinning. I can hear their soft beat. And so I know it must be windy two hundred feet above my head. It must be a different day up there in the low sky, than down here, on the road.

Works about Wind, again, I test myself: Allora & Calzadilla, *Half Mast / Full Mast*, 2010. A split-channel video upon which a procession of acrobats take turns to hoist themselves up a flagpole. Each body holding itself momentarily perpendicular, in imitation of a flag, flying.

I think it might be about a disputed territory somewhere, a legacy of military occupation.

Or maybe it is just about hauling yourself up again. Holding fast for as long as possible.

The radio usually sits on a shelf in my grandmother's kitchen, above the whistling kettle. But I have made a habit of carrying it with me from socket to socket, adjusting the dial according to room. It has so much dust on it I'm surprised the airwaves are able to penetrate wherever it is.

Now a presenter is interviewing a nun from an enclosed order. Her voice is light and tinkling; her take on the world exhaustively optimistic. She makes me wonder what the submission process is like; how difficult it would be to fabricate a vocation. The faking of a quite different form of craziness.

Now a woman roughly my own age is being interviewed. 'I'm glad,' she says, 'that the stroke happened to me.' She speaks in a faltering, toneless voice. She speaks this way because she is brain-damaged. 'It made me a better person,' she says.

Not a happier person, I think, but better.

The village shop is attached to a bungalow with a glass porch and its own garden gate. On the gate, there's a BEWARE OF DOG sign, and inside the porch there's a life-size model Labrador as if the sign's only a joke. In the shop I buy a bread roll, a banana, a box of juice. I wait several minutes at the counter before the shop woman notices I'm standing there and comes in from the back smelling like cigarette smoke.

'You should have given me a shout!' she says. But then you would have been annoyed, I think, whereas now you are apologetic.

The bread, fruit and juice are my crappy picnic and I am going on a cycle.

I pedal, trying to make it to the top of hills without having to dismount and push. I concentrate on furiously pedalling and try not to think about where I'm heading. After roughly an hour, my old primary school reveals itself.

It seems tinier than I remember. I've already witnessed this shrinkage – of places, objects; even people. Yet the old school seems an extremity, so clownishly dinky. I register the empty car park and drawn blinds of half-term break. I jump the gate and skulk around the doll-sized school, cupping my palms to peer through the classroom windows, the narrow gaps between blind and wall, blind and sill. I reach up and tickle the basketball hoop with my fingertips, stamp down the daisies on the soccer pitch as if I am an exiled giant. Finally, I settle on the bank at the edge of the playground and eat my lunch there, just like I used to. I ask the banana a question even though I don't have a knife with which to neatly slice the butt of its peel for an accurate answer.

'Is William Shaughnessy happy now?' I ask, and have no choice but to bite it.

The mark is somewhere between a Y and an indecipherable smudge. No matter what way I look at it, I can't seem to decide.

I read somewhere that children have an innate flexibility which diminishes as they grow. Slowly, slowly, adulthood deadens us. Muscles are forgotten, slacken, waste. And one day we realise we can no longer hoist ourselves parallel with the ground to fly from flagpoles. Unless we are acrobats, or digitally generated.

Every August when I was a child, a large pile of school copybooks would appear at the end of the supermarket checkouts, and once all the groceries had been blipped through, the cashier would dole out a free share in proportion with my mother's shopping bill. For the four summers before I turned five, I barely noticed the copybooks. School was just some abstract place my sister attended alone. For three years she'd been sent there without me and I'd grown accustomed to being the unchallenged centre of our mother's attention for most of each weekday. It hadn't even occurred to me that I might, some September, be sent off to school as well.

Why do I never use my sister's name? My sister is Jane. Jane is her name.

One day in the August of the year I turned five, after the groceries had been unpacked, Mum took a supermarket copybook for herself, and sat down next to me at the kitchen table, and started dipping in and out of the repurposed margarine carton where Jane and I kept our crayons and colouring pencils and felt-tip pens. All day, she refused to show me what she was drawing, but the next morning, after Jane had been dropped to school, she sat me down at the kitchen table and opened the front cover of her copybook.

'Now it's time for you to begin speaking properly,' my mother said.

Because I didn't speak properly. I jabbered too fast, bleeding words together, mispronouncing the ones that began with an 'F' or 'S'. It wasn't that I had a speech impediment; I just couldn't be bothered. My mother and sister and grandmother were able to understand my jabber perfectly well and it didn't matter to me whether or not anybody else could; there was nobody else with whom I wished to communicate.

But my mother knew I wouldn't get away with this once I was in school. In her copybook she had expertly written and illustrated a series of stories. There were Flower Fairies with names like Stacy and Sammy and Philly and Fanny, and they all lived together in a Fairy Fort in the Forest, eating Strawberries and Sugarcubes, and so on. Sitting at the kitchen table with her copybook open in front of me, I read out every line slowly, clearly. I faultlessly pronounced each word. Then, as soon as we got down from the table, I resumed jabbering exactly as I'd always done.

Works about Intelligibility, I test myself: Gillian Wearing, *10–16*, 1997. A video piece in which adults lip-sync the voices and affect the mannerisms of children. It's a work about the loss of childhood, about the pervasiveness of gibberish, about the insuperable difficulty of articulating what we honestly feel. It's a work about how, even as adults, most of our fears remain so petty. So inadequate.

When I finally started school, I refused to speak at all. Jane must have been so mad at me. On the final evening of my first week, she told our mother: 'Teacher says everybody thinks Frankie's stupid.'

For roughly the first three years, I cried every weekday morning in the car on the drive to school and refused to forgive Mum for making me go. I was so young, and yet, I had already established an unshakeable sense of priority. I knew precisely what things I wanted to do – and when and why – and I was deeply resentful of other people's attempts to enforce structure on my days.

I don't remember the jabbering, nor when I stopped. These are just stories my mother has told me over the years: the legend of how I first struggled with expression. As the years passed, I cried less and less until I didn't cry at all. I fell, carelessly, into the habit of speaking properly. I became one of the regular, unremarkable children. No special abilities or disabilities, neither a bully nor bullied. I made friends and scored decent marks and never once stood alone by the rubbish bin in winter without a coat.

On the cycle home, pedalling up the hills I freewheeled down and freewheeling down the hills I pedalled up, my ears recklessly plugged with headphones, I listen to Cat Stevens on repeat. I listen to 'Wild World' until I cannot stand it any longer and switch to the radio.

A man is talking about how he is saving to purchase his own grave. He confesses he is not terribly old, dying or sick. Nor does he have an exclusive graveyard in mind, a pre-eminent plot. All the same, he is saving to buy his own grave and he talks about this as if it's perfectly reasonable. As if death ought to be life's foremost preoccupation.

What a waste of water and light and oxygen this man is, I think. What a tragedy that so many others who are trying so frantically to continue to live, will die, while he's still saving.

It's dinnertime once I'm back at the base of the hill. I've nearly pushed my bicycle all the way to the top when the upright figure of a man becomes visible. Jink. Standing in the road outside the bungalow's gate, perfectly still with his

big-eye-small-eye fixed on the window of the front bedroom, a vase of hydrangeas on the sill. Those petals used
to be moist and baby blue. Now they're bone dry and
brownish. The curtain is open, the window slightly ajar. Is
Jink watching for me? How miserable he looks.

I drop back and press my bicycle into the ditch and
crouch. I don't want to say hello, nor do I want him to
know that I've seen him and failed to say hello. Only days
ago I wanted to be the old man's friend, and now here I
am, hiding from him.

I think: You might be like that man one day.

I think: Old? Lonely? Born again?

After a couple of moments, Jink turns around and begins,
down the opposite side of the hill, the limping descent to
his cottage. I remain as I am until he is good and gone. Until
there is only the turbine to welcome me home.

My Brazilians are gone now too. The unrestrainable weeds,
the irrepressible lushness, replaces the daffodils and their
pickers, as it replaces the mud, the wood, the brambles.

How long ago was it that packets of pancake batter and
plastic lemons appeared in a display at the front of the posh
supermarket? Shrove Tuesday. Back then I hazily contemplated giving up some vice for Lent, not in the name of
religious observance, but just to practise asserting will-
power. I tried to think of a vice I want to sacrifice, and
ended up reasoning that I need my bad habits, desperately,
just to coax myself through each day.

Now, from the appearance of chocolate rabbits in the

village shop, I determine it must be almost Easter. Mum phones to invite me for dinner. I want to refuse, but I have never missed an Easter Sunday in the famine hospital, and I need my mother to believe I still feel like doing the things I used to. I don't want her to know about how it has become necessary to coax myself.

Works about Deprivation, I test myself: Tehching Hsieh, *One Year Performance*, 1978–79. The artist erected a cell inside his studio and remained there for a year, confined. Every day, he did practically nothing. He did not allow himself a radio or television, or to read or write or talk to the people who came in to see him. An image I find on the internet shows Hsieh in his studio-cell, its spare interior. A sink, a waste-paper bin, a bed, a bare bulb, a very small window. On one wall, the artist has drawn rows of short, upright lines. Each has been crossed off, indicating that some length of time must have passed before this picture was taken. Hsieh sits on the bed dressed in a pale, plain uniform of trousers, shirt. His chin is tipped to the ceiling, his spine supported by pillows. One of the foreground bars intersects his head. But enough of the artist's face is visible to see that Hsieh's eyes are open, that he is not asleep.

Blown, painted, fractured eggs. A sponge cake with primroses glued into the icing. Chickens made out of pipe-cleaners and real one in the oven. Headless, footless, oozing ambrosial juices as it roasts. Easter dinner at my parents' proceeds exactly as it always has. We sit around the kitchen table saying too many meaningless things, eating too much fat and salt and sweet.

I stay until I sense it's acceptable to leave. At the garden gate, I tell Mum I've booked myself in for a haircut next week. I want to say something to give the impression I am okay. As pathetic as a hair appointment is, it's all I can come up with.

Mum crumples a fifty-euro note into my pocket as I leave. Perhaps for the haircut or perhaps because she knows I am the adult-child who always needs and accepts sneakily crumpled fifties.

Alone in the car, I realise I have lied again. I drive back via Lisduff, to make amends. I slow and stop on the main street at the first hairdresser's I see. Park on the double yellow lines, take out my mobile phone, punch in the number on the door and promise myself that next week, I will make a real appointment.

On my grandmother's sofa, I bash the chocolate orange my sister gave me until I feel it loosen, give.

I eat every bit, right down to the chocolate pith: the piece that appears to serve no practical or aesthetic purpose, a formless chocolate mistake between segments.

When the hairdresser asks me what style I would like, I realise I don't know any styles; I've never had one before.

'Just . . . short,' I say.

The floor is tiled and strewn with clippings. The air cloys with chemicals and the sound of taps rushing, dryers roaring, teaspoons tinkling. In spite of the black cloak everybody is obliged to wear, there's something especially naked about people in salons. Hair hosed back, or in a bag, under a hood. Stripped of the frame around their face which defines their face. Here in the hairdresser's, we are all ill-defined, inchoate. We are all but ankles and shoes, wet necks and wet foreheads.

'Would you like a cup of tea or coffee?' the hairdresser says.

Her own style reminds me of a portrait of Marie Antoinette in my Junior Cert history book. A great, stacked mop with waves and rolls and flicks and highlights, tall enough to conceal a whistling kettle. I can't resist staring at it in the mirror. I think about the time it must take to get it positioned in the morning.

'I'm okay, thanks,' I say.

On the ledge below the mirror in front of me, there is a well-thumbed woman's magazine. I pick it up and it falls open at a page bookmarked by a tuft of vibrantly blonde hair. I skim an article about female friendship. About how if females are especially close to their female friends, they menstruate in synchronisation and get fat by osmosis.

'Did you do anything nice over the weekend?' the hairdresser asks.

'Um, not really . . .' I say.

'Are you going anywhere nice on your holidays?' she asks.

'I don't really . . . um, I suppose not . . .' I say.

'Are you sure now you wouldn't like a nice cup of something?' she asks.

I am running out of different ways to phrase refusal. I feel like such a disappointment to my hairdresser.

'Don't you ever get sick of asking all that stuff?' I say, very quietly.

I see, in the mirror, a raised eyebrow. She doesn't reply, keeps snipping.

'Do you get up every morning,' I say, 'and do that to your hair? Do you undo it at night and then, the next morning, do you get up and do it all over again?'

She hesitates, but still says nothing, keeps on cutting. I can see her glowering at the back of my head, the wet gaps where my pallid scalp peeks through. The skin there is so curiously white, a ghost head hidden beneath my hairline.

'Doesn't that leach at your soul?' I whisper. 'Even a little bit, even at all?'

The ability to talk to people: that's the key to the world. It doesn't matter whether you are able to articulate your own thoughts and feelings and meanings or not. What matters is being able to make the noises that encourage others to feel comfortable, and the inquiries which present them with the opportunity to articulate their thoughts and feelings and meanings, the particulars of their existences, their passions, preoccupations, beliefs. If you can talk to other people in this way, you can go – you can get – anywhere in this world, in life.

The hairdresser is finished. Now I see I should have tried to be a bit more specific. What I meant by short was drastically longer than what she meant by short. I stay in my seat as she brushes the clippings into my eyelashes and down my collar, indignantly, and it's a good little piece of revenge for

my conversational insubordination because on the way home
in the car I can feel them disseminating down my shirt.

Scratch, tickle, prickle.

People don't like it when you say real things.

I have not had a dead creature in some time now. I don't
want anything to die, of course; I only want to make good
pictures, a good project. With only a robin, rabbit and rat
it hardly seems like a series yet; I could hardly call it art.

Sometimes, when I'm in the car, I think maybe I should
consider accelerating when I come upon dozy pigeons. Only
once in all my driving years have I created my own piece
of roadkill: it was early autumn, the height of harvest season.
It was pecking spilled grain from the tarmac, and I must
have been concentrating on something else or not concentrating at all, because my unthinking instinct was to
accelerate. I hope that I also unthinkingly assumed the
pigeon would fly away safely before I reached it, that its
untimely death was no more than a tragic miscalculation.
I'd like to believe, as everyone does, that I am innately good;
innately wired to do good.

But maybe I innately wanted to see the pigeon burst
against my windscreen, a miniature piñata.

It left two smears across the glass, one of blood and one
of shit. Or maybe the shit had already been there; maybe it
belonged to some other pigeon and the one I hit merely
smeared it. Afterwards, I refused to clean my car. I left
the blood and shit there as a reminder of my instinctive
brutality, as a caution. And every time I looked through my
windscreen during the weeks before the rain rained the

smears away, I thought about the Second World War; how pigeons used to carry messages across cities and seas and mountains; how they are navigating geniuses whereas I can't even remember what side of the road I'm supposed to keep my car on.

I have decided to lay down some ground rules for my project. I'm not allowed to photograph a creature I kill myself; this would only encourage unnecessary barbarism. Or a creature which is wounded but still alive; this would be unnecessarily irreverent. Such creatures, I decide, will not count.

Tehching Hsieh. Confined to his studio-cell. I think about what he thought about for all those unsleeping hours. I wonder if he managed to teach himself not to think, and if a mind can ever be rehabilitated after an experience like that.

This morning it is May. An item of post arrives, the first to find me since I moved to my grandmother's bungalow. I can see it was originally addressed to the famine hospital and has been forwarded by my mother. It has a Health Board logo on the envelope and so Mum will have guessed what it is, and will soon phone to make sure it has arrived. I open it. Lisduff Mental Health Centre. My assessment is Wednesday, 3 p.m.

The appointment letter throws me off kilter. I lose even the puny, haphazard purpose I normally maintain. The day prostrates itself before me, the same cruel length as it always is. Immoveable, intractable.

I cycle to the shop and buy a bag of popcorn because

even though I haven't eaten popcorn in years, I experience a specific craving. In the evening, I eat toast and Marmite for dinner, and only once my insides are glutted with salt do I desire sweet again. So I finish with feeding and commence to drink. It's too warm for red wine; now I mix gin and tonics instead. I find they make the ordinary sensation of living lighter, less ruffled.

Tonight, the radio interview about the enclosed order of nuns rematerialises in the form of a television documentary. Here are the nuns' faces: uniformly homely, placid. Old-seeming if they are young and young-seeming if they are old. I sit in my spot on the sofa sipping a G&T, my fourth, and expect to agree with their espousal of a simple, spiritual life lived close to nature. But I don't. Instead, it angers me that they attribute credit for everything fine and splendid to God. 'WHY CAN'T YOU LIVE A GOOD LIFE FOR ITS OWN SAKE,' I yell at the telly, 'INSTEAD OF IN DEVOTION TO A MYTHICAL BEING?' I sip my drink. Now one of the nuns describes seeing a salmon jump in a stream, light bouncing from its scales, what beauty.

'That was the magnificence of God,' she says.

'BOLLOCKS TO GOD!' I yell at the telly. 'THAT WAS THE MAGNIFICENCE OF NATURE!'

But the nun cannot hear me, none of the nuns can hear me. And even if they could, they wouldn't listen. They are programmed, incapable of thinking for themselves. I might as well reason with a toaster.

I suddenly remember a Sister of Mercy who, when I was eight, told my class at school that if God called we would have no choice but to answer him, and how, for the next couple of years, I lived in fear of God's call, until I was old enough to realise that I could simply ignore him.

She is still talking, the salmon nun. 'We want to be here in prayer for people,' she says, and I yell at the telly: 'HOW DARE YOU ASSUME TO PRAY FOR ME FROM YOUR DECADENT REFUGE FROM THE WORLD? WITH ITS TALL TREES AND SALMON STREAMS AND SHEEP FLOCKS.' I sip my drink. 'PRAYING IS AS USELESS AS DOING NOTHING AT ALL. PRAY-ING IS WORSE THAN DOING NOTHING AT ALL BECAUSE YOU ARE PRETENDING TO DO SOME-THING. YOU ARE PRETENDING!'

I sip my drink. God is an abdication of personal respon-sibility, I decide. I like this phrasing. I sip my drink. He is an excuse for escaping the hardest parts of life. I sip my drink. My third, my fourth? God is history's most successful scapegoat, I think, and this is good phrasing too. How good I am at phrasing tonight.

When Jane and I were small, our pet cats were semi-wild, and always fluffy. They'd deliver litters in ditches and discard them there too. They'd carry home dead sparrows and shrews instead, lay them out beneficently on the welcome mat. They'd climb the pigeon-post beside our father's vegetable patch and gnaw out the downy meat between bone and bullet and twine. We'd hear our toms yowling in the night, and in the morning the tips of their ears would have gone missing, and sometimes the whole of a cat would go missing for weeks and weeks, and sometimes forever. There was one morning,

I remember, a neighbour found a cat on the road. It had been hit by a car. She knew it belonged to us because it was fluffy, and she phoned the house just as we were about to leave for school. Mum went out with a bin bag and spade and I cried so hard she allowed me to stay at home for the day. This was back when I still cried every school morning and begged her not to make me go; this was the first time she yielded.

But in the end, it only lasted as long as every day lasts. Immoveable, intractable.

Here is another rule for my project: no pets, only wild things. So it can be about the immense poignancy of how, in the course of ordinary life, we only get to look closely at the sublime once it has dropped to the ditch, once the maggots have already arrived at work.

Works about Killing Animals, I test myself: Hermann Nitsch, *Orgien Mysterien Theater* or *Theatre of Orgies and Mysteries* or *Orgy Mystery Theatre*, or something like that. Since 1962, Nitsch has staged it tens of times, over tens of years, with tens of variations. Generally, the performance involves animal sacrifice, the kneading of flesh, the drinking of blood, sex organs, entrails. Generally, it's organised in the style of a pagan ritual, and the general point being made has to do with how mankind has forgotten its inborn proclivity to violence and slaughter. How, instead, we are all too busy washing our hair, our car. Plucking our guitar strings, our eyebrows.

I haven't seen any of the small and beautiful and stupid birds splashing in their basin for a few days now. This morning when I go out for my bicycle, I notice the reason why. There's something floating on the surface of the rainwater. I lean in and my face appears reflected in the green, and square in the green of my face, a mouse.

Floating on its belly, paws and tail extended. Ears inflated, eyes scrunched, nose submerged, whiskers pencilling frail lines through the green, a perfect drawing.

Works about Drowning, I test myself: the most apposite artwork for my mouse, the most exquisitely macabre. *Ophelia* by Sir John Everett Millais, 1851–52. A diaphanous redhead lying in a picturesque pool of water. Half above, half below the surface. Her face is chalk, her petticoats billowing. There are wild flowers strung around her dead wrists and spilling from the pool banks. Bindweed, foxgloves, reeds.

I picture the mouse trying to swim, to scrabble back out. Slipping down the sides, a spider in a bathtub. Beneath the surface, the pads of her paws are pale and bald like the palms of tiny hands. Her back legs are splayed as if she had been kicking at the instant her heart stopped. As if, in the instant which came before the stopping of her heart, she learned to swim, a second too late.

I should have emptied the basin weeks ago, turned it over.

Because this Ophelia mouse is a casualty of my careless-ness, I don't know where she fits within the rules of my project.

I fetch my camera anyway; she makes my most impeccable picture so far.

5

ROOK

The last and only time I was inside Lisduff Hospital was when I was a third-year student in secondary school, and a member of the junior choir. It was Christmas and the choirmaster had escorted us on a trip to the part of the hospital which is a nursing home. He divided us into groups and assigned each group a ward. Then he abandoned us to croon at the old folks. Due to diminished size, we didn't sound very good. The strength of voice in numbers was gone; the good singers no longer plentiful enough to drown out the bad.

None of the patients seemed to care either way. Some of them weren't even conscious.

*

Lisduff Mental Health Centre is located at the very back of the hospital complex. Despite its rearward location, it's an inviting building. Stone-faced, creeping ivy clinging to the coarse bricks. From the outside it looks peaceful, almost appealing, but inside it's too dim, too clean, too clinical.

The receptionist takes my letter and directs me to the empty waiting room. I sit down and open my book at the page I last marked. I read a paragraph, reread the paragraph, re-mark the page and place the book back in my bag. I sit still and worry about bumping into someone I used to know. How could I possibly hide what I'm here for? It's nowhere near Christmas, and I'm all on my own, and I've never been able to sing anyway. I only joined the choir to avoid PE and I was always amongst its weakest members. One of the ones who sheltered in the lee of stronger voices.

From down one of these snaky corridors, behind one of these closed doors, the sound of somebody moaning.

My doctor is a black woman in a purple shirt. I hadn't expected that. Byzantium purple, checked. She gestures for me to sit down in the chair beside her desk. I hand her the letter from Dr Clancy and she hands me a questionnaire on a clipboard, a blue biro. It's eight pages long. I am still ticking and scribbling as she places the letter down and starts to lean back on her chair legs like a jaded child, to fiddle with the personal items on her desk. A hole-punch, a beeswax candle, a photo frame. Her chair legs creak. I am stuck on question number fifteen: *Do you see or hear things that others do not see or hear?* How am I supposed to know what other people see and hear? It's multiple choice so I just tick the one I know I'm supposed to tick. I tick *NO*. I rush to the end, hand the clipboard back to the doctor.

She places it down on the desk between us and raises a new biro, red.

My attention straggles to the wall behind the doctor's head. The light switch, a clock, a painting of a bushy red floret in an ostentatious frame. Hung at her eye level, above my own. A difficult-to-name floret like the one I found pressed inside my grandmother's Lowry book, as if the dry, dead bloom has somehow reconstituted itself and followed me here.

At ten minutes to four, the doctor lowers her biro, glances at her wristwatch, folds the palms of her hands across the belly of her shirt and puffs out her cheeks to stifle a sigh.

'Why would you say you here?'

I try out a few different answers in my head: I'm here because my mother made me come. I'm here because I accidentally cried in the doctor's surgery. I'm here because I thought that attending counselling might mean I won't be forced to take mind-altering drugs. But in the end I don't say any of these things, I say: 'I'm here because . . . I'm just going through a . . . adult life isn't . . . and I'm just . . . a bit . . . you know . . . lost.'

Works about Lostness, I test myself: Stanley Brouwn, *This way brouwn*, 1960–64. A performance and its documentation. The artist would stop people on the street and ask them to draw him a sketch to a particular point. Most of the maps don't have any words, only wiggly lines and circles, Xs and arrows. Perhaps more so than any piece I have ever encountered, *This way brouwn* is an apt and forcible metaphor for living. For how: we start out trying to decipher other people's plans for us, a process which might last decades. For how: throughout all of this time, these decades, we have no choice but to obtusely, optimistically, follow.

On the website for the Richard Saltoun Gallery, I found a page bearing the artist's name, and on it a declaration. 'Since 1972,' it read, 'Brouwn has asked that no biographical information should be given about him and that no works be reproduced.'

How forcible, how apt, I thought, again. That he does not want anyone to know where he eventually ended up.

The doctor doesn't reply. I am strangely pleased with my answer. Yes, I think, that's it. I am not sick, just lost. And lostness is an entirely fixable state. Whereas sickness – mind-sickness in particular – is entirely contrary, intangible, unfixable. And I am calmed by this idea, encouraged. And so I go on.

'There really isn't much wrong with me,' I say, 'it's just that, well, I'm not like other people; I don't want the things they want. And this is not right, I mean, in other people's eyes, and I feel as though they feel they are duty-bound to normalise me, that it isn't okay just to not want the things they want, you know?'

I realise I've been leaning forward. I lean back. 'So it's as if,' I say, 'I'm okay in my own bones, but I know that my bones aren't living up to other people's version of what a life should be, and I feel a little crushed by that, to be honest, a little confused as to how to align the two things: to be an acceptable member of society but to be able to be my own bones both at once.'

A pause which stretches into an uncomfortable silence. Finally, the doctor speaks, says:

'You have job at present?'

'No,' I say. 'I don't have a job.'

'You think you feel better if you have job?'

I lean further back again. I try not to show how disappointed I am by her response.

'Do you think you would feel better if you had a job,' I say, correcting her. 'You're missing the little words that hold it all together.'

Somebody passes through the corridor outside, the hollow clonking of sensible shoes. I realise I can't hear the moaning from inside this room, or maybe the moaning person has gone silent. I notice the compartment beneath the doctor's hole-punch is packed with tiny, multicoloured circles, like old-fashioned confetti, the sort which took too long to disintegrate. So long they had to invent a new sort which disintegrated instantly.

The doctor doesn't take kindly to my correcting her English. She picks up a notepad and starts to write a prescription instead. 'You on dole?' she says.

'No,' I say. 'I have . . . a benefactor.'

'Excuse me?'

When my grandmother knew she was terminally ill, she opened a special bank account and deposited five thousand euro. The money was for Joe, because she did not know then that he would die so shortly after she did. Joe had an extravagant lifestyle, for a dog. Because he was morbidly obese, he ate only specialised low-calorie kibble; because he was ancient, he required pills to keep his heart going, elixirs to soothe his arthritis. By my grandmother's optimistic calculations, five thousand would allow him to outlive her by two years. But he survived only two months, and so the account remained almost untouched. My aunts agreed my mother should have the money, as she was the one who had always dog-sat. And then Mum gave me the account book and said I could use whatever I needed, that Joe always loved me the best anyway.

And this made me feel terrible because I don't think I liked Joe when he was alive. I think I've only convinced myself of this since they both died, because I liked my grandmother so very much. I've blocked out of my mind: the way he smelled of genitalia, the stripe of stained fur below his asshole, and all the times he stuck his slimy muzzle into my crotch and I smacked it away as soon as my grandmother had left the room to refill the teapot.

But I don't tell the doctor any of this, and she doesn't ask me to elaborate. She hands me the slip of paper.

'You present within the bracket of moderate to severe depression,' she says. And suddenly she's using the little words again, as if reciting something learned by heart, as if using someone else's lines, like Jink. 'You require to be started upon a programme of antidepressant medication as soon as possible.'

I hold the slip in my hand; so I am able to do mental illness properly after all.

I say: 'I don't want to take this.'

The doctor drums a finger against the surface of her desk and begins to release a new sigh. A little through the lips, the rest through her nostrils, an exasperated wheeze. 'If you don't take the antidepressants, you won't be eligible for counselling. You will get steadily worse. Every patient I treated who initially attempt to get better without medication come back to me after a couple weeks begging for the drugs.'

'Okay then,' I say. 'I refuse. I refuse to take them.'

The doctor drums a second finger, a third, all of her fingers, puffs a massive sigh out through every orifice of her face at once, tells me: if I haven't already been started on the programme of medication by the time I have my first counselling session, her boss will be very angry with her. 'You want me get in trouble with my boss?' she says.

I laugh. A single, high, completely inappropriate cackle. 'I don't know what they call that in your country,' I say, 'but in my country we call it emotional blackmail.'

I take out my wallet, and from my wallet, the prescription which Dr Clancy gave me. I place both the prescriptions down on the surface of the desk between us. One crumpled, one smooth.

I tear them up and drop the torn pieces into the wastepaper basket on my way out.

Works about Lostness, again, I test myself: Vito Acconci, again, *Following Piece*, 1969. The artist selected strangers on the street at random and pursued them. For as long as he could, for as far as they went. Until they lost him, or he lost them. It's a piece, again, about aimlessness and point-lessness. About how selecting a total stranger to determine your path is every bit as reckless and jeopardous as trusting yourself.

As I leave the centre, my hands are shaking. Sometimes they start to wobble when I haven't eaten enough, but this is different. I place my shaking hands upon the steering wheel and grasp. Start the engine. Pull out of the hospital car park. Indicate in the direction of turbine hill, of home.

My heart is racing, my mind is racing; I race a bus back through Lisduff. As it pulls in at a red pole and I am over-taking, I suddenly remember to wonder what the doctor will tell her boss. Will she say I threw a tantrum, stormed out? Will she write in my file that I made racist remarks, that I am a racist? By the time I reach the back road, I am deeply appalled by the 'your country/my country' remark, and how it came to me so naturally. Would I have been as rude to a white woman? Would I have located some trait other than her foreignness, her imperfect English? Am I a racist after all?

But now I remember: I am mentally ill. Properly, officially. And cannot be held responsible for my actions, my words.

And I wonder – if this is the case – will the centre phone and tell me to come back? Will they send someone, some vehicle, to come and fetch me?

When Jane and I were little kids with semi-wild and fluffy cats, there was this thing we used to do to them, for a joke, a joke only little kids would laugh at. We used to hold them in our laps and stroke their heads, and as we stroked, we'd tug back the skin and fur of their faces, pulling it gently until their eyes went slitty and small, and then we'd cry out: *HING-HONG CHINESE PUSSYCAT!* And giggle uncontrollably.

In the car, through the town and out the other side, onto back roads again, I remember this and think: I am a racist after all.

My heart is racing, my mind. My hands are shaking, my vision. And so, it is strange that, in spite of everything, I notice the rook.

In the ditch at the side of the road. Lying splayed but still. It appears to have been hit by a car which passed before me.

'This is not a good time,' I say aloud. My camera is in the glove compartment but I'm in the worst state of mind to attempt the making of art. And besides, it's raining.

But I don't have a crow and I like crows. Their skulls significantly smaller than that of a dog, a cow, a horse, and yet they are so much smarter – so smart they can solve puzzles on YouTube.

'This is not a good time,' I say. And yet, I indicate.

The air is thick and wet even though I cannot see any individual droplet. They slip from the sky and join with the ground invisibly. They leave their trace in the way the tarmac glistens; in the way the new leaves and grass blades are ruthlessly green. The only surface which seems to hold them is the rook's broken wing. His outstretched feathers are electric black. The drops sit like diamanté just for a second before dripping on, or being replenished and merging into fatter jewels, quivering. Up close, I see that beneath his broken wing, the rook is struggling to draw breath. He opens an eye and his pupil swivels around and registers me. His hindered breathing quickens but he does not caw; he does not shift. He's lying on a shallow heap of straw, the yellow and the black in bold contrast.

I climb back into the driver's seat, but I don't start the engine. I'm not allowed to photograph things which are not dead. And so, I must wait. I take out my book and open it at the page I marked in the hospital waiting room. I stare at a sentence, and then the next, the next, the next. After a quarter of an hour, I get out and check the rook. He is still breathing, slower now. Again I go back to the car. I don't try to read this time. I rest my head against the headrest, sink my eyes shut.

In the farm behind my parents' house, when I was a child, the farmer used to string crows across the entrance of the meal shed, dangle them from the guttering by their throats, a grisly length of bunting. It was much worse than my father and the pigeon-post because the crows were still half alive, at first. Until they accidentally strangled themselves in a frenzy of thwarted flight.

After a while, it starts to get dark. I hadn't realised it was so late, but it's a dull day, of course, more vulnerable to dusk than most. The leaves blur into shadows. A horsebox rumbles past. The silhouette of pricked-up horse ears.

My sleeve is rolled back and I am fingering a scar which runs from my wrist in the direction of my elbow. A rook gave me this scar, years and years ago, one of the farmer's examples. Dad warned me not to interfere with them. So I waited until everybody went out at once. Then I sneaked into the farmyard and approached the meal shed carrying my mother's shears. There were three shot rooks and only one still flapping, and smart as they are, this one could not seem to understand that I was trying to help. It took a swoop and with the sharp tip of its beak split open the skin of the arm I had extended in order to free it. I pulled back, stood shocked. Then ran away and left the rook there – still shot but flapping – still tied. I hid in the bathroom until the bleeding stopped. I bandaged it up before my parents got home, and when my mother noticed the bandage, I told her one of the cats had scratched me.

I fully expected to contract some horrible disease, but I didn't. For at least a day after, I couldn't bring myself to look out my bedroom window and into the farmyard, and when at last I did, I saw my rook was upside down. Wings fallen back and open. But the wind continued to toss it about in simulated flight, and so I could not tell whether it was still alive or not.

The car is warm. The sound of soft rain on tin is soothing. I fall asleep and when I wake again my stomach is grumbling and the light is almost completely lost. No cars pass and every house is far in the distance. My hands have stopped shaking and the rook is dead. Or at least, I tell myself he's dead. In the spool of light cast from my headlamps, I don't look too closely. I'm tired and hungry and don't care about my own rules any more. I just want my picture and to be gone.

I find the rook is still enough; I find his stillness will do for me.

6

FOX

Sometimes when I wake in the morning, I find I don't know how to swallow. It isn't that I am not able; it's that I can't remember how. If someone were to ask, I wouldn't be able to describe it. Even if they were spluttering, gagging, retching, turning purple, on the brink of drowning in a mouthful, nose-full, throat-full of their own spit. Whenever this happens, I am grateful that my body is able to swallow without my brain's authorisation. In the same way as it continues to breathe, whether I will it to or not.

Always when I wake in the morning, I marvel at the autonomy of my anatomy, its belligerence. I take a breath. I swallow. I get up.

*

Works about Getting Up, I test myself: On Kawara, *I Got Up*, 1968–79. Every day the artist sent at least two different postcards to people he knew. All they said was: I GOT UP, and the time he arose at, and the address of the place where he happened to have slept. On Kawara got up at many different times in many different places over the course of the project, which, to my mind, diminishes its potency. Had he left the same bed every morning for eleven years at the same time in the same place and recorded it, this would have affected me more. This would have made it a work about drudgery, about incuriosity. About, again, workaday despair.

I report back to Mum on the phone: 'It went fine. They told me I'm fine. No need for a second appointment.' She replies, hesitantly, that this is great news, that she is glad, but it's hard to tell how she really feels when I cannot see her face. I should have embroidered my report, but I've lost the will. If she does believe me, I know it's only because she desperately wants to.

I tell myself, I promise myself: this is the last time I will lie to my mother.

Downloading the rook's picture, I feel compelled to adulterate the colour balance in Photoshop. I fiddle with the contrast until his feathers are unrealistically blue. Why must I blue my crow, I wonder. What does a blue crow mean?

Another item about brain damage on the radio. A man whose 24-year-old daughter has been a vegetable her entire life. She is 'high-dependency' he calls it, 'non-communicative'.

She isn't able to use her spit like a normal person because she cannot talk, and so she produces too much of it. She drools and drools. He talks about how her days, his days, the whole family's days, play out in a state of 'suspended animation'. I am surprised by the elegance of his phrasing. It makes me wonder if living under tragic circumstances inflects a person's sentences, irresistibly, with poetry. He explains how his daughter will never get better even though she will continue to grow. Until she is old; until she dies of oldness like most people.

Works about Suspended Animation, I test myself: Xu Zhen, *In Just a Blink of an Eye*, 2005–07. Performance or installation? Living sculpture? I've only seen a picture in a book. Several people dotted around a gallery. Frozen into several different inconceivable poses. Falls, faints, flings. The first time I saw the picture, I stared and stared, trying to figure out how such positions could possibly be held – and sustained – without falling. But the caption betrayed the artwork, explained its ambiguity away. Each performer was rigged to a supporting structure beneath their roomy clothing. They were not holding their bodies up; they were allowing their bodies to be held.

Even still, art remains the closest I have ever come to witnessing magic.

I change the radio station. On the new one, they are talking about wildlife. Oh good, I think, this should be devoid of hideous tragedy.

'Merlins,' the expert says, 'are the smallest of the raptors.

They hunt by chasing even smaller birds until they are exhausted. They literally fly their prey to death.'

This morning, I put away my laptop and unpack my box of paint tubes and brushes instead, my strongest sketchbook, the one of cartridge paper pages. At the sun room table, I take up my limp and soft and pliant weaponry.

But I cannot think of any shapes. All I can manage is blobs. Of yellow, red, blue. I squeeze the tubes. Watch the blobs drop, plop, and sit on the cartridge paper, expectantly. I close the sketchbook, press it. The painting paints itself.

A Rorschach blot. Teasing me, testing me.

Well then, what does it resemble?

A butterfly, of course.

I put my paints away, restore my laptop to purpose. On the internet, I look up Rorschach. I find this is exactly what everybody thinks his blots resemble.

Days go by. The Mental Health Centre doesn't phone, or send an emissary to retrieve me. There isn't even a letter of discharge. I am relieved, but also a little taken aback. What if I were ill in a normal kind of way, in the way the doctor wanted me to be when she asked all her standardised questions? A danger to myself. To others.

Tomorrow is my birthday, my twenty-sixth.

The night before almost every one to date, I always expect I will wake up the following morning feeling somehow different, somehow transformed. I never do. I feel exactly the same, and am disappointed. But by the time my birthday comes around again the following year, I've forgotten the unchangedness and disappointment, and the night before, I always expect to feel different all over again.

But twenty-six is not the same as the other birthdays. Twenty-six troubles me more than any of the others since I turned ten.

Ten brought with it the gravity of having existed for an entire decade, the emblematic jump to double figures. I could never be a single, solid digit again. In the final months of being nine, ten seemed to represent the death of childhood.

Did I feel different when I woke up on the morning of my tenth birthday? Did I look around my bedroom and momentously condemn the Monchichi Family and the My Little Ponies? I think it might have been roughly the age at which I stopped playing with monkey-and-horse-shaped toys, and instead, started to join organisations for the prevention of cruelty to real animals.

I flattened an empty box of Shreddies and painted a fox on the unprinted side. The background was brilliant red to represent the ruthless shedding of the fox's blood. The foreground was emblazoned with the words: STOP THE HUNT! Then I propped it in one of the playroom windows which face the front of the famine hospital and the road along which, on the occasional Sunday and bank holiday, the huntsmen and their horses passed. Nobody told me to take it down. Dad was oblivious; Mum didn't want to crush my reactionary spirit. Jane was mortified.

Twenty-six is not significant in a good way. It's the age at which I become irrevocably closer to thirty than twenty. I wake on the morning of my birthday, and think at once: now I know, with certainty, that it's too late to be a genius.

My mother phones. 'HAPPY BIRTHDAY LOVE!' she shouts.

'Oh fuck off, Mum,' I say. And hang up. I feel immediately terrible, but if there's one day in the year I can get away with telling my mother to fuck off, I imagine it must be this one. I get up and dress and fetch my bicycle exactly as I always do. My only chance is to pretend it's a day like any other; to keep the despair only as great as on all the others.

A birthday gift from the capricious countryside: a fox.

I see foxes often, but always they are crossing fallow fields in the distance. Gold flecks on faraway expanses of green. Magnetic to the meandering eye. Enigmatic, unreachable. But not this one. This fox is almost nearby. Sitting still and facing forwards, just like the picture I painted on a placard when I was, roughly, ten.

Only it isn't. There's something not-quite-right about it, something misshapen. I can only see it because I am elevated above the level of the hedge by the height of my bicycle. It glances in and out of sight between the hawthorns and blackthorns as I freewheel, such that I can't figure out exactly what the something strange is. At the next gateway, I squeeze my brakes, stamp my feet down.

It's wearing a tin can on its head. I stare at the tin-can fox. I feel as though I recognise this scene from somewhere. I stare and start to wonder whether or not I should try and help. But the fox doesn't give me a chance to decide. It trots off towards the corner of the field as though it knows exactly where it's going, as though there are eyeholes in its tin can.

As though my birthday fox has built itself a helmet.

My mother arrives in the evening. I hear her Ford Estate climb turbine hill. I know the sound of its engine, like a dog who waits every day for his owner to return home from work. Now the clack and whine of opening gate, the tyre-crunch of gravel. And last, the curious vibration in the living room ceiling triggered by arriving cars. As if there is a seam which runs from the driveway up through the walls of the bungalow, ending in the light fixture.

My mother has never rung this doorbell; when my grand-mother lived here, she'd let herself in through the back, knocking cursorily. 'HALLO MUM!' she'd shout.

'Hallo Mum,' I say as I meet her on the step.

She smiles, worriedly. She is carrying a paper gift bag and a cake. I see that she has made a healthy cake especially: carrots and apples and spelt flour. Sunflower oil instead of butter; maple syrup instead of sugar. I look at the cake in my mother's arms and think: here stands the only person in the whole world who'd go to such trouble for fractious, ungrateful me.

There's only a handful of candles. I count them. 'Eight?' I say. 'Why ever eight?'

'Two and six,' she says, 'for twenty-six.' And we laugh.

I make tea and we sit out in the windy garden, watching the redcurrant bushes jitter. In the gift bag there's a jar of Manuka honey, a book about Navajo Folk Art, a six-pack of Marks & Spencer cotton-rich socks and a birthday card with two fifties pressed inside, crisp this time.

'Why not go for a trip to Dublin?' Mum says, indicating the fifties. 'Buy yourself something nice, catch up with a few friends?'

I get up and give her an awkward hug of thanks. I flick through the pages of my new book. I see her watching the movement of my hands.

'Your fingernails have grown very long,' she says.

I look at them. They have.

'I'm trying to make a tiny bird.' I have to stop myself from saying aloud: Works about Tiny Birds, I test myself. 'There's this artist called Tim Hawkinson,' I explain, ' . . . he made a bird out of fingernail clippings and glue. A bird skeleton, I mean. Like a tiny exhibit in a natural history museum.'

'Bird bones are fine as fingernails,' she replies. Because my mother always understands.

There is one last thing in the gift bag. Overlooked, almost. It's a tiny timber box in the shape of a circle. Mum shows me how the lid works like a hollow screw. Inside, it's half filled with a fine grey powder. Instinctively, I lean in to sniff.

'Ashes,' Mum says. 'A small share of Grannie to keep, if you would like.'

They smell like earth and wind and fire.

'Of course I would,' I say.

Works about Motherhood, I test myself: Mary Kelly, *Post-Partum Document*, 1973–79. For the formative six years of her son's life, the artist documented his development, from feeding regimes to language skills. I look it up. The pictures I find are of charts and diagrams, wool vests and nappy linings mounted in frames. Was it Kelly's first child? I wonder. I flick, flick, flick. Was it a celebration of the astounding initial stage of existence which everyone forgets? Or was it a means by which to salvage some artistic purpose from the chaos and disruption of child-rearing? I see that the project ended around the time the boy started school, the commencement of his sovereign self. And this makes me less curious about the artist than I am about her son. I try to find some reference to what became of him. I can't. And so it's fair to presume, from the age of six to date, he has had a perfectly ordinary life, one in which the internet is not interested.

I place the timber-screw-box on the chest of drawers in my grandmother's bedroom. I shunt it a few inches to the right. Now she is in the place where I last saw her; the exact spot where the dog lay down once we had let him back in after the wake.

The Dublin train is four carriages long with a disconcertingly wide gap between its position on the rails and the station platform. There is a very fat woman a few seats down and across the aisle. She is wearing a lilac blouse and a velvet scrunchie, but it's her fatness which prevails over every other potentially defining feature. Apparently, there's a specific point of fatness beyond which it's virtually impossible to ever reduce back to normal. Apparently, very fat people are only ever able to lose one tenth of their volume, no matter the weight they start at, no matter how hard they try.

The worse things get, the more onerous they are to put right again. But this applies to every aspect of life. How can it be that the very fat people didn't know?

It's Friday. Because Friday is the sort of day upon which you're supposed to do this sort of thing. Go on nice trips, buy nice stuff, catch up with nice friends. As the train sets off, I realise I have positioned myself in the wrong direction. I am facing backward as we move forward. Now I will feel ever-so-slightly disorientated for the entire journey.

Almost as soon as the station is gone, the train enters a long tunnel and I am forced to assess my reflection in the window. I see how I decided upon completely the wrong clothes in spite of all the time I devoted to the decision. Until my reflection vanishes back into the grey cement city, I feel thoroughly awful.

I may have booked my train ticket, saved up the coins I needed to feed the station parking meter and decided, poorly, on what clothes to wear, but I don't want to be here. This trip is nothing but a small concession to my mother. I agreed to go and I must not lie again, but there will be no niceness.

After everything was organised, I thought about the people I know in Dublin. I realised that almost every one is only a casual acquaintance. Ex-housemate, ex-classmate, ex-workmate. I suppose these acquaintanceships might have budded into something had I not been so stubborn about Facebook. Instead, to them, I am but a banal email address, a tiny profile picture of a taxidermy hedgehog. And it would be strange to phone or text and attempt to arrange a meet-up. They might agree but they'd also be surprised, and the meeting itself would be uncomfortable.

Jess and I haven't spoken since the last night in my bedsit, but this is only because I haven't answered my phone on any of the occasions I've seen her name appear on the screen as it is ringing. Each time, I've told myself: don't be stupid, it's Jess, it's only Jess. And once it has stopped ringing, each time I've promised myself I will call back, I have prepared myself for calling back, and once I have failed to call back, I've promised myself I'll answer it the next time.

As for Ben, there was never any question. Whether or not I want to see him, I do not want him to see me.

The cement is gone now. Instead, there are grassy banks, ten feet at least, rising up on either side of the tracks.

Every time I take the train, I buy a coffee from the snack trolley and the trolley attendant asks me the same question: 'sugar or milk?' And I reply: 'no, neither, thanks.' And he or she then presents me with, alongside my coffee, a stirring stick. I probably wouldn't have noticed if it had happened only once, or if it was always the same attendant, but this is not so. Whoever it is, every single time, they make the same mistake.

I've been gathering these sticks for seven years now. I keep them all together in a paper bag. They don't seem to take up much space even though they are too many to keep count. They are a project. I have not yet decided how to display them, but they are a conceptual art project about the way in which people don't listen, don't think.

In the final approach to the city, the banks give way to

the view of people's back gardens, sandpits and decking and trellises, so many trampolines.

Trudging the quays towards the city centre, familiar footpaths channelling familiar streets, flanked by familiar buildings. This woman wheeling a pram of bananas, this halal kebab joint, its conical rotisserie slow-twirling in the window like a gruesome ballerina, a grease-clogged music box. And the same old loose paving slab to shoot rainwater up my trouser leg.

On the main drag, a rip tide of jaywalkers. Outfits and hairdos and polished shoes, as if everybody were on their way to a wedding. I bump and trip between them. My bag strap snags an elbow. I stop a fraction short of colliding with a lamp post. It's as if I cannot steer myself through the city as nimbly as I used to. As if I have lost the knack of this place.

Seven years I lived here. From north side of the miry river to south, box-room to bedsit.

I break away from the faces, head for the quieter streets I know best, take shelter in the covered market. I leaf through a box of vinyls at the record stall, even though I don't own a record player. I spin the jewellery stall's rotating earring rack, hypnotise myself with silver loops and multicoloured beads. In front of a shelf at the second-hand book stall, I stand close to the spines for a long time. I realise I am not able to read words when they are in a vertical line, but I don't turn my head on its side. I don't pick anything up. I move on.

It must be lunchtime. I walk to the salad bar where I always used to go for food. I hold a cardboard tub in one hand and hover the other over the buffet. Each bucket brims with verdant greens and beans, cooled grains and seeds and tofu. I recall the salads I used to choose, and how I'd arrange them in order of preference: my favourite at the bottom so I could save it for last. I lift a plastic scoop. Other customers dodge around and lean across me, just as they used to in the posh supermarket. Come and pay and go while I'm still here. I move from salad to salad, robotically, taking a tiny scoop of each until my tub is filled.

As I circle the park in search of a free bench, I chant the old sentence inside my head: *I want to go home, I want to go home, I want to go home.* But my train is almost the last one of the day; I am a prisoner of this city until evening.

I squat beneath a tree. The wet of the earth soaks through the seat of my trousers, the pigeons start to close in. Unkempt and aggressive. They coo with an exclamation mark, demanding something.

Coo! Coo! Coo! I toss a forkful of quinoa.

Now an old woman in a shabby winter coat with a plastic bag of broken bread shuffles up and my pigeons desert me.

I know I have to do something; something always has to be done. I try to remember my old enthusiasms as if they were an instruction leaflet, a shopping list. I must allow them to lead me around the city, to bridge this gulf between the present and the train.

I spot, coming down the footpath, a girl who was in my class in college. I duck into a shop and pretend to browse party shoes until she has passed. I am heading for an art gallery, but not the one where I used to work. If I go there, the assistant curator will pop out of the office for a chat; the invigilators will ask how I am, what I'm up to. Only Jim-the-security-guard will leave me alone to drift between paintings. Maybe he'll whisper an unobtrusive hello; maybe he'll tell me how his cats are doing.

I picture Jim in his invigilator's chair, rustling his *Daily Mail*. I wonder how his cats are doing. I hope they are okay.

In a different gallery, I ascend a timber staircase up to a concrete floor. It's empty; they are always empty. My footsteps echo. There's a table with some catalogues and a guest book in the corner; there are artworks. Today, I need so badly to be inspired by them, even though I hate that word: inspiration. It crops up in too many advertisements, politicians' speeches, Disney films, its meaning obliterated. I refuse to be 'inspired' in the same insipid way that ad executives and politicians and Hollywood producers suggest I should be. What I need from these works is to be reminded of why I used to care about art — so much that I'd try and make it for myself.

I begin slow-stepping around the concrete. A series of black-and-white photographs. Each printed large as a door. Depicting a dry-stone wall or a section of dry-stone wall or a vista of dry-stone walls. But size is not force. My pace picks up as I weary of walls.

Works about Walls, I test myself: Lin Yilin, *Safely Maneuvering across Lin He Road*, 1995. The artist raised an un-cemented barrier of cavity blocks at the edge of a wide, main, hectic thoroughfare in Guangzhou city. Twelve high, five across. Then, for hours and hours, he moved the wall across the road. Progressing one block at a time. Taking from the back end, building on to the front. Traffic roaring all around as he assembled, dismantled, assembled, dismantled, assembled, dismantled.

I come to a stop in front of the guest book and leaf back through its pages. I see how every visitor who preceded me has noted only their name and the date of their visit. Four pages of people content to register no opinion; nothing more than the fact that they came, and saw. I pick up the guest pen.

Stack up your own damn walls, I write.

Sitting on a tall stool in a café window, looking out at the people who pass. Most of them move in fast, short skips. Some stride or lope, roll as if set on miniature wheels. Often two come up against each other and the weaker-willed walker must dodge to the side and stand a second and watch for their chance to weave back in. We are all an enormous waltz, I think. Our limbs know how to follow the rhythm, like throats to swallow, lungs to breathe. Even though there are no fixed moves, no steps. The waltz is spontaneous, speculative. Some get to join in; others don't. Some end up waltzing against their will.

I suck the lip of my coffee cup, watch the passing people who never appear to see me back; as if the window glass is one-way. Whereas I see everything. The mouth which spits a blob of chewing gum onto the street, the shoe which picks up the blob and carries it away. I finish my coffee. I am spooning up the scum of milk when I see Ben.

He is walking down the opposite side of the street. He is with a girl.

I don't know the girl but she looks like one of the art crowd; she seems faintly familiar. Once they have passed I see how she has her hand rested in the small of Ben's back and he has his in the small of hers. I watch as their crossed arms and resting hands move away down the street. I watch until other members of the crowd waltz in front of them, waltz them away.

Well then, I think.

Well then that's that then, I think. Of course.

When I first started working in the gallery, I was an intern, and there was never very much for me to do. Every couple of hours I asked the curatorial assistant: what now? What now? What now? Ben was an invigilator and so it was acceptable for him to sit at the front desk alongside the radiator in the bookshop all day, leafing through art magazines, doodling in the back pages of the memo book. I was always jealous of the invigilators.

Ben would take at least one cigarette break for every shift he worked. Roughly halfway through, he'd get up and stand at the edge of the partition which separated the bookshop from the office. He'd do a smoking mime and point at the exit; that was my cue to cover for him. I relished the warmth and the magazines, but most of all, the opportunity to sit in Ben's squashed-down coat. It was khaki green and canvas. It smelled like dust and smoke. It had no buttons, and I never asked him why he'd cut them off. I feared there was no reason, that it was an affectation, in which case I preferred not to know.

I covered the front desk on everybody's breaks. I sat in jackets and macs and blazers and furs, but Ben's coat was inviting, and consoling, in a way that nobody else's quite was. Left alone, I'd scrunch down and inhale the lining.

We rarely saw each other outside the walls of the gallery, but inside its glaring white spaces, to exorcise the tedium of the tasks we shared, Ben and I often ended up talking, and time and time again, he would say things that resonated so powerfully with my uneasiness about life, and back there and then, I believed it was an uneasiness unique to us, and that we were somehow bound by it.

But no, now I see I never meant to Ben what Ben meant to me. If there was anything I said which resonated in return, he found a better speech elsewhere. My romance went no further than his coat.

I take out my sketchbook to jot down this small revelation. But now I see a woman in the corner of the café in the corner of my eye. I remember that whenever I linger over coffee, it's in the kind of café where people take out notebooks as they nibble and sip, and gnaw on their pen-lids and gaze around and jot things down, ponderously. They almost always wear the same sort of clothes as me. Eyeliner, slightly weather-beaten faces, and a scarf, always a scarf, even in summer. And now I wonder why the fuck I bother, when there are already so many versions of me, writing down my thoughts.

Is this why Ben's girl was familiar? Because she is me. Only better.

*

I leave the café strangers to their jotting and walk a circuitous route to the gates of the Natural History Museum. I
used to come here as a student, after classes had ended
for the day. When my fellow students were all in the park
sitting around on one kind of grass and smoking another,
I used to come here with my pencil-case and sketchbook
and crouch on these timber boards and draw. I have never
been any good at fur. I just can't figure out a shortcut to
the right effect; I only know how to depict every strand
individually. And so my fur drawings are the ruined pages.
The Tasmanian Devil, a tousled macaque. My successes
are reptiles and fish and birds and skeletons, the elk's antlers,
the toucan's beak, the rhino head with missing horn.
And the conjoined pikes. The larger of which tried to
swallow his slightly smaller compatriot and killed them
both in the attempt.

But today, I don't have the right pencils.

In front of the rumpled hide of a calf elephant, beneath
a reconstructed whale's worth of yellow bones, I wonder
why I came here instead of going to the zoo. It didn't even
occur to me to go to the zoo.

Works about Zoos, I test myself: Peter Friedl, *The Zoo Story*,
2007. A stuffed giraffe. Seams wiggly, posture somewhat
slack; more giant toy than living animal. He was called
Brownie. He was killed in Qalqilya Zoo in the West Bank
in 2002. Startled by the sound of gunfire from the advancing
Israeli army, he ran into a metal pole and struck his head.
He fell down and his heart failed. Because giraffes are not
supposed to lie flat, or so I've always believed, and if they

do, they die. Later on, the local vet, who was also an amateur taxidermist, shoddily stuffed him.

But this is Brownie's story; where is the art? The artist came across the wonky giraffe, identified his force, and placed him in an exhibition.

The art was the appropriation.

I have to run for the train. All the time I spent idling, and now I must run. On James's Street, the length of footpath beneath the dodgy flats, between the Adult Shop and the hospital, some kids launch a water balloon off their balcony. It hits me square on the crown, blasts its icy load across hair, clothes, bag. I curb my reaction. Don't scream, don't stop, don't even look up. It's just a balloon, just water, just strangers. I am still late.

I reach the station just in time, sprinting a final stretch along the platform. I notice a marshmallow lying on the tracks. It looks like a tiny, lost penis. I launch myself into my carriage, triumphing over the departing train. The automatic door closes as I land.

Gradually the body heat of running dwindles, replaced by the chill of my wet clothes and hair. I start to shiver as I sit. There are a couple of students in the booth in front of me. I follow the byways of their conversation, study their reflections in the opposing glass. They are my age. But no, of course. I forget I am twenty-six, closer to thirty, whereas they are each closer to twenty for sure. They talk about the future and the litany of impossible things they expect from it. In American accents even though they are not American, they earnestly tell each other that they are great, that things will turn out great.

Works about Penises, I test myself: Rudolf Schwarzkogler. For years, I believed he had bled to death in the 1960s in the aftermath of a performance piece in which he amputated his own penis, inch by inch. Recently, somebody told me that this is not true; that he died after falling out a window, in a perfectly decent, respectable sort of way.

I sit shivering. I play Björk at full volume. Out the window, there are flat fields and forests, sweeping racecourses, llama farms. All obscured by the almost-dark except for where the rape is flowering. These expanses are not utterly yellow, but faintly glowing. Like the painted-over star stickers on my childhood bedroom ceiling. Water towers, treehouses. A flock of swans in a huddle next to a wide pond, their necks folded down like deckchairs. And I remember walking home through the city from Jess's flat one night, my stomach sodden with cheap wine, and along the canal side in the dark, the city swans all huddled asleep, pretending to be soft, white boulders.

There isn't a single night cloud and the sky above the midlands is flecked with aeroplane lights, as if the whole central clod of the country lies beneath hundreds of parallel flight paths. Every time I spot a blinking set, I think of the missing aeroplane, missing still. On the radio, just yesterday, the newscaster said: beyond all reasonable doubt it crashed; every last passenger dead.

*

Works about Blinking Lights, I test myself: Atsuko Tanaka, *Electric Dress*, 1956. A gown made out of strip lights with a train of wires. A Christmas tree, a wraparound sleigh. Only the artist's hands and face were visible; the rest of Tanaka entombed within clinking, winking, twinkling illuminations.

How easy to be electrocuted. How fine the line between beauty and peril.

I wake. In the bed I wearily selected last night. The one with an almost white duvet cover. A pattern of dandelion seed-heads so faint it might be that the flowers are real and sprouting inside my duvet, pressing ghostlike against the cotton. Björk is all gone now; replaced by the *I want to go home* chant. I push myself up in fury. Because I went away yesterday, and now I'm back, and there are only two directions, remember? I beat about the bedroom in frustration. Up-scuttling my drinking water, clocking a wrist off the door frame, pulling one sock on inside out and failing to find the other.

I am so terrible at socks.

Today it is June. This morning, summer has broken out like a plague. The garden filled with quarrelling butterflies, more on each flower than flowers on each bush. Rorschach blots rising, dipping, gliding, flitting.

Now I'll open every window in the house every morning. Hose the herb garden, tend the strawberry patch. I'll make a home in my routine. And this will be enough for me, and I will be right again.

I pack yesterday away. I flip down the faces in the crowd

of yesterday's street as if they are the tiny plastic panels in a game of *Guess Who?* I place the lid back on the *Guess Who?* box in my brain.

In the bathroom, I floss until my gums bleed. On the mirror, speckled by diluted blood and spit and tartar, there is a brindled slug. I follow his glitter trail down the wall and over the carpet. Out of the bathroom, through the study, all the way to a crack in the sun room door. I follow his trail but I leave the brindled slug where he is. I assume he knows why he wanted to be there, what business he has with the bathroom mirror.

It's a calm day as I am calm, but brighter than me. On with tracksuit, out with bike. Tie the dog string. The real seed-heads of real dandelions lie in drifts along the ditch like frost. They are waiting for a breeze to parachute them on.

And now, a fox. My birthday fox.

Pelt matted with dust, rear quarters indented with the mark of passing tyres. Hind legs twisted, paws flattened into novelty slippers. A gash in its side from which its entrails have slipped, already bloodless and writhing with flies.

And on its head, the tin can. Yellow label of Pedigree Chum, no eyeholes. So the tin-can fox couldn't see where it was going after all, nor what was approaching it.

Maybe it was a whole year ago: the last rambling conversation I had with Ben. In preparation for the arrival of a collection of Japanese tea bowls, I painted the walls of the small exhibition space from brilliant white to grey. But the artist decided that my shade of grey was not warm enough, and Ben, who was taller and faster and neater than me, was called in to repaint.

After I finished my office chores for the day, I went down to the small gallery to see if I could help and to say sorry, for even though it wasn't my fault, I felt responsible, and I cared a lot about what Ben thought of me. I found him with splashes of warm grey on his shoes and trousers, clinging to the strands of his hair like grey glitter. I fetched a second roller and soon I was all warm grey too.

We stayed on after the other staff had left for the day. The exhibition opened the following evening and the walls needed to be dry enough for tea-bowl shelves to be erected in the morning. We painted attentively but talked aimlessly. At some point we stumbled upon the subject of infinity. Perhaps it was the natural response to so much greyness.

'I remember when I first realised about the universe,' Ben said. 'About how it was too vast and complicated for me to contemplate, that I'd never be able to contemplate it. I was just a kid and it scared the crap out of me. Infinity. I couldn't sleep at night.'

I can't remember what I replied, but when I thought about it afterwards, it struck me as a fear which made such perfect sense that I couldn't understand why I had never thought of it, why I hadn't been frightened too. What was it about Ben?

That is it now. Stop now. I will not think of him again.

Works about Blinking Lights, another, I test myself: Felix Gonzalez-Torres, again, *"Untitled"*, 1992. A chain of lightbulbs, bound to one another by extension cord. The artist gave permission for curators to display the piece however they wished. He wanted it to bend and change according to circumstance; the only thing he did not allow was for his bulbs to be renewed during the run of each exhibition.

He wanted them to live out their natural lifespan and die, the way a person does.

I pull the tin can off the fox's head. Restore its handsome face, and take my photograph.

Lying on my back in my wilderness, I kick out my legs and squash down the flowers. I make a crop circle even though the grass isn't a crop and the shape I make is nothing like a circle.

And now a prey bird soars overhead, chasing a sparrow. It is only tiny, and so must be a merlin.

It must be a merlin flying its sparrow to death.

7

FROG

My grandmother's strawberry net is in the shed, balled up. I shake the spiders out. They land, like cats, on their feet, and spread out to find new black crevasses.

I must chase the rabbits and pigeons off the patch before I can lay the net down. I pace, trying to stretch it to cover every corner at once, but it's too skimpy, too balled. Every time I tug it over one part, an opposite part is exposed. Now a summer breeze swishes the leaves, wafts the net up again.

I gather the biggest stones from between the mud and weeds, weight its perimeter. Only now do I notice the slugs, brindled and beige and liquorice black. Trapped beneath my net and already gnawing with their gummy lips on the unripe fruit.

My father would put down pellets. My mother would scatter the rows with crushed eggshell. But I know I will do neither; nothing. I have all the time in the world, and yet, I can't be bothered.

Works about Ineffectuality, I test myself. There is a picture in my head. Of a man in a stream in a row boat. And he is trying the smooth the surface of the water with his oar, to level the ripples. I can't remember the name of the piece, or the artist. Maybe it wasn't even an artwork. Why must I automatically assume that every strange object is a sculpture, that every public display of unorthodox behaviour is an act of performance?

An uneven arrangement of timber planks on the verge of a dual carriageway: art.

The sound of oboes from a decommissioned trawler lilting along a quayside in the dead of night: art.

But what do ordinary people think these things are? Is their world more generally mysterious than mine because they are not so easily able to identify public sculpture?

I think: I can read into anything. I think: I can read into nothing at all.

On the news, a baby girl found abandoned in a rural gateway, freezing, but still breathing. She would not have been discovered at all, the newscaster says, but for a man who pulled his car into the ditch and climbed out at that exact spot, to have a piss. But the radio newscaster doesn't say 'piss'; he says the driving man stopped to 'answer a call of nature'. What a pretty way of describing such a mundane, mandatory bodily function. In the face of immense tragedy – yet again – unexpected poetry.

I wonder if I'd been the one to find the baby in the gateway, would I have presumed she was art? And left her there.

The phone rings at the same time in the evening that my mother usually calls, but tonight it is my sister. I wonder have they consulted on how to cause me the least possible disruption. Because I am the complicated, creative, cantankerous youngest child, my family have always afforded me dispensations from the petty responsibilities of life, from the conventional social graces. Every year, in the days approaching my father's birthday, my mother buys me a card to write, stamps and addresses the envelope, puts it in another stamped and addressed envelope and posts it to me so that I can post it all the way back again, to him. In the days approaching Christmas, she always reminds me of the previous year: 'Jane crocheted you an entire poncho, and all you gave her was a bone-shaped beach stone.'

But nowadays I feel guilty that I am granted the immunity of the artistically gifted, having never actually achieved anything to prove myself worthy.

'I have a favour to ask,' Jane says after a few minutes of chitter. 'I was wondering if you'd mind Graham for me while we're on hols?'

Graham is her guinea pig; I should have guessed. Pet-sitting is the only task anybody ever trusts me with.

'I'll drop him over to Grannie's for you. It's only a week so he won't need to be cleaned out or anything and I already have a bag of carrots and a cabbage.'

'Of course!' I say. 'I'll be glad of the company.' Though really, it's the distraction I'll be glad of. Or maybe they both mean the same thing; maybe loneliness is idleness, nothing more.

There's an almighty bang from the kitchen, followed by the clatter of fractured matter colliding with the lino. I had been preparing dinner when the phone rang. Now I remember I left a porcelain plate to warm on an electric hob.

'What the hell was that?' Jane says.

'Um. A bird-scarer,' I say, not wanting her to know I live so negligently as this.

We arrange a time for her to drop Graham, and after an awkward moment of goodbyes, hang up in unison. We used to share the same bathwater, I think, and yet now, somehow, it has become awkward just to say goodbye.

I take a new plate from the press and place it on the warm hob. Sweep up the shards of the broken one.

I've always been prone to domestic mishap. My fingertips and wrists bear many faint burn-scars from leaning against the rims of hot pans and grabbing hold of baking dishes without oven gloves. In the first house I shared which was not home, I set the grill on fire by neglecting a toasting tray of sunflower seeds. An Australian bodybuilder called Rick, one of my housemates, put it out with a wet tea towel, disabled the alarm, ruffled my hair and called me a 'firebug'. Later on in the year, after Rick moved out, I found a stack of porn magazines underneath his bed, a copy of *For Whom the Bell Tolls* and a billfold of Turkish lire.

The pattern on the broken plate was a row of daisies. How appropriate. The crack has cleanly severed every one of their heads.

A thing I know about flower-heads, even though I've never witnessed it: they shut up their petals and go to sleep at night. So, tonight, I wait until after dark. I go outside and find the poppies and daisies and marigolds have all tucked themselves into ragged buds.

The black garden makes me remember my last night in the city, Jess wobbling away between the street lamps on her bicycle. Those suburbs were old, their front gardens established. There were low trees, hedgerows, shrubbery, and though I cannot distinguish blossoms – cherry from apple from plum – I remember how blossom was every-where that night, hovering over the walls and railings like immobile snow. Why hadn't all the tiny flowers gone to sleep? It was so late. Instead it garlanded the scene as Jess cycled away, as if it knew it was a special occasion.

There's something pleasant about standing here in the dark amongst the trembling greenery and dithering moths. I study the silhouettes of the bushes and trees, the steaming lumps of reclining cows. I look up to the turbine, which doesn't appear to go to sleep as the flower-heads do. It stays up at night, continues to spin. Two white lights glow from the generator at its axis, a set of cat's eyes, but each of the blades remains unlit. They disappear into the night sky and

I only know they're still spinning from the thrum-thrum-thrum. How is it that owls and bats and helicopters don't get cut down by the indiscernible blades and plunge into my straw-berry patch, my wilderness? I know bats have echolocation. They use their extraordinary voice to feel objects through the dark. But I'm not so sure about owls, or helicopters.

It feels as if the cat's eyes are looking down, looking back at me. Watching over the garden, the bungalow. But I've never been good at judging the distance or size or position of objects in the sky. I remember riding in the back of my mother's Ford Estate: I was four, it was night-time, and the moon was full. I was gazing out the window, and I couldn't understand why it moved through the sky at the same pace as the car along the road, why we never managed to leave it behind. 'Drive faster!' I commanded my mother, but refused to tell her why, and so, she didn't.

I turn my attention back to the tucked-up petals.

How do the flowers know it's night-time? Why is the moon everywhere?

On the radio, nobody comes forward to claim the ditch-baby. An engineer talks about how there is a special type of micro-phone which can be slotted into the infrastructure of a building to record the conversation between brick and cement. Cement and glass. Glass and floorboards. An unemployed man talks about how he makes a hobby of posting unusually shaped items to himself, the most-difficult-to-post things he can think of. A loo roll. A dice. A jigsaw puzzle which the postman had to piece together in order to read the address.

*

I can't hear the thrum-thrum-thrum of the turbine from every room inside the bungalow. Instead there's a gentle domestic burring which never goes mute. Today, I try to switch everything off. Even the things that never get switched off: the kettle, the radio, the fridge. I troop from room to room. Sliding my hand behind wardrobes and mattresses, drawing it out dust-covered, sticky. But the burring remains. As if the house is a body working. As if the electricity is stalled in its wires, anxiously jittering, impatient to be allowed back in.

Tonight, a book open on my lap, and an episode of *Dragons' Den*. I half read and half watch until I am only pretending to read.

A would-be entrepreneur wheels out his demonstration trolley, strokes a flip chart with a long stick, passes around a sampling tray. His shoes are sleek and pointy; his shirt is buttoned right up to the collar. He asks the dragons for fifteen thousand euro for ten per cent, thirty thousand euro for fifteen per cent, one hundred thousand euro for fifty per cent.

Another and another. Each accent is different but they all speak with the same rhythm and intonation. Voices and hands shake; necks flush. Those who manage to remain level through to the end are praised for their bearing, the canniness of their money-making ploy.

'THERE'S NO INNOVATION, NO CREATIVITY –' I yell at the set, because I've had a few gins '– IN MONEY BEGETTING MONEY!'

And yet, here they all are, placed upon a television

pedestal. I look back to my book, finger the pages. But who am I pretending for, when no one knows what I am doing at any stage of the day or night anyway?

I am pretending for myself.

I cannot bear to be the kind of person who simply watches television.

I used to get so angry with my father, for the way he is so cynical about everybody on the news, and so quick to insult. But now I am beginning to understand that we all become tyrants beneath our own roof slates. Or maybe we don't; maybe it's just my father and me – the tyrannical gene I inherited from him.

'Life's a bitch and then you die,' he always says.

Works about Television, I test myself: William Anastasi, *Free Will*, 1968. A set on the floor in a corner of a gallery, a video camera sitting on top. The camera is filming the corner obscured by the set, which is being broadcast directly onto the screen. It's a preposterous piece about the preposterousness of what can pass for art. But also, about the preposterousness of television. How it circumscribes our sightlines, restricting us to corners. How it feigns showing us real things, when it is in fact obscuring reality.

Is the title meant to remind us that we are free to look around, to look away?

The entrepreneurs are only about my age, probably even younger, but they don't seem so. Their tailored clothes and unbending hairdos, their clipboards and laser pointers, make them seem like real grown-up people in a way I have never been.

When I was two, or maybe three at most, I was slightly afraid of my father. He left for work early in the morning and returned home late at night, and so I didn't see him very often. At the weekends, he worked shorter hours, and I remember how he used to lean against the kitchen countertop smoking rolled tobacco, using the sink as a gigantic ashtray. He had a single trick to entertain Jane and me: an impression of the Incredible Hulk. He'd button his grubby work shirt right the way up to the collar. Then he'd bellow and squeeze his biceps, puffing out his muscular beer gut. One by one, the buttons would pop off his shirt and skip away across the kitchen floor. Under the table, the washing machine, the fridge; into the spider's black crevasses. It was both wonderful and terrifying.

Now I wonder if maybe my father's Incredible Hulk impression is the reason I've never shown any respect for fully buttoned shirts.

Jane and I had agreed she would come around four. It was me who suggested afternoon: the stage of day I find most difficult to endure. In the morning, I am generally purposeful. In the evening, I am content to be purposeless. It's in the afternoon, every afternoon, I despair.

Today, at five to four, I open the gate and sit down on the front step.

When I was twenty and Jane was twenty-three, she went to study French for a year in Marseilles. Early in the summer, I flew over to visit, and for five nights we slept side by side, feet to face in her stuffy bed in a stuffy dorm of the stuffy student accommodation complex. I'd never bunked with my sister before. She wore earplugs and an eye mask. A pop-sock over her head to flatten her hair. She lay very still with her arms crossed over her chest. She made no sound, and every night I woke up alone and feared she had died, and every morning we woke up together and she asked me what I wanted to do for the day.

During the family dinners which mark Christmas and Easter and birthdays, I automatically compete with my sister, vying for our parents' attention. I disagree, disapprove. Because I am the artistic one, with my artistic temperament. Because there were only ever the two of us, and we were always too similar.

But in the south of France, we ate croissants and walked around Carcassonne and visited Cézanne's house. We'd never spent so much time together so far away from everyone else; I had never been the sole focus of my sister's attention. I loved that trip better than any before or since.

Marseilles smelled like lavender.

Or maybe it was Jane who smelled like lavender, when she lived there. Maybe it was just the glue-stick she rolled onto her temples at night, in the hope that it would make her perpetual headache go away.

Together we carry Graham's hutch from car to house. Now we go back for the paraphernalia. I've cleared a space on the surface of the living room table. I stow the food mix, salt licks and leash underneath, adjust the hutch until it's parallel with the window.

'This way he can look out at the rabbits,' I say. As if the guinea pig had specially requested a view which might allow him to make-believe he is a wild animal.

In the kitchen I put Graham's vegetables in the fridge and fill the kettle for tea. It's strange having my sister here in this house where we have always been equals, and yet now it's somehow my territory and not hers. I must be the one to set the mugs and jug on the Lowry tray, to offer the biscuit box.

'I'm okay for a biscuit,' Jane says — 'any sign of strawberries?'

'There should be ripe ones by now; I haven't checked in a few days. Will we have a look?' I take a bowl from the cupboard and we walk down. Chase the rabbits and pigeons off the patch, peel back the net, pick off the slugs.

'You don't mind a slug's leftovers?'

'Good protein in slug-slime.'

'I hear it tastes like chicken!'

Back in the kitchen, I divide the strawberries into two smaller bowls. 'Apologies,' I say, 'no cream.'

'That's okay. Just like when we were kids, remember?'

My sister and I weren't allowed cream as children. I suppose it had something to do with decadence. Cream was for grown-ups, like olives, like wine, like Viennetta. Fruit was served alongside the sugar bowl. Sitting at the table in the sun room, Jane and I help ourselves to conservative spoonfuls, and after a couple of strawberries, go back for more. The flesh of the fruit is tough and tart, with a hint of chicken-slime.

*

Apart from those four days in Marseilles, there was one other time Jane and I were alone together very far from home. For my twenty-first birthday, I asked Mum and Dad for the price of flights to and from New Delhi, and Jane was gifted the tickets as well. For three weeks in India, she was to be my guardian.

Delhi in June was a kind of hot we could never have imagined. The first day we walked around outside, the painted wooden beads of my necklace melted a rainbow across my chest. We got into an auto-rickshaw to escape the immobile air, but even when it was gusting, the breeze was still hot. So we took a bus into the foothills of the Himalayas, a fourteen-hour trip. Rising up a long and winding forest road, there was a lay-by with a chai stall and a fridge-freezer full of Anglo-chocolate bars. We stood on a roadside in northern India and ate frozen Dairy Milks. In the town there were temples and flagstones painted in red and yellow script and monks who drifted the narrow streets in billowing robes as though being carried by the hairdryer breeze. At first, we adored it. But then, of course, we ate or drank something dubious, and got sick.

I remember lying on a trolley in a corridor of the Tibetan Delek Hospital. Watching a swallow who had built his nest in a pock high up in the shoddily plastered wall. I could hear chanting in the distance, the crashing of enormous cymbals. I watched the swallow flying to and fro, and the great mound of poo on the hospital floor underneath his home, how it grew and grew.

Though our bodies recovered, our spirit of adventure had perished. For what remained of the trip, we went barely anywhere, tried barely anything new. We stayed in the same hotel and ate in the same restaurant and bought the same brand of bottled water from the same tobacco shop. And with every bottle of water, we checked to make sure the seal hadn't been tampered with.

When we returned home from India and people asked what it was like, I would always say: breathtaking.

It's a glarish, muggy day and soon grows stifling inside the sun room. A bell jar, a fish bowl, a cannabis grow house. Jane and I finish our strawberries and carry fresh mugs of tea outside to sit on the bench by the shed.

'I put Graham's leash in,' my sister says, 'if you feel like taking him for a turn around the garden.'

'What if he squirms out and runs away with the rabbits . . . ?'

'Ha! He's not much of a squirmer. He probably won't get beyond the first tasty tuft of grass.'

Jane slides a pair of sunglasses from her breast pocket, rests them between her ears. I always feel like a vagrant alongside my sister. Her hair shiny and straight; her outfit neat and stylish. Whereas most of the clothes I own came from market stalls and fit me ill, and smell like strangers. Even now it is shorn, my hair is knotted, my fingernails bitten, and I usually have at least one toothpaste blob, if not more, down the front of my jumper. White badges of slovenliness.

But I work hard never to think about what I look like.

What I look like will not be left behind; only what I make.

*

Jane finishes her tea, points at the lawn. The dandelions are dead and dying, but the daisies should endure until the end of summer; the clover, too.

'How long's it been now . . .' she says, '. . . since Grannie . . . ?'

'Coming up for three years, believe it or not. I'm still always expecting her to pop out from behind a bush in her gardening duds. There's something weird about this place and stuff still being here, when she isn't . . .'

'I know I don't come very often any more, but still . . .' Jane says, 'I don't know how I'm going to feel when it sells. It'll be a bit like a second death.'

'Like a third death,' I say. 'The dog.'

Jane smiles, but sadly. 'Oh yeah,' she says, 'Joe.' She leans forward on the bench and tugs her sleeve back to reveal her wristwatch. I know she should be leaving, and I cast around for something which might keep her here. To chip away at just a tiny bit more of the endlessness of my afternoon.

'Jane,' I say, 'do you still remember Grannie's voice?'

My sister looks at me. 'Of course I remember. *Oh hello* she'd say, never just *hello*, always *oh hello*, and when she called Joe, she'd do it in threes. *Joe Joe Joe* and then when he didn't come because he never came, she'd call *Joe Joe Joe* again.'

'No, but, I don't mean the things she said. I mean the sound of her voice. Can you still hear it in your head?'

'Yes, of course. Can't you?'

A bird-scarer goes off in the distance. It chooses this precise moment, which is strange, because I've never heard it before.

'No. I don't think I can. I keep trying but it's gone. It's like I didn't think about her enough over the past couple of years, like I was too busy with my own stuff and I didn't think about her enough, and now I really want to remember, it's too late, it's gone.'

My sister looks at me. She lifts her empty mug. She smiles her sad smile. 'I really have to go,' she says.

When I was a child, I was able to wiggle my ears. None of the other kids in my class could do it and so it was my party trick. But throughout secondary school and college, I had no cause to wiggle my ears. And when I remembered and tried again in adult life, I discovered I couldn't do it any more. From the internet, I learned that everybody possesses muscles with the potential to flex the cartilage of each ear. But most people don't use them and so they seize up early in life. If you are able to wiggle your ears, you have to keep doing it, or the ability will eventually be lost.

'Of course,' I say, 'of course you do.'

Stalled at the gate in the aftermath of my sister, I see, down the valley, a man standing on the roof of his bungalow. He seems to be stripping the slates off, exposing a paler layer, the wooden beams beneath. It looks as if he has stopped and is staring up the valley towards the turbine, towards me, but in truth the man is too far away for me to tell which direction he is facing, or if he has a face at all.

I trail my gaze to Jink's cottage. A grey rod of smoke rises from his chimney even though it's a warm day. Muggy, glarish. I wonder why Jink has his fire lit in summer. I wonder if he is spying on me through the trees.

*

Works about Time, I test myself: Christian Marclay, *The Clock*, 2010. A 24-hour film, a collage of extracts from several thousand other films, the complete history of cinema. Each extract represents a minute of the day. Mostly, though not exclusively, by means of a clock face. Wherever the film is screened, it is played in sync with actual time. But I have never seen it for real. Right the way through from beginning to end. I don't imagine many people have. Nevertheless, I love this piece. I love the idea.

I love that an idea can be so powerful it doesn't matter whether I've seen the artwork for real or not.

Graham is roughly the size and shape of a travel pillow, the colour of woodstain. He makes a sound like a squeaky wheelbarrow whenever I pass. This is his way of summoning me for food. But he is already nibbling hay as he squeaks. So I put him into his harness, clip on his flimsy leash, carry him out into the garden for some exercise.

In the garden, I find that Graham does not want to exercise. He wants to eat. Just as Jane predicted, he stops at the first patch of grass and commences to munch.

'But look!' I implore him. 'It's such a great big garden out there!'

But no. Graham is apparently not a Shackleton sort of guinea pig. I watch as he takes down several blades with each swipe of his buck teeth and sucks them through his tiny mouth like green spaghetti. Chews and chews. I watch and try to guess whether he is standing or sitting or lying down. His amorphous belly drags the ground, making it impossible to distinguish between positions. I plonk myself next to Graham and tickle the fur on his back and begin to examine it, strand by strand.

Now, suddenly, I want to draw.

It happens so seldom; I must catch and keep this slender yearning, a rare beetle in a jam-jar trap. But mustering will is not the same as wanting. I lie in the garden and think about all the footsteps between my body on the grass and my pencil-case and notebook on the table in the sun room. All the muscles I'll have to flex and relax to get myself there.

'Make yourself,' I command my muscles. 'Just fucking make yourself.'

I rip up fistfuls of Graham's blades and weeds; he can finish them inside. He keeps chewing as I lift him, continues to chew as we cross the lawn, the kitchen, the hall, to the hutch. He is still chewing when I return from the sun room with my drawing tools, as I spread them out across the table.

How I adored to draw as a child, a teen; all my life before I began to try and shape a career out of it. As soon as I started college, art became a pursuit I might succeed at, and so it followed that I might also fail, that failing was the easiest way. Drawing and making meant more to me than ever before, but I was no longer able to immerse myself in their processes as I once had. Their processes no longer made me solidly happy.

In college, I used to weigh and measure everything in my whole small world for its potential as an art project. In the studio I'd burrow my headphones deep and hew away at whatever I happened to be hewing. The gluing of kindling to plywood, the whittling of old Christmas trees, the scratching of tableaux into eggshells, the carving of balsa birds.

And in the rented beds of rented rooms, I surrounded myself with the pictures and objects I made, and then I made myself up as if I were art too. A ring through my lip, a ring through my nose, a pair of oxblood Doc Martens.

Works about Validation, I test myself: Jennifer Dalton, *What Does an Artist Look Like? (Every Photograph of an Artist to Appear in The New Yorker, 1999–2001)*, 2002.

My held up, held out, hovering pencil reaches, touches, caresses the paper. In the reflection of my grandmother's living room window: no dreads or wraps or rings or Docs. Now I look like a perfectly regular person, definitively not a genius.

It took me five years of formal education to figure out that what I truly wanted to be was an outsider artist, and that it was too late. I'd already put five years into generating a career out of solid happiness. I wanted both and ended up with neither. Like the pike in the museum; the one who died in the process of eating a weaker member of his own kind. And there's no going back – now I'm closer to thirty than twenty – condemned by formal education to rationalise, conceptualise, interpret. Not just think, but rethink. Not just look for meaning, but make meaning all by myself.

Art is the only thing I am able for. And yet here I am. All day every day. Doing nothing. Feeling worse.

*

Tonight, it rains. Soft rain. I dabble in the shallows of sleep, listening to the rain-murmur, the turbine's beat.

I like the night, I try to persuade myself. At night, I am immune. There is no onus to fill hours; nothing I should do or feel like I have to. Night is a nothingness to be savoured.

But on the radio today, an expert talking about how a person needs at least eight hours of unadulterated unconsciousness in every twenty-four so that the brain can adequately repair itself in readiness for the next day. If brains spend the night-time necessarily repairing themselves, this must mean they spend the daytime involuntarily depleting. Now I lie awake and try not to think about this.

When I couldn't sleep as a child, my mother would bring me two cream crackers and a glass of milk, and if that didn't work, she'd tell me it made no difference whether I was actually unconscious or not, so long as I was resting. But now I know this isn't true. Now I know that a tiny piece of my brain is annihilated by each moment of missed sleep, and the only solution is oblivion.

I look down the bed at my protruding foot, the left. Spread my toes, bend them all together. Now I try to bend them one at a time, as if I were playing toe piano. But they won't, I can't. I stick out my other foot, the right, and try the same. Better, but no. I try to remember if I wasn't ever able to play toe piano, or whether I have recently lost the ability, as with my ears. Another small part of me which has seized up, because I neglected to practise.

*

In this morning's paper, a story about a burned-out car meticulously covered in Christmas wrapping paper and abandoned on a beach: art.

A pine forest in the midlands where several tiny houses with tiny timber doors and tiny panes of glass and tiny floral-patterned curtains have been found built into tree trunks: art.

I tear yesterday's guinea pig page from my sketchbook, start to scrumple it.

Stop scrumpling. Unscrumple. Smooth. Start to fold instead.

I bend and tuck the failed fur drawing into a miniature paper hat. I open the door of the hutch and balance it between Graham's satiny ears.

It began like this, with Make & Do. Rockets out of Fairy Liquid bottles and castles out of cereal boxes. Wigs out of shredded newspaper and superhero costumes out of old underwear and glitter-glue and sequins. Make & Do was my introduction to art, and my signature technique has never changed, never matured. All those years in the studio with power saws and welding rods and kilns – all the hours I put down in the hope that time might make up for talent – and still, instinctively, I reach for the sticky-tape and crayons and scissors. I end up with a paper hat, when it should have been a masterpiece.

And the hat falls off the guinea pig, into his bedding straw.

Lying face-up in my wilderness, music pressed as close as possible to my brain, playing at full volume. I skip, skip,

skip. Every song it contains is etiolated. Every singer bored, every note flat; my music a drug to which I've grown resistant.

The sky stopped up with sooty cloud. But after a while, a blue vortex. I watch it creep into my line of vision. Creep across, creep from. I watch for something to tumble out, or to be sucked in. But the vortex passes, the sky restored to soot. I close my eyes.

It's Friday. The Friday of the June bank holiday weekend. The director of the Road Safety Authority comes on the radio to tell me that today is the day of the year upon which more people die in car accidents than on any other, as though if he tells me this I might postpone the car accident I had scheduled; I might remember not to be so common, so vulgar, as to die today.

There's a sign on the gate of the quarry where my father works. ACCIDENTS DON'T HAPPEN BY ACCIDENT, it reads. But of course they do. That's what the word 'accident' means. Who are the people who decide what signs will say and where to put them? And how many times have I obeyed a sign without considering the sign-makers, how they are fallible humans too, doing a job they are humanly bored by, making human mistakes?

Evening settles in, the pigeons and rooks flap off to roost and I have not died on this popular day for dying. I feed Graham when he squeaks. I make him a new paper hat. I go to bed much earlier than usual, eager to have woken up in the morning and survived.

*

Works about Signage, I test myself: Gillian Wearing, *Signs that Say What You Want Them to Say and Not Signs that Say What Someone Else Wants You to Say*, 1992–93. Wearing flagged down strangers on London streets, presented them with a sheet of blank paper, a black pen, and asked them to write something, to hold it up. Then she took a photograph. I HAVE BEEN CERTIFIED AS MILDLY INSANE! reads the sign of a man with a snake tattooed on his face. I'M DESPERATE, reads the sign of a man in a snazzy suit, with soft features and yellow hair thinning at the peak. But my favourite photograph shows an archetypal nerd: bad haircut, thick-rimmed glasses. His sign reads: EVERYTHING IS CONNECTED IN LIFE THE POINT IS TO KNOW IT AND TO UNDERSTAND IT. And he is smiling, as if he does.

The Saturday of the bank holiday weekend. Standing in my grandmother's garden, I can hear, in the distance, my neighbours' mowers and strimmers and power-washers being brought to life. A man passes the gate riding a tractor lawnmower. Driving it along the left side of the road as if it were a vehicle like any other. He stares straight ahead and doesn't see me. As if he still has a very long way to go.

By noon, I can smell other people's freshly cut grass. I can see pollen hanging in the air. Now a small bird shoots a white blot to earth. It lands in the grass, millimetres from the spot where my head lies in the wilderness. On my brow, I feel its microscopic backsplash.

Works about Pollen, I test myself: Wolfgang Laib, but I don't know what the piece was called, or if it even had a name.

I was seven or eight or nine. My mother brought me to a great concrete art gallery in the city. What were we there for? I think perhaps I'd had a hospital appointment. When I was seven or eight or nine, Mum suspected I had a heart defect, which turned out to be only arrhythmia. But I don't remember the hospital that day; I only remember the gallery. How the walls were blank and blinding white. How there was nothing but a rectangle of pollen anywhere on the whole of the vast floor. It was so insubstantial, so easily harmed, and yet, so arresting. It made its patch of floor throb. It made everything else dim and deaden.

The artist gathers the pollen himself. I learned this years later. Where it comes from matters to him, matters to the artwork. Hazelnut trees, wild flowers, pines, or perhaps, all of these mixed together. Collected bloom by bloom, plant by plant, season by season.

The old battery in my mobile phone is so weak I avoid carrying it around, as if physical motion might weaken it even more. This afternoon, from the sunspot on the kitchen windowsill where I leave it to rest and regenerate, it signals the arrival of a text message, a noise which is supposed to mimic a released spring. The message is from Caitriona. Caitriona with whom I used to compare fathers. She is staying at her parents' house for the long weekend, she explains, just down the road from my grand-mother's. She has heard I am around and wonders whether I'd like to have a drink. Maybe tonight, maybe tomorrow.

The last time I saw Caitriona was on a lunch date roughly two years after the end of secondary school. There were

five of us, my old clique of friends, and we met in a restaurant in the city, to compare notes on our differing college
courses, our diverging new directions in life.

The restaurant had slippery leather seats, a single lily in
a glass flute on every table, an enormous painting of a cup-
cake. It was the sort of place I'd never dare walk into alone;
the sort of place in which I'd be more comfortable serving
others than being served. And yet, my old classmates seemed
at ease. Two out of four had acquired incredibly blonde hair
and looked almost exactly the same as each other. Over
seafood salads and transparent soup, they talked about their
science and business degrees, compared the starter salaries
of their respective careers and speculated as to what sort of
a lifestyle might be afforded in accordance with each.

I'd never heard the term 'starter salary' or once considered
how I might earn money after college. Uh-oh, I thought, staring
wistfully into my bowlful of unusual lettuces, contributing only
the odd 'hmm' and 'yeah' and expressionless inquiry. By the
time the lettuces had been taken away, it had dawned on me:
we were no longer the kind of people who would be friends.

And yet, if there had been an exception that afternoon,
it was Caitriona. She still had her original hair. She was
studying geography and cello and Japanese. She and I had
shared the most subjects in school, and I had always
expected Caitriona to be the one to go to art college, and
I was unfairly glad when she didn't. I'd felt then that only
one of us could be the artist.

At lunch that day, I was pleased to be confirmed as the
outsider.

*

I know that if I put off replying to the text message, I will only end up saying no, and I know that I should go; should see someone; should test if normal behaviour might yet be a possibility. For just a few hours.

So I text back; we set a time.

I prepare an early dinner. Carry my bowl of dahl down to the sun room, seat myself between the slimed panes. It's only once I'm chewing and swallowing I start to think: if Caitriona knows I'm back from the city and living in my grandmother's bungalow, then maybe she also knows why. I assume she heard from her mother who heard from my mother, and so what does my mother tell neighbours when they ask after her children? I try to imagine what it might be like to talk to her if I wasn't me. Would she state outright that her youngest is having a breakdown, or would she have some cryptic way of putting it? Frankie is unwell. Frankie is struggling. Frankie is a little out of sorts. Would she go so far as to solicit Caitriona's mother to solicit Caitriona to text me, to suggest a meet-up to check if I'm okay?

If this had occurred to me earlier, I'd never have replied. I curse myself for being rash; I try to think up last-minute excuses.

Caitriona is still not blonde; this is a relief. We hug, limply, order half-pints of lager and squabble over who will pay, as if we are our mothers. Finally we pay separately, and settle onto stools in the corner of the bar, as if we are our fathers instead.

Over the first drink we talk about her life and just a little about mine. I steer the conversation around me as tactfully as I can. With the second, we move on to people we were in school with and what they are doing now. I don't know anyone any more, but I'm happy to receive Caitriona's gossip; I'm having a nice time. She fills me in on who has married, reproduced, signed up to a forty-year mortgage. With the third drink she reveals who is cheating on who and who has had a clandestine boob job and whose new baby is ugly as a baked potato. With the fourth, I wonder aloud who has had a nervous breakdown.

'What do you mean, exactly?' Caitriona says. Her tone is concerned.

I lose my nerve, mumble excuses, make a beeline for the toilets.

On the seat, I stare at the timber slats of the cubicle door. The small bolt and the coat hook, the blades of light which splinter through and stripe my white legs.

I think: well then it must just be me.

Caitriona and I do not have very big tanks, as my father would say. My father measures a person by the size of their tank. In the aftermath of the fourth drink, we are both pissed. The stone bricks of the gable wall blear together into scabrous brown. The bar lights throb and glister, seeming suddenly terribly far away. Caitriona's bottom lip goes wobbly and she starts to tell me how, all her life, everything she's ever been good at, I've been good at it too – I've been better.

Through the drunkenness, I register her meaning. Now

I remember how, back when we still shared subjects, Caitriona was the first person who made me consider the possibility that my dreams were not singular, not even unusual; that there were countless other people out there who wanted precisely the same as I did, with equal force, and they put equal effort into achieving it. And they stood equal chance. In the years since, I've met ten more Caitrionas, and understood that for every one I meet, there are ten more I never even will.

But I had not once considered that I might also be somebody else's better version of themselves. I try to tell Caitriona I know what this feels like; I understand. But my words blear together like the stone bricks, and maybe this is for the best. Maybe it would not be particularly helpful for her to learn that there are many much better versions even than me. That the world is rifting at the seams with Caitrionas and Frankies. They are jotting notes in cafés and making beautiful speeches and wearing summer scarves.

Our farewell hug is warmer than the greeting one. I walk a hundred metres before remembering I brought my bicycle. I go back and find it and start again in the direction of home, careening through the dark, convinced my head is disconnected from my shoulders, paragliding alone over the hawthorns and hedgetops to the base of turbine hill. Now I crash spectacularly into the ditch.

I don't think I'm hurt. I check for my head. My body is too flaccid. I didn't brace it in preparation for impact and so my four lagers have saved me from serious injury. Only a gash in my leg; the skin split even though my trousers aren't. How curious.

I get up and push.

I remember a nature documentary: a beetle who traipsed around all night every night searching for a dead thing to eat. Because he could not kill for himself, the beetle. And he could not eat things that were still alive.

In my grandmother's kitchen, in the dark, I press the light switch. But no light comes on. Have I somehow managed to do it wrong? Is there some trick to working light switches which, in my drunkenness, I have forgotten? I press again and again. Nothing. So the bulb must have expired, though there was no clink and blink before the black. But then I am drunk; my perceptions jumbled. Maybe I just missed the clink-blink.

Sometimes things happen that give me cause to believe I no longer exist. Car park barriers which do not lift when I drive towards them, automatic doors which do not open automatically as I approach. Maybe that's all this is.

I stumble across the lino by the light of the screen of my weakly phone. I pat the wall until I find the hall switch. I press. Nothing. How can it be that both bulbs have expired at once? Maybe it's a power cut, but there have been no storms and no notice from the County Council. I stumble on through my grandmother's rooms, pawing switches. By the time I reach the end of the hall, I've established that every light along the east-facing side of the bungalow is out, whereas on the west, they are all still working.

But this is even more confusing. Now I'm thinking about who might know I'm staying here alone and went out drinking this evening, and be lying in one of the darkened rooms in wait. Jink? The man on the tractor lawnmower who drove past my gate this morning for no obvious reason? The man who stood on his roof for a whole day last week? Glancing up the hill, pretending to strip slates.

Suddenly sober, I do what I always do in times of catastrophe. I phone my mother.

Works about Light, or maybe Dark? I test myself: Martin Creed, *Work No. 227: The lights going on and off*, 2000. Lots of people were, again, so angry about this piece. Though I have not experienced it in a sterile gallery space, I have recreated it in my own tightly furnished, highly coloured, dust-coated rooms. It is, primarily, boring. And yet, like *The Clock*, like so many artworks, I love what it might mean. The light and dark in everything, the reaction to every action, the prodigious unpredictability of life. And I love the possibility – the audacity – that it might mean nothing at all.

My mother's voice is a mix of grogginess and alarm.

'I'm so sorry for calling so late,' I jabber, 'it's not an emergency or anything, I'm fine. It's just the lights, half the lights in the house have gone out. I don't understand why they would do that, why would they do that?'

I hear the rustle and creak of my father waking beside

her. Twisting around, propping himself up on the mattress springs. His voice is saying my name, asking it: 'Frankie? Is it Frankie? What time is it? What's the matter?'

My mother, calmer now, tells him what I have told her, asks him why. 'It's just the circuit,' I hear my father say. 'A switch will have tripped the whole circuit. It just needs to be stuck back up again.' Now my mother repeats it into the receiver, and after I've heard it for the second time, I'm calmer too. I start to clarify the details. 'Stick what back up? Where? Might I electrocute myself?'

How easy to be electrocuted. How fine the line between mundanity and peril.

I carry my phone back to the kitchen, open a cupboard I've never opened before. A cupboard which holds nothing, but displays two rows of electrical switches, jam labels bearing the names of rooms. A whole row has snapped down. I use the handle of a wooden spoon to snap them up again. I walk from room to room along the eastern side, watching the lights wink back to life. I thank my mother, apologise. I tell her I'm alright now; that I'll be alright.

'Frankie,' Mum says, 'have you been drinking?'

Now I am ambushed by a yawning fit. I know this is a sure sign that I will soon begin to faint and puke. Tonight, I am grateful to my body for obliging to wait until I am back beneath my grandmother's roof, until the crisis of the failed circuit is over and done with. I yawn first on the phone, yawn again as I am standing at the kitchen counter waiting for a slice of bread to pop up, yawn again as it pops up, transformed into toast. I have mistaken the queasy feeling in my gut for hunger. As soon as I bite into the toast, I know it's the opposite, that instead of desiring to consume substances, my gut was preparing to expel them. Now a different set of lights – the ones inside my head – begin to go out, as if someone is filling a vial of ink behind each eyeball. I lean against the fridge, slither to the floor. A selection of alphabet magnets fall down after me. I lay my head against the lino and raise my feet to try and swoosh some blood back to my heart. I forget that I'm still holding the toast. I clutch it into crumbs.

As soon as I can see again, I check what the letters are. A, P, C, R, T. Spelling nothing in particular, or at least, nothing meaningful. I crawl from the kitchen and along the hall in the direction of the bathroom. It seems as if a lot of time has passed before I feel the bathroom carpet beneath my grappling fingers. I collapse upon its clammy warmth.

A wave of relief, followed seconds later by a wave of puking.

For the rest of the night, I alternate between cowering over the toilet bowl and lying prone beneath it. Each bout of vomit comes as a relief, but almost as soon as it has ended, the dreadful nausea begins to accrete inside me again. I try lying in different positions, hauling myself up to the tap and gulping down mouthfuls of cold water. I try distracting myself by studying the details of my grandmother's shabby bathroom. The cord on the bathroom heater blackened by years of finger filth, the pubic hairs – presumably mine – woven into the pile, and the slug on the mirror who is dead now, slightly desiccated. But no detail can make the cycle of puking cease. It persists until natural light blobs through the frosted window and a blackbird pipes up from the garden beyond. Until the muscles of my throat ache from retching, and there's nothing left to project from mouth to bowl but leaflet-coloured stomach bile, and my body is too exhausted to retch any more.

Have I puked up my deadness now?

Only dahl, only lager.

I haul myself to the closest bed. I lie awake and feel more alone than I have all the days and nights I've been here alone so far.

I fall into a treacle-sleep and hallucinate the swelling world.

When I wake again I know, from the constrained intensity of the light and the subdued tone of the birdsong, that morning has passed into evening. Even though I am too hot I do not flail my legs for a patch of cold somewhere beneath the duvet. I do not move. I know with unqualified certainty that I want to die. But I also know with equivalent certainty that I won't do anything about it. That I will only remain here and wait for death to indulge me.

But now, from the living room, I hear the furious meeping of a guinea pig, delirious with hunger and anguish. I remember that I have not fed Graham in over twenty-four hours.

And so I get up.

And so I go and feed the guinea pig.

*

Works about Death, or maybe Life, or maybe Misunder-
standing, I test myself: Jo Spence and Terry Dennett. From
a photographic series called *Final Project*, 1991–92. A picture
called *(What 1991 felt like . . . (most of the time))*. Which shows
Spence standing on a narrow plank laid across a channel.
The surface so thick with green sludge that it barely resem-
bles water. Spence's face turned away from the camera, cast
down upon the sludge. The first time I saw the photo, I only
glimpsed the writing underneath, and when I thought about
it later, I misremembered the title as *What life feels like . . .*
and I thought I understood it utterly. Later I learned that
1992 was the year of Spence's death, and for two years
before, she had known she was suffering from leukaemia,
that her chances of survival were as murky as that water.
And this new information made it mean something tremendously different, and it made me feel tremendously guilty
and tremendously stupid for recklessly empathising with a
condition, a state of mind, a level of existence of which I
am, in fact, of course, utterly ignorant.

Out on the line where I hung my washed clothes several
days ago – three pairs of pants to every peg, no peg at all
for the socks – I find a long streak of bird-shit down a trouser leg, more shit than I can even imagine a bird-body
producing. I went to all the trouble of washing them in the
avocado bath, against a chopping board, like making some
stringy kind of guacamole. Now my eyes fill with stupid,
unnecessary tears and I think: even when I wash my clothes.
Even when I try to be good and tidy.

*

All week after the bank holiday, it rains. Frogs come out into the wet. I find one on the road early in the morning. Thin skin grated off, legs vastly distended, organs buttered across the tarmac. Still I am able to see how small it originally was; it must be a new-season frog. It's too annihilated and would barely show up in a photograph. I can only hope there'll be another, intact. A frog that died of cancer, perhaps, or cardiac arrest.

Jane and I used to steal frogspawn from a field-stream every year at the start of March. We loaded it into flimsy plastic castle-shaped buckets. Crumbs of last summer's seaweed and shale floating amid the polkadot jelly. We lugged it home under electric fences and over stiles, then we slopped it into an old fish tank in the greenhouse. The tadpoles, once hatched, would eat their own spawn, nibble by nibble. After it had run out, we fed them aquarium flakes and mashed fruit flies.

The black flecks fortunate enough to survive to froghood were few. As soon as their tadpole tails were shed, Jane and I transplanted them to a water barrel in the garden. But the froglets rarely stuck around for more than a fortnight, fleeing to the countryside beyond our trimmed lawns, clipped hedges and artificial pools. A staggered exodus home to the wilds whence we pinched them, somehow capable of remembering a place they encountered only as spawn. As well as the way back.

Mum comes at the weekend. I hear her nearing, like a dog. And stand in the doorway as her old Ford climbs turbine hill, and wait while she parks. I can tell she is worried. I can see she has an overnight bag. She arrives in the afternoon, and I am grateful.

'Well,' she says. 'How do you feel you're doing?'

I try to smile and nod; instead I well up.

'Oh Frankie,' my mother says, 'you've got this far.'

'I know,' I gulp. 'But something's given way.'

She suggests I go back and see the doctor. 'To get something just to take the edge off?' she says.

'But Mum,' I say. 'I need edge. Edge is my only hope.'

She cooks dinner with my unwashed pots. We talk about the book she's reading, the other members of the family. We go out and stand in the garden after dark. We are looking for shooting stars.

I think I have spotted one, but Mum says it is too slow.

'What we really ought to do,' she says, 'is put on big coats and lie on our backs in the wilderness.'

But we don't. Because we don't have big coats. Because it is summer and neither of us really live here.

Now I spot another slow star, another and another. Until Mum says maybe they are shooting after all.

This morning, the perfect frog. Miles from turbine hill. I have forgotten my camera.

The surface of the laneway is more moss than road. Gorse presses in from either side, closing it to a dark and prickly passage. I cycle all the way back and turn around again. My knuckles numb into a handlebar claw. I'm afraid a car will have passed by the time I get back again, split and pulped my frog, or a song thrush swiped and scoffed it. But no, it's

still here. I drop my bicycle to the ditch and kneel. I have to shake the feeling back into my fingers before I am able to press the button.

Jane returns from holiday with a small package of strange gifts. Cinnamon-coated walnuts and sea-salt-flavoured chocolate. A wooden honey spoon and a miniature porcelain plate hand-painted with a scene of geese in a cobbled farmyard, a maiden carrying a wicker basket. I make tea again. As the kettle boils, I hold the plate up to the window. 'It's so pretty,' I say.

'I think they're a foie gras flock,' my sister says, 'so I suppose the maiden must be force-feeding them.'

Graham is packed and ready to go. I am sorry to see them leave. Both the guinea pig, and my sister.

I go back to the kitchen and lift up my porcelain plate

and drop it into the bin. I hear it break against the last broken plate I dropped in there.

I go to the living room and sit at the table where the hutch sat and finger Graham's paper hats. I remember how every picture and every sculpture I ever made died at the very moment I finished it.

I finger Graham's paper hats. I think about all the dead things I've made.

8

HARE

From the sun room radio, an expert is telling me that there is poison in my water.

My pipes are made of lead, he says, and so, every day, I am drinking it. But how can I not have noticed that I'm being poisoned? Because it will take years and years, the expert says, before all this lead I drink actually begins to harm me. It is building in my blood, but only very slowly. And so, of course, I did know this after all: that I am, slowly, being killed.

From the sun room radio, the newscaster is telling me that a body has been found in a suitcase in the Grand Canal, but that the Gardaí are unable to distinguish whether the person was a woman or a man, old or young, black or white or some colour in-between.

I am digging.

Crouched beside a sand heap on the outskirts of the dunes. Back to the sun. Shoulder caps reddening. Fine hairs at my temples yellowing. But as fast as I am able to dig, the sand caves in and refills my hole. I make a clearing, pushing back the dry top layer of grains which cover the beach. If I am to stand a chance, I must set a pace of emptying faster than it refills. I must begin wide and delve narrow. Why is my hole against me? Even my hole.

I drove to the beach this afternoon. A perfectly reasonable thing for a perfectly reasonable person to do on a fine day in summer. I parked the car and walked as far as I could walk from all the perfectly reasonable people on the beach.

The tide is out, and I'm not sure whether or not my way back will be cut off once it comes in again. My grandmother would be proud.

In the dark, coarse, cold, firm layer, the sand starts to hold itself up alone and I am able to make progress. My mother used to tell me that if I dug down deep enough, eventually I'd arrive in Australia. 'It's right down through the middle of the Earth,' she'd say, 'and directly out the other side.' When I was a child, I believed in Santa and the Tooth Fairy and the Easter Bunny until I was embarrassingly old. I believed that nougat was made out of old chewing gum, that teabags were filled with dried and minced cowpats, that telegraph poles were God's discarded toothpicks. And so, I saw no reason to question this shortcut to Australia.

Now I am down as deep as the length of my digging arm and I'm not sure I can reach any further. Every time I plunge, my cheek rests a second against the surface of the beach, adding extra grains to my lopsided sand beard. Every time I raise my head, I check the tide hasn't barred my way. I check my Fiesta is still waiting for me beyond the dunes. And I check the old man in the sea, the solitary old man.

No matter how far I try to travel from people, people always appear. Either they follow me, or they're already there, and I followed them, unwittingly. His wrinkled and bronzed paunch is bared to the ocean and he is wading-swimming his way along the length of the strand and back again, seemingly unruffled by the freezing water, the burgundy balls of bladderwrack bumping beneath the surface, the plague of transparent jellyfish. The water is shallow. The old man's knees must be grazing the seabed as he kicks his legs, and when he stands to wade again, his trunks drag precipitously low on his hips with the weight of their wetness. The curls on his chest are fiercely white against his tanned skin, and every now and again, I see the old man checking on me too.

I suppose I pictured that, in Australia, I'd pop out through a trapdoor in the sky, spot the crowns of koalas' heads swaying in the topmost branches of the gum trees and hear the distant whingeing of didgeridoos. Then I'd drop down, landing squarely with the bush on one side and the beach on the other and Alf and Irene from *Home and Away* waiting to welcome me. My child imagination had it all nicely rational-ised, until, one day, I stopped to study a diagram of a cross-section of the Earth in my geography book. The molten rock, the blazing magma, the fiery core.

Did it do me any good, early in life, to believe so many things which were not true? Or did it damage me? Pouring a foundation of disappointment, of uncertainty.

The sky grows overcast. Even though it's still warm and dry, the crowd by the car park begins to dwindle. In this country where the sun shines so infrequently, I find it strange that most reasonable people remain so fussy. That they leave with the arrival of the first cloud, thinking they'll return on a sunnier day which is unlikely to ever come. That they expect so much from life and will not compromise.

I am digging.

Until I can dig no further. Creeping forward only to be gently wrenched back. Until there is nothing but dark and rock.

I withdraw my arm and clamber into my hole and stand. I stand in my hole and pretend to be a dwarf. Now the wading-swimming man and I check one another at exactly the same moment. He registers my dwarf and looks away. I climb out and begin a new hole.

Works about Digging, I test myself: in 2007, Urs Fischer had the floor of Gavin Brown's gallery in New York's West Village dug up and out. Drilled, torn, removed. Leaving only dry dirt and rubble, a sign by the entrance warning that the installation was dangerous to the point of risk of death. The title of the piece is baffling: *You*. But who was this 'you'? Somebody who, the artist felt, imperilled his solid grounding, even his life? And now I wonder did he get his secret message across; now I wonder if each artwork is in fact utterly inaccessible to everybody but the person to whom it is secretly addressed?

Five holes later, each an exact arm's length deep, I realise there's someone standing over me. A woman in sunglasses and a baseball cap. I've no idea how long she's been there because there is no sun to cast a shadow. 'Excuse me,' she pipes up, 'what are you doing?'

I brush my yellowed hair from my eyes, scratch my sand beard. 'What does it look like I'm doing? I'm digging holes.'

'I just don't think it's appropriate,' she says. 'What if my children were to come running down here to play? And trip into one of your holes? And break an ankle?'

'A knee.'

'Excuse me?'

'Well, unless your children are unnaturally tall, I expect a knee is what they'd break.'

Her expression is astonishment, and then, disgust. 'What's wrong with you?' she says.

'Wrong?' I get up from my knees and climb out. 'Just because I don't give a shit about your children doesn't mean there's something wrong with me.'

The woman begins to back off. I watch her watching her footing as she goes, picking between my ankle-breaking holes, back along the beach to her windbreak and her picnic rug and her precious, breakable children. I stand up and shout into the wind: 'WHAT THE FUCK IS WRONG-NESS ANYWAY?!'

Works about Wrongness, I test myself: Henrik Plenge Jakobsen, 1996. A tall-as-man circular wall painting cut through its core with the sentence: *EVERYTHING IS WRONG*.

A gull the size of an albatross soars overhead, screeches. A bee emerges uncertainly from the dunes and commits suicide in the slosh of my inaugural hole. My mother says there are twenty different species of bee in Ireland, but that the average person divides them into only two: bumble and honey.

I gaze out at the blue and vast. My mother says that every seventh wave is supposed to be large. In the same way as a succession of shallow breaths necessitates a deep one. As if the sea is breathing as well as counting.

But today, there's something the matter with it. The tide goes out and out and out, when surely it ought to have turned around again by now.

Maybe it isn't going to come back this time.

A world without sea.

I think about how this wide openness is the view I love best, and yet, if I was out there, how quickly it would kill me.

Drive again, home again. I can feel the grains in my socks and sleeves and pants sandpapering my sunburn. I stand in front of the bathroom mirror and lift my T-shirt and twist about. I see how my shoulder caps and a patch of skin at the top of my back and back of my neck is shocking pink. Fluorescent.

I remember a thing I used to do as a child after a day at the seaside. I'd drop my chin, stick out my tongue to lick my chest and taste the salt on my skin. I used to wait until I was home again in the bathroom or my bedroom and alone, as if there were something indecent about it, in the way that children are able to sense indecency, without fully understanding.

I stand on my grandmother's carpet. Alone in her bathroom, alone in her house, alone on the summit of turbine hill. I drop chin to chest, stick out my tongue and taste the flavour of sea on skin, relish it. I close my eyes and wish I'd stayed there on the shore's edge in front of the wide openness. And dug all my holes into one, and given myself a pirate's burial.

I go to my grandmother's room and lie down in the place where the bed borrowed from the hospice had been before a man came to reclaim it. I lower my cheek to the floor. My eyes fill as my head falls.

People are most likely to die in bed; I suppose I heard somewhere. But what bed? At home in their own, or in a hospice? Or maybe, like my grandmother, at home in a hospice bed?

Now I wonder how many more people have died in that borrowed bed since my grandmother.

On this carpet, again I remember the old one. Its cider-shade and the tin soldier who lived beneath and how he used to drum on his furniture. He was quite brilliant at it. With only his hands and domestic surfaces, he drummed up an endless variety of rhythms, and it wasn't even annoying; it was curiously lovely. What bothered me was that he was the one who was supposed to have purpose; purpose enough for both of us. What bothered me was all of the time he wasted by drumming, and all the time I wasted by listening to him drum, by taking pleasure in it, for pleasure is almost always a waste of time.

It was forty-four wooden spoons long, my bedsit. Even though I kept a steel ruler in the desk-tidy on my tabletop, I insisted on measuring the length of my bedsit in wooden spoons, and spoon by spoon, from the old fireplace across the tacked-down lino, as I measured, I saw how filthy my floor was, and I found a toy car with the figure of a tiny man inside, a thing that didn't belong to me and that I'd never seen before.

I suppose that must have been shortly before I momentously phoned my mother, but I can't remember for sure. I can't remember what happened to the toy car and toy driver either. Did they get left behind, again?

When I first arrived here, it was morning, and my grandmother's bungalow shimmered with healing potential. It wasn't until after the sun set on my first night that I noticed the signs of decrepitude, as if, in daylight, weathered objects are inexplicably repaired: fissures resealed, colours reconstituted. All afternoon I'd been distracted by the process and possibility of the move. It wasn't until my belongings had been put away that I'd looked – really looked – and registered: the mould on the weighing scales scoop, the chopping board, the table legs. The webs in the window frames so thick you could have called them hammocks and cradled kittens there. The stench of abandonment.

*

On the radio, gardaí and pathologists are piecing together a little bit more of the suitcase body every day. Now they say it is a man, white and young. They are appealing for information.

Check your wardrobe for suitcases. Your life for the space a young white man used to take up.

At the beginning, I refused to acknowledge the decrepitude. Because this phase of my life was supposed to be new; I was supposed to be rejuvenated. But as the weeks pass, even the things which initially seemed intact have revealed themselves to be faulty. The knobs dropped off the cooker; now I'm down to the last one. I have to cook either all in the same pot or in rotation, or sometimes I use a pair of pliers to force the metal spike beneath the broken knob. Then there's the beautiful old armchair where I sit in the evening to read. It was part of a suite, every other part of which is missing, and I couldn't understand, at first, why it had been overlooked, until one night I lifted the throw-blanket draped across and found the place where Joe used to scratch his back: an ineradicable black stain from the grease of his coat.

The first night I spent here, I sat up until dawn in the dog-stained armchair. As surely as the sun had set and the decay shown itself, at the moment I stopped shifting about, the house started to shift instead, to creak and clunk and squeak and twitch. Even though I don't believe in ghosts, I believe utterly in robbers and rapists and murderers, in those who make the scrutiny of defenceless people their specialist subject. So I sat up in the armchair until dawn.

Then I moved to the floor of my grandmother's bedroom and lay down there, as I am lying here now.

I need you at this moment, more than I ever did when you were alive, I implore my gone grandmother. *If you come now I promise I won't ever ask again.*

And I remember that this is something I used to say to God, back when I thought there might still be a chance he existed.

And my grandmother doesn't come, just like God didn't.

Works about Ghosts, I test myself: James Lee Byars, 1969. An empty room, except for the audience, a bewildered audience. The title of the artwork: *This is a Call from the Ghost of James Lee Byars.*

'I write the world's simplest poems,' the artist said, and I transcribed it in black ink and capital letters to the back of my left hand, and watched as it washed away, letter by letter.

The summer days continue to arrive in spite of my indifference to them. If I was my sun, I doubt I'd bother to rise and fall so incessantly with such scant acknowledgement. But then nature acknowledges it, of course. Everything leafing, blooming, bushing, teeming. The redcurrant bushes fruit and the fruit falls and gets scoffed by the rats and bugs. The baby birds learn to fly and fledge and fuck off. Only the air is dead and so only the turbine is on my side. Its somnolent blades barely managing to turn.

I lie on my back in my wilderness, watching the grass blades erupting into feathers above me. I remember how, when I lived in the city, I used to hear strangers sneezing in the distance. Now there are only the farmer's recently

weaned calves in the field which wraps around my grandmother's property. They bawl and bawl, which is infinitely
worse than sneezing. Sometimes, when I am not gazing at
the grass stalks, I gaze at the dip in the garden step and
contemplate all the footfalls it took to wear, and I find my
grandmother in that dip. Or I gaze at the same spot in the
sky; I wait for something to pass through it.

Today, a lone goose, gently honking. A honk for each flap,
like a lorry reversing. Mindful of others, issuing a gentle
warning. I watch the patch the lone goose intersected until
the sun reaches it. Reducing the blue and cloud to stars and
flashes, forcing me to close my eyes.

I do almost nothing, just barely enough to keep myself from
turning to stone. I perform only the most necessary tasks
at the basest level of involvement. Shower without soaping,
eat without cooking, read without concentrating. I still go
out and cycle, but only just. I push the pedals down and
down and down. They push themselves back up again. I
don't take my camera. I don't look for dead things and when
I find them anyway I cycle past and leave them there.
   I miss rats and rabbits; I miss a hare.

I go to my bags and boxes in the spare room, the ones I
have not unpacked yet. I turn them out onto the carpet. In
the last – always the last – I find it.
   The toy car which doesn't belong to me, but which I
didn't leave behind.

*

I tell myself that so long as I eat and sleep and wash and cycle and talk on the phone every other evening in an emotionally stable tone of voice, on emotionally stable subject matter, then she will not notice how nearly killed I am.

But of course she does; she is my mother.

Mum in summer, when I was a child. Because the famine hospital is at a crossroads, it marked a logical meeting point for the neighbouring children. On sunny days there would always be several of us frolicking in the rockery, clambering the straggled pines, sploshing in the paddling pool. It was during summer that Jane and I realised our mother was less motherly than the others' mothers, and this was a great blessing. She'd ignore our amateur acrobatics on the swing-set, our tendency to turn the guinea pigs loose and chase them. She'd drive us to the beach and carry all the seaside paraphernalia herself, the cool box and windbreak and picnic basket. Rubber rings, bodyboards, rug. She'd even buy us all ice lollies on the drive home.

The swing-set acrobatics, as precarious as I imagine they appeared, had been carefully devised. They began the summer of the Barcelona Olympics, after Jane and I became obsessed with watching the gymnastics. The Americans who always cried and the Russians who always won and the Chinese who never had any boobs. The rules of our contest were more concerned with landing than swinging or leaping. The object was to hit the ground with arms out straight and feet planted evenly apart. We often twisted ankles or got kicked in the head, but were not discouraged. Because it was quite challenging to accomplish a perfect land, we remained interested; we continued to play.

Like all the best games, it was pointless and difficult.

Like all the best games, it was about pretending to fly.

What does my mother do in summer now? She goes to work. But what about the other days? I've no idea. I never ask.

'HOW ARE YOU?' I shout down the phone this evening when she calls. 'What did you do today? What's that noise?' She's on her mobile at a classic car rally in a seaside town with my father and his vintage Jensen. In the background, I can hear bandstand music.

'Jimmy died last night,' my mother says, 'so we've got to do the removal on the way home from here.'

'Who's Jimmy?' I say.

She tells me where in the parish he lived. Alongside the parochial house, with red hot pokers in a bed by the front wall. But I neither recognise nor absorb the information. Another faceless old man, perhaps the one who used to ride on a Honda 50, perhaps the one who used to loiter around the crossroads on hot days trying to catch a glimpse of my sister and me and our little friends messing about in the paddling pool.

I don't keep track of them any more: the old men who die.

Now Mum starts to talk about a new book she is reading. It's about famous hypochondriacs. Marcel Proust, Andy Warhol, even Florence Nightingale. My mother says: 'People who suffer from anxiety are usually those with the most vivid imaginations.' A gentle accusation disguised as consolation, as compliment; this is how I know she knows that I am struggling.

'How would you feel if I phoned Beth?' she says.

My aunt Beth is a Buddhist. 'Buddhist Beth' my father calls her, sometimes even to her face. She is the member of our family who is mobilised whenever any of the rest of us run into emotional turmoil.

I remember that the hare was Joseph Beuys's spirit animal. I go back with my camera. It's still there, just a little bit more battered.

A hare is a rabbit crossed with a horse. All limb and no fluff, an air of prudence. One of the cars has somehow managed to split the bowel and draw out a strand of shocking pink intestine, the colour of sunburn. And to flick a piece of its own shit into its frozen open eye.

This is how it will be for all of us, I think. Even the ones who do no harm.

Back again. To the famine hospital. We sit opposite each other on the floor of the room which used to be the playroom, my aunt Beth and I, cross-legged. We are having a go at meditation.

'Should I close my eyes?' I ask.

'However you feel comfortable,' she says.

With them open, I feel deeply uncomfortable, so I close them. But it's just as bad.

I feel Beth's hand on my right leg. It is jiggling my leg, or rather, my leg is jiggling her hand; this is my habitual right-leg jiggle. I force it to be still, which makes me even more uncomfortable.

Already I know I won't be able to do this.

Right here on this same floor, when Jane and I were small, Beth would lie on her back and raise her legs up into the air and we'd take it in turns to have her balance us on the soles of her feet. It was a wonderful game. Of course. It was about pretending to fly.

So I open my eyes again and trail them around the room which has now been repurposed as my mother's study. In my unemptied mind, I peel back the changes my parents have made since I left home: the computer desk and built-in bookshelves, the brilliant-white wall and its tasteful abstract paintings, the sofa bed and its multi-patterned cushions. In my mind, I put it all back the way it was when it was still meant for play.

The most horrible wallpaper of all used to hang here in this room. A stripy pattern the colour of peach yoghurt, and every second stripe was of a spongy material which was curiously satisfying to sink my fingernails into. But Mum used to find the tiny half-moon prints and tell me off, and so I had to be sneaky about it. I'd shunt the furniture forward to poke the wall behind; I'd shunt it back again once I was finished.

I close my eyes and see the peeled room. The toy houses lining its perimeter, toy cars parked in toy driveways, toy grocery shops and toy cafés. Jane's roller-skater doll lived in a moulded plastic mansion and my Monchichi family lived in a moulded plastic campervan and all of the others lived in renovated cardboard boxes. We had designated the open expanse of carpet in the middle a lagoon, though sometimes we'd forget, or run out of space elsewhere and locate our games in the invisible lagoon anyway, ignoring the fact that the toys ought to be drowning. Jane would always give her dolls the names of nobody we knew or had ever known in real life; American names inspired by the characters on *Baywatch*. And I copied her; I always copied her. My cuddly cats and bears and monkeys were called Ricky and Shauny and Erica. And we gave them ages. Our toys were sixteen or seventeen; only the very eldest were in their early twenties, because, apparently, I didn't envision anything of particular interest in life beyond twenty-five. And now I am a greater age than any of the toys were allowed to reach, older than I even cared to imagine as a child.

I peek at Beth. Her eyes are closed and so I close mine again too. But I cannot make the doll town go away. Ricky and Shauny and Erica are rising out of the carpet-lagoon and dancing inflexibly around my meditating aunt. Kicking their stumpy legs up, shaking their rigid elbows and fluffy bellies about.

'It's important,' she says, 'to pay attention to the nothings and appreciate them.'

Alone in the car again. Passing the about-to-be-harvested fields, stuck behind a harvester. I think about what Beth said. 'Don't feel guilty,' she said. 'Nothing good comes of guilt.'

She said it after I admitted how frightened I am that all this stupid sadness is chewing at my intellect.

'It's time to let this go,' she said.

She meant: it's time to postpone – if not entirely abandon – my burden of unrealistic ambition. To start churning the intellect I have left into simply feeling better; to make this my highest goal. It's time to accept that I am average, and to stop making this acceptance of my average-ness into a bereavement.

'Do you remember the story of when you were born?' my aunt said.

I was born blue and breached. Half-strangled by my own umbilical cord. The very thing which kept me alive for nine months tried to kill me as soon as I started leaving it behind. The same name had been written twice on a blackboard in the delivery room. It was spelled once for a boy and once for a girl – Francis and Frances – and for a moment my mother must have thought I'd never get a chance to be either. But then the midwife diligently un-strangled me and a nurse arrived wheeling an incubator.

'You were resilient,' my aunt said, 'right from the off.'

I was, at least, above average at resilience.

Works about Misguided Resilience, I test myself: Robert Morris, *Untitled (Passageway)*, 1961. A floating entrance inside the exhibition space. Leads to a passage. The passage leads on and on, narrows and narrows. The passage becomes so narrow it's impossible for the person trying to walk down to keep going, but still, the person persists in pushing and pushing. Determined they are heading somewhere; determined to refuse to accept that the passage is the point.

What else did Beth say? I try to focus on the nothings. The air – all of this air I fought so hard to take in as a newborn and have spent every moment since completely ignoring. Now I notice the scuffing of the inside of my clothes against the outside of my skin. How can it be that I have worn clothes every day of my life and never noticed this sensation? It feels as if the labels at my hip and collar are scratting flesh away to bone, as if the elastic band of my pants is sawing a slit towards my organs. And now I notice the trembling. Not just my right leg, but everywhere. Very slight but irrepressible. Have I always trembled? I can't remember. Was I born breached and blue, and trembling?

*

Gorse blurs past. Trees, cows, houses. At the bottom of turbine hill, I notice all the stray balls and plastic plant pots in the hedge at the bottom. I see how every rolling thing that ever rolled down turbine hill has lodged here. There seems to be an awful lot for so few houses. How strange I haven't noticed until now. I drop to second gear and feel the change which occurs in the engine, a mechanical sigh of relief. I reach my grandmother's bungalow, park in the driveway and walk back to close the gate, to tie the dog string. I notice how frayed it has become. With the force of a few more tugs it will snap and I'll have to choose between replacing it with an utterly needless new length of twine and accepting that the dog is gone.

I go in the back door to the kitchen. Open a cupboard, click. Take out a tin of tuna chunks and close the cupboard, thunk. Pull the ring on the can, click, again; a smaller, sharper click. Open the cutlery drawer, jangle, and select a fork, clink. Pick an ant off my sleeve and flick it down the sink. I breathe. I breathe. I breathe.

And all of this time, I am trembling.

I eat my tuna chunks with red wine at the sun room table, dripping brine into the keyboard of my laptop. I drag a duvet off a bed and onto the sofa, trick myself into sleeping by trying not to sleep.

I dream about pneumatic drills and Himalayan earthquakes. I wake up thinking about the Tibetan Delek Hospital and why I ended up there. It wasn't because of the stomach thing, not initially. Jane, initially, called an ambulance because I thought I could not breathe; because I was so scared of the thin air and the vomiting that I forgot my body knows to inhale and exhale on its own and does not require my brain to initiate every breath; I panicked. And as soon as the fuss had been made and we were both in hospital I felt like such a fucking eejit. The doctor who X-rayed my chest gave me the photograph to keep, the one which showed my lungs were perfectly fine. I rolled it up and carried it home over land and sea, through sky, and nailed it to my bedroom wall as a reminder of what a fucking eejit I'd been.

When people ask what India was like, still I always say: 'breathtaking'.

In the morning, they are all still here; the under-appreciated nothings. Pulsing, bleating, blaring, swirling. Once in a doctor's waiting room I overheard two old women talking about the irritation of how, when they have their hearing aids switched up to full volume, it results in an unsettling din of white noise. Water hissing through pipes, mice twitching in their sleep, the whirr of light fixtures. Now I recognise what the old women were talking about, the deafening silence.

This morning, I see the lead in my glass tumbler. A slim, bright glint, a silverfish. I feel it collecting in my blood, papercutting the lining of my veins.

There's a queen wasp in the sun room, beating her fragile head against the glass, crushing her antennae down. 'Why can't I go on,' she is thinking, 'when there's nothing here to stop me?' I watch, and wait unnecessarily long before I open the window.

When I do, I see the flies which have built up in the frame

and on the floor. Houseflies and horseflies and bluebottles, dead and dry and crispy. What do so many mean? They are time, of course. All the time I've been here, neglecting to open the windows, to clean up like my mother told me.

I will leave the flies where they have fallen, as a unit of measurement.

What is it about crying? As if my body believes that squeezing all its salt out might somehow quell the sadness. As if sadness is a parasite which suckles on sodium chloride.

After a few days of dry heat, a huge shower. The thrust of descending rain so strong it guns my unpegged socks down from the line to the sodden grass.

Rising from the earth and through the open sun room door: the scent of a chemical reaction between the heated ground and the cold cloud's water; of summer thunderstorms.

I hit the radio switch and assume foetal position on the mouldy sofa. On the radio, lone joggers are being devoured by wolves, because the way the wolves see it, running away is a sign of vulnerability, an open invitation to give chase.

There's a toad who is able to predict earthquakes, a cat who got locked in a freezer and lost his tail and ears to frostbite, a man who is able to hypnotise squirrels.

On the radio, at last, there is a head to fit the suitcase body.

The storm stops fast. The sky unclenches, a blanket lifted from a birdcage. I go outside to survey the damage. The rain has battered down the tall grass of my wilderness as well as my socks, erased my crop circle. I bend over and begin to stand the stalks back up again. But one by one, they resist me, refusing to be repaired.

The inaugural thunderstorm heralds more rain: a whole monsoon season in the space of a week. On behalf of the green world, I am glad. The grass had started to develop jaundice, the flower-heads to droop. The strawberry patch surrendered the last of its crop to the indomitable slugs; the leaves of each plant withered, whorled. I suppose I should have watered the garden, but I didn't think of this until the clouds stepped in on my behalf.

And yet, the early mornings are always fine. The sun climbs into a clear sky and burns away the dew, as if the dawn is a perpetual optimist.

Every afternoon, clouded mood beneath clouded sky, in foetal position on the sun room sofa, I listen.

There's the one-in-one-thousandth donkey that has given birth to twins, a man who was charged with public drunkenness because he was found administering the kiss of life to the corpse of an opossum, a woman on a waiting list for gastric band surgery followed by a spokesperson from the Size Acceptance Movement whose members prefer the term 'fuller figured'. This makes me think about how there's a counter argument for everything: every single thing I thought I knew – there's someone out there who can discredit it.

I lie on the sofa and tremble, until the radio stories jumble into nonsense. The toad that lost his tail and the donkey twins that can predict earthquakes.

*

I stay up late and watch a foreign film on the Irish language channel. It is spoken in Hungarian, subtitled in Irish. I can't understand either, but I still have all the little gestures and noises and faces people make in order to express themselves; I still understand the film, enough. How prosaic words are, I realise, how insufficient.

After the Hungarian film, the late-night news. A woman walking her dog has found thirteen pilot whales beached on a long strand of the north-west coast. The reporter is talking to an angry environmentalist who is doing an interview when he ought to be dragging sea mammals into the falling tide. The JCB can only take them so far; there are teams waiting in the shallows, towing them into deeper water, dressed up in wetsuits as if to better resemble the creatures they are trying to save. The angry environmentalist implicates fleets of Dutch and French trawlers which have indiscriminate access to our waters; the signals from their enormous boats interfere with the cetaceans' sonar, he says, causing them ferocious, unknowable trauma from which they cannot recover – from which they see no means of escape but to throw themselves on the mercy of the treacherous dry land.

The camera lingers on a whale stretched out in the sinky sand of the shallows, the sort into which my sister and I used to plant our feet and pretend we'd had them amputated. Every now and again, he pushes a great gust of air through his blowhole, out and out and out, and never in again. The environmentalist says they are called pilot whales because they like to crest the wave created by a ship's bow, as though they are piloting it. He says that, of all whales, pilots are the ones which most frequently strand. The ones with the most sensitive hearing, or perhaps, the closest listeners.

The ocean is a cacophony of noise. I'm guessing David Attenborough said this at some point and it stuck with me because it's so hard to believe. I've held my nose, plunged my head beneath the surface on summer days at the beach, and heard nothing but the suctioning of water. But now I understand that this isn't because the ocean is silent; it's because I am ocean-deaf.

A final monsoon shower. The clouds recede into a watery rainbow. I watch it through the sun room roof, fading as fast as it coalesced. I go outside to stand in the centre of the garden, the openest part. This is my ocean lawn. The other parts of the garden – the wilderness and flower beds and compost heap – are only seas. The bungalow is only an island. The birds sing and the calves cry and the turbines' blades thrum. And yet, it's peaceful. Here is the peace I craved all the years I lived in the city, shushing my sneezing neighbours.

How could I have known that peace could become so boring?

In only my socks on the lawn ocean. Beneath the throbbing turbine and the fading rainbow. I shut my eyes, raise my hands up and my elbows and shoulders raise after them. Slowly, methodically, I sway. Like a hammock. A pendulum. The clapper of a church bell.

9

HEDGEHOG

The doorbell, slicing through my reverie. I sit up on the sun room sofa. Why would my mother ring the doorbell? Because it isn't my mother, obviously. Because it's somebody else; somebody who is obliged to request entry.

It takes another couple of moments before I remember I am obliged to respond.

There is a man standing on the front doorstep, a second a few paces behind. They are carrying identical briefcases and wearing identical suits and formal coats which are ludicrously black and heavy and long for a day like this, the end of July. They are young to be dressed so formally, younger than me. I stand mute on the other side of the threshold, dazzled by their clothes, by the unlikeliness of their presence. I don't see and didn't hear any car, or the gate creak or approaching footsteps; there is something fantastic about how they've appeared here on turbine hill on an ordinary Tuesday and pressed my grandmother's doorbell.

'I'm here to ask you whether you know God by name,' the closest man says.

Of course. They are Jehovah's Witnesses.

'His name isn't God?' I say.

A short section of the rubber seal which runs around the inside of the door frame has come loose at the top and is dangling. Waggling gently, licentiously, in the space separating us. The man who has spoken is slim and bearded. He holds out a leaflet and points at the capitalised heading word by word as if I might be slow at reading. DO-YOU-KNOW-GOD-BY-NAME? I reach up past both our heads and begin to poke the seal back into its nook.

'Do you have any understanding of why we go door to door like this?' he says.

I know this one. I say: 'Because they make you.'

Both the young men shake their heads and smile, regretfully. They look at me as though they can see right through my T-shirt and my pimply chest, my ribcage and lung tissue, my bronchi and bronchioles and alveoli, right through to my enfeebled soul.

'It's because of the Bible,' he says. 'I'd like to encourage you to read your Bible.'

*

There's a policeman's hat hanging from a hook in the porch, a foot from where the Witnesses are now standing. It used to belong to a garda who was in the same painting group as my grandmother. The garda and my grandmother and several other amateur watercolourists would come together every Wednesday to paint wishy-washy still lives and portraits and landscapes-from-photographs. When she moved to turbine hill, the garda gave my grandmother one of his hats to hang in her porch. This seems to me a cavalier way to deter burglars, but in the twelve years she lived here, nobody ever broke in.

Both my Witnesses are fair and willowy. At first I wonder if they are brothers; now I remember to wonder if they are robbers or rapists or murderers who've hired suits and photocopied leaflets in a cunning ploy to insinuate themselves into the quiet bungalows of defenceless strangers on hills in middles-of-nowhere, and I realise it would be very stupid to invite them in so they can see for themselves there's no garda here. That's if they haven't already guessed from the twelve years' worth of dust which has collected on his hat.

'I don't suppose I have a bible,' I say. A holy neighbour gifted me one for my first communion, but I lost it immediately, almost two decades ago.

'Would you like to keep one of these?' he says, the one who seems to do all the speaking. His hand is still outstretched, the paper flapping in the breeze like a tiny flag. It makes me think of Jink, Jink's leaflet. It makes me wonder what it is about me that invites conversion.

'Okay,' I say, and take it. It's roughly the same size and

shape as the pieces of paper I used to make Graham's hats, and so I am compelled to fold, and fold, and fold again, and open. I hand it back to the speaking one.

'It's a boat,' he says.

'Okay,' I say. 'If that's what you want it to be.'

Works about God, I test myself: Adam Chodzko, *God Look-Alike Contest*, 1992–93. The artist placed an ad in the classifieds appealing for people who believed themselves to look like God. The artwork is a collection of the photographs he received in response. What's interesting is that very few of them are old white men with beards. Instead there's a boy in denims, a clean-shaven young man in a collar and tie, a woman in a red corset. 'God is in everything,' the priest told us at mass when I was a child. And so I used to check in my pencil-case and coat pockets, under the bed, over the hedges, for God.

A smudge of cerise trickles from the silent one's beard, down his white neck. Evidently, he is more sensitive than the speaking one, who simply places the boat/hat/leaflet into his briefcase and turns to go.

'I encourage you to read your Bible,' he murmurs over his shoulder.

Before the Witnesses have reached the gate, the door seal works itself free again, uncoiling slowly from its nook. I watch its creeping descent; I watch until it comes to rest against the concrete step.

Because the famine hospital is at a crossroads, it has always attracted unexpected callers. Not alone the parish children, but salesmen, politicians, preachers. And my mother, in her infinite open-mindedness, always used to invite the Witnesses in for tea. I'd sit with them at the kitchen table, watching Mum listening patiently to the predictable speech before asking several sensible questions perfectly politely. Now I can't remember exactly what she asked, nor what the Witnesses answered, only that they did not adequately satisfy her doubts because I can still hear her making this statement: 'You have not adequately satisfied my doubts.' I've never asked her why she gave them tea and let them speak in the first place; I haven't thought about it in years. Was it amusement, or curiosity, or was my mother deliberately making an example of the Witnesses for the benefit of Jane and me? To show us how fundamentalism is always tolerable, yet fallible.

Jink returns to my thoughts. Back in the sun room, I wait while my laptop awakens itself. I look up 'Born Again Christians' on Wikipedia. 'To be born again,' it says, 'is to undergo a regeneration of the human soul or spirit from the Holy Spirit, contrasted with the spiritual birth everyone experiences.' What a nice idea, I think, to have a second shot. Now I feel bad I was so furious with him. Only for wanting to believe in somewhere better than here, in some being better than us; only for believing in what I cannot, and being comforted when I am not.

I urge the old man from my mind, because I know I've been unfair to him.

But as if there is a means by which the person I am thinking about can know I am thinking about him, can sense that my ill feelings have subsided, Jink knocks on my back door. He is carrying an egg box which doesn't appear to close properly. Instead it is secured by two elastic bands: one yellow, one red. He holds it out to me across the threshold.

'Some eggs,' Jink says. 'If you'd eat 'em? The ducks are only laying like mad this time o' year. Hard to keep up with them meself.'

I take the box and thank him, even though I'm not so keen on eggs. He asks me how I'm getting on and I say something trite – something untrue – and cut to asking him how he's getting on. I don't offer tea; afraid that if we sit down together he'll start bending the conversation in the direction of his personal obsession, like perverts bending towards sex. Only Jink's sex is Jesus. Instead I am effusive in my enthusiasm for these eggs-I-will-not-eat, and hope this will do well enough to show that I am sorry.

I watch him limp away down my grandmother's driveway. His shoulder bones are knolls beneath his jumper and his white hair is squashed flat, like a baby which can do nothing all day long but lie on its back in its crib. I try to imagine Jink in a meeting hall filled with uproarious evangelicals. Clapping, singing, proclaiming. I can't. And I wonder if it's true. And I begin to think it isn't.

He seems so much like the kind of lonely old man who has always been old and lonely, even when he was young and surrounded by family.

I am surprised by my box of eggs. They are weirdly large and pale; not simply white but almost translucent. Now I remember what Jink said – that they are duck eggs in a hen egg box; this is the reason for the elastic bands. They make me think of a scene in *Jurassic Park*. The one in the laboratory where the baby dinosaurs are hatched. I lower the lid, replace the yellow and red. Now I know for sure I cannot eat them.

An update on the stranding: most of the whales are dead. The angry environmentalists managed to push them all back out to sea, but nine came in again with the next tide. Nine had already made up their minds; the impenetrable resolve of a deranged penguin.

On the sidelines of the trembling, more specific parts of me have started to malfunction. A bruise at the site of my tail-bone which refuses to fade. A vague loss of sensation in my smallest toe. A tender lump in my scalp. A fly which entered my eye cavity when I was freewheeling, and doesn't appear to have come out again.

Works about Body, I test myself: Giuseppe Penone, *To Unroll One's Skin*, 1970. The artist took more than six hundred photographs of every inch of his body, using a small rect-angle of glass as a guiding device. Pressing it against his flesh, framing each shot according to its proportions, dis-playing the prints in grid formation. But he must have asked someone to help him at some stage. For the parts of the body which are difficult to reach?

The parts of my body which are difficult to reach; I'd forgotten all about them.

*

I open my eyes to find the morning adjourned. There's all the light there should be. Green carpet, white wall, pine door. But no gentle ticking of my bedside clock; no rustle of duvet as I shift my limbs about the bed; no chittering of birdsong or bawling of calves – not even the turbine's heartbeat.

Of course, I understand completely. I am deaf now. To the Earth and sky as well as the ocean.

I roll from my side onto my back and some of the morning sounds are miraculously restored. I sit up and stick a finger in one ear and listen. Now the other, and listen. I realise the right is fine, whereas the left is completely blocked. I relax for a second before remembering to worry about what it is that's blocking my ear. Maybe just wax but maybe not wax, maybe a massive brain tumour and the tender lump in my scalp isn't just the bump from where I clocked it off the corner of a cupboard door, but the rear end of the same massive tumour which is bunging my left ear.

You're okay, I whisper, all of this is only Wind Turbine Syndrome, remember?

But I can barely hear myself.

Works about Deafness, I test myself: Joseph Grigely, who is deaf, started his career as an artist and critical theorist as a painter, but at a certain point in his painting career realised that the paper scraps of scribbled conversations he used to communicate with people who could not use sign language, mostly strangers, were more interesting, as artefacts, than his paintings. Or perhaps more honest and concise, as philosophies, than that which he was trying to paint.

*

The precarious silence inside my head is a beach shell: the sound my mother told me was the sea but was actually the wind. I brush my teeth and spit and dress. Fetch my bicycle, tie the frayed dog string, select boreens and back roads at will, swerve around potholes and drowsy pigeons, pedalling faster in pursuit of rabbits, as if I am a fox.

I'm so absorbed in being a fox, it takes me a while to notice the vehicle stuck behind me. When I do, I've no idea how long it's been there, across how many hundreds of metres of narrow back road it has been forced to tailgate my bicycle. I don't hear it, because I am deaf now. But, eventually, a sixth sense compels me to turn around.

Now I see: it is the minibus.

Everything is very nearly over. And so none of the normal rules of behaviour apply. And so none of my actions can have consequences.

I do not move out of the way of the bus. Instead I dismount and turn around. I raise my hand to make it stop.

On my right side only, the sound the door makes as it opens: the release of the lid on a colossal bottle of pop. As I climb the steps into the pop bottle all eyes cling to me, like bubbles. Only the driver speaks. He is asking who I am, what I want, where I think I'm going.

I'm going past him and down the aisle, scanning faces. Some of the passengers have taken their seatbelts off and are giving me a standing ovation. I pass them and keep going. As soon as I see him I say his name.

'Willie,' I say. 'It's Frankie. We were in school together. Do you remember?'

The driver is climbing out of his booth. Some of the standing passengers are clapping, calling. Willie is the only motionless person. His are the only pair of bubbles drifting away, out the window.

'Willie,' I say. 'You're not like these people; you don't belong on this bus. You should get off; you should come with me.'

But he doesn't look up. And now the driver places his large hands on my shoulders, softly.

'Come on,' he says. 'Enough of all this.'

Alone on the road. Arms flopped to sides and hands held open, empty. My bicycle is lying in the ditch with its front wheel crushing the thistles and its back wheel uselessly spinning. Where does the spinning wheel think it's going? Does it believe it's able to cycle in air? And it isn't my bicycle; mine vanished into the city with the person who stole it, or perhaps the person to whom the person who stole it sold it. All I have left from the last day I saw my bicycle is the scar on my chin in the place where it gashed against the footpath. The doctor glued tiny metal hooks to my teeth, wired my mouth shut for five months. And what would I have done if Willie had come with me? What do I know of Willie, really, all these years gone by?

My open, empty hands recommence trembling. Because you're not supposed to initiate confrontation with vulnerable members of society; I've only just remembered this. Old people, children, the mentally or physically disabled. I have never been skilled in the peculiar intimacy of conflict, and now, I've crossed a line.

I draw my bicycle up from the ditch. I know I will not be able to steer straight, so I only steady myself against the handlebars, and push. At the bottom of turbine hill, a rogue wave of lassitude crashes over the back of my head. I drop my grandmother's handlebars to the ditch and her bicycle falls into all the balls which ever rolled down turbine hill.

I was very small, three at most, and sitting in the shallows in an oversized sun hat. My mother didn't see the salt water gathering height behind me. Was it the wash from a distant yacht? Did a jet ski flash past, a pilot whale breach? Whatever created it, the wave gushed over my face, my shoulders.

'You were fine,' Mum told me years later. 'You just got such a fright. You screamed and screamed and couldn't swim again.' Because like all babies, at the very onset of life, I knew intuitively how to swim. But then the wave hit and washed away my intuition as surely as it did my hat.

I didn't learn again until I was eleven and Mum insisted that I attend lessons in the Spastic Clinic. Nowadays the Spastic Clinic is called something else, something politically correct. I'd already tried and failed at the swimming lessons organised through school and I was lucky that the Spastic Clinic didn't discriminate because I wasn't a spastic, and that the instructor was significantly more patient.

Still, I was so slow to learn. Wary of straying out of my depth.

How is it that we're born able to swim? Like gazelles. Who know how to stand up and walk moments after they've dropped from their mother's uterus onto the savannah. Who know to fear hyenas though they've never seen or heard a hyena, never been informed what a hyena is. How is it that we are born able to swim, but as we grow and subsume a glut of conventional wisdom, we forget, and have to learn again?

That wave was the onset of consciousness. The moment it broke the moment at which I realised I was not indestructible, that the world was filled with forces separate to me, hostile to me, horrifyingly beyond my control. Just the same as a gazelle's.

Innate flexibility fades; muscles seize up.

How many more small injustices of adulthood are still to be discovered?

For six full swimming lessons, I paddled and splashed. It wasn't until the seventh and final week – the last day, my last chance – that I spontaneously understood how to float. You have to lie, not stand but lie, in the water. You have to picture the part of yourself which isn't your body, the weightless part. You have to picture it breaking off and rising away, as if you are just about to die, and this is your out-of-body experience.

But why hadn't any of the instructors told me? They showed me how to position my arms for the different strokes. How to kick my feet in such a manner to create minimum splash, maximum motion. But I already knew how to move in the ways that would make my body swim; it was the ineffable part I struggled with.

Works about Weightlessness, I test myself: Piero Manzoni, *Artist's Breath*, 1960. A series of inflated balloons fixed to wooden stands. And as if he somehow knew his breaths were numbered, Manzoni died young.

The strangled birth, the broken wave, the swelling dream. But these aren't things which constitute a troubled childhood; not even close. In the newspaper, the story of a boy raised by drug addicts. Routinely starved and slapped about by strange junkies who wandered in and out of his home. He grew up to become a psychiatric patient, hospitalised for persistently swallowing small implements. A pair of nail scissors, a miniature stapler, a napkin ring.

And yet, here I am. Perceiving everything that is wonderful to be proportionately difficult; everything that is possible an elaborate battle to achieve. My happy life was never enough for me. I always considered my time to be more precious than that of other people and almost every routine pursuit – equitable employment, domestic chores, friendship – unworthy of it. Now I see how this rebellion against ordinary happiness is the greatest vanity of them all.

I think of my aunt and her 'self compassion'. But it isn't fair to forgive myself so easily.

In the final weeks of being nine, how could I possibly have guessed how many more years of childhood were yet to come? But the last dreg has left my system now, abandoned me to my intellect.

Another day of partial deafness. I miss the thrum-thrum-thrum, the gentle domestic burring. I jab my blocked ear with a cotton bud, just to see what will happen. It becomes sore and inflamed. Of course. How stupid of me.

She stands in my grandmother's kitchen, an empty canvas shopping bag with a ladybird motif in one hand, a tinfoil-covered cake plate in the other. Not just on the phone any more but right here in front of me. It seems like a very long time since I've seen my mother, even though it isn't.

'Why ever did you stop the minibus?' Mum says.

She claims to have come for the duct-taped boxes in my grandmother's bedroom. She doesn't mention who told her about the minibus, though I'm not particularly surprised that she has heard. In the ladybird bag there are vegetables from the garden, new potatoes still coated in mud, cour-gettes still wearing their flowers, and things from the health food shop – dried figs and toasted wheatgerm and smoked tofu – and the arts supplements from the Sunday papers. She unpacks it all onto the kitchen countertop before she asks me again, about the bus.

I rest my spine against the frosted glass of the back door and slide down until I am hunched on the welcome mat, beside the shoehorn. I cry. Because my mother is the only person in the world with whom I can, I cry.

'It's my ear . . . it was because of my ear. I can't hear anything out my left side. It's just blocked I think, but I can't think clearly. I can't think consequences.'

Mum crouches down and stretches an arm around me.

'Oh Frankie,' she says, 'it's probably just wax. How long has it been like that?'

'I don't know. Maybe a week, maybe less than a week, maybe just a couple of days.'

My mother rubs the palm of her right hand up and down, from my shoulder to my elbow, over and over. The soft weight and warmth is like a sedative. I try to remember the last time somebody touched me.

Works about Contact, I test myself: a kinetic sculpture by Conrad Shawcross, 2010. A wall-mounted electronic machine with three spindly metal arms, each bearing a light at its furthest point. In uneasy coordination, the arms extend, spin, and then come back in again to meet at the centre. Sometimes the lights touch, sometimes they fail to touch. And there is something agonisingly tender about their failure, about the human imperfection, and capriciousness, of machinery. The title of the piece: *The Limit of Everything*.

This wonderful sedative, I remember, is my mother. My mother has other people, other things to do, a past, even a future. I had forgotten that my mother has a future too.

My mother likes odd numbers and is suspicious of the even ones. She reads a new book every week and is bewitched by black holes in the universe. She describes herself as an optimist but she worries about everything – worries incessantly – worries on behalf of others when she feels they are not worrying adequately for themselves.

And my mother misses her own mother, my grandmother, immensely, who only has a past now; who is only allowed to be as we remember her.

When the hug is over, Mum ruins it; she says: 'I can feel all your bones.'

The chemist's is very bright but not in a warm, yellow kind of way. The light is blue like the inside of a fridge, a public toilet, an ambulance.

The waiting chair is already occupied. I linger at the door, pretending to examine a display of dental hygiene products as Mum goes to stand beside the cough lozenges and chewy vitamin tablets and condoms in the queue for the counter. The person in the waiting chair is an elderly woman. In spite of her elderliness, she has a wholesome appearance; straight shoulders, ruddy cheeks. The chemist calls her up and she receives a paper bag of pillboxes, and I wonder if it's actually her bundle of medication which keeps her looking so wholesome. Do old women live too long now, beyond the point at which good health is sustainable by natural means, to the point at which a monthly bag-load of pillboxes is the only option for survival?

I think: by the time I'm old, pizzas will be delivered by drones and sensors will be able to detect when we break the law.

I think: by the time I'm old, nobody will be able to die any more.

But now I remember, of course, I'm never going to be old.

I can't believe there are so many different types of floss. Not just waxed and unwaxed but some other kind called 'silk ribbon', as well as multi-packs of miniature two-pronged plastic forks with a short length of thread stretched from prong to prong. What kind of person buys a specific type of floss? What could possibly happen in life to cause this person to develop a preference? Or maybe everybody has a preference. Maybe I am the only person in the world who doesn't give a fuck about floss.

My mother comes at me through the lip balms and travel sweets and mosquito candles. She is carrying a small, red box.

'This'll do the trick,' she says.

In the bathroom, I stand in front of the mirror and Mum stands behind, like the scalp examination all over again.

'Tip your head to the right.'

She holds the dropper over my earhole. Releases three drips of the liquescent decongestant and stoppers it inside my head. There isn't any cotton wool so we use a minced-up tissue.

'What in God's name is that?' my mother suddenly says.

'That's my desiccated slug,' I say. 'I suppose it must have been checking its belly.'

Now I watch as she peels it from the glass, tosses it into the toilet bowl. Splosh. And flushes.

I expect that Mum will tell me I have to return to the famine hospital. Instead, at six o'clock, she phones my father and tells him she won't be back to make his dinner this evening. She goes to my grandmother's kitchen instead, and starts to prepare a vegetable stew.

On my own in the sun room, I feel something rolling around inside my head. I root out the tissue and a great clot of wax emerges in its wake, a nugget of soft gold. I stare at the wax and tell myself: I will be good and grateful from now on. I will stop with all this dying.

We eat off our laps in the living room, in front of *Coronation Street*. As we eat, my mother tells me all the things that have happened since I left home and stopped watching it. Seven years of fake births, fake deaths, fake marriages and fake love affairs between the fake walls, around the fake bar. Afterwards, on the news, they are preparing to bury pilot whales in the blackmost layer of sand. The angry environmentalist is now only sad. 'Hope has been abandoned for the final four,' he says. They are being left to lie on the beach. Just one has made it back to sea.

'Well that's good anyway,' Mum says, in her perpetual optimism.

'But is it really?' I say. 'Now the surviving one is alone in an enormous ocean, perhaps wishing he hadn't been rescued after all.'

'But he'll find more whales,' she says. 'Join a new pod.'

Neither my mother nor I remember the boxes in my grand-mother's bedroom until she is about to leave.

'What's inside them anyway?' I ask on our way back down the hall.

'Didn't I tell you already?' Mum says. 'It's her photos, pretty much all of them, from when I was a child right up to when you were. Just after she died I sorted through everything with the sisters. We meant to divvy them up but we only put them in order instead. I suppose we decided they couldn't be separated; they only make sense all together.'

'Can I look at them?' I say. Because I suspect my mother will be more lenient on me after today, that she'll trust me where I shouldn't really be trusted.

I sit on the shabby sun room sofa and flick through the magazines my mother brought. All the wristwatches in wristwatch advertisements say the same time. I've never noticed that before. They all say ten past ten, as if the clock face is smiling.

This morning, the sun endures past dawn. I realise that it is August: the summer's last stand.

At a distance, I spot it. A prickly auburn mound by the side of the road. The sky blazing a chemical blue backdrop to its broken spikes. I squeeze my brakes.

Over the hedge from where I pull up, an unplastered house sits atop a plot of freshly seeded grass. A father and son knock a sliotar to and fro.

Now they stop. Lower their hurleys. Walk to the gate to watch me.

'What's he doing, Daddy?' the boy says. The father stares, suspiciously, in my direction.

The hedgehog's mouth agog. Front teeth splintered, tongue half eaten by giant slugs. I fumble several shots, return to my bike as quickly as possible. But the spokes of the back wheel have managed to become caught up with a clump of flowering groundsel. I stand in the ditch and struggle to untangle my entangled wheel. A Corn Flakes reflector falls off. I swing my leg over and leave it behind, push off and pedal fast to the corner and before I turn, glance back. The hedgehog has shrunk to a thorny dot; the plastic cockerel catches a ray and winks. The boy and dad remain at their gate, waiting for me to disappear.

'I think he was a she, okay?' I hear the dad say.

Hedgehogs aren't supposed to die in summer. They have such little time already. Their whole year is only two seasons long, and so they have to squeeze everything they need to do into the warmish months. They aren't supposed to die in summer when they are at their most awake, when there's so much to attend to. And especially now, in August, when they've very nearly made it through to the end of another hedgehog year.

They are supposed to die in winter, in their sleep. Winter

is supposed to carry off the old and weakly hedgehogs. Peacefully, painlessly.

Now I know: for every whale which survives a stranding, there is a hedgehog that never makes it back to hibernation.

I open the first box. The box labelled ONE. I rip back the duct tape as if it's a sticky plaster, an old wound I can't bear to expose. I pour the contents onto the floor, a sepia ava-lanche onto the green carpet. Sea green; I have decided now – not flora after all, but the unmistakeable shade of deep water beneath lightless sky. Now TWO, THREE, FOUR and there's colour amidst the avalanche. Faces I recognise, my face. I make piles, like the chimp who thought he was a human. I spread my piles into islands on the sea floor. I nudge my islands, collide them into continents, as if I am their drift.

In the shower, I examine my bones, the ones my mother mentioned.

I used to try so hard to be this thin and now I find it bittersweet that I am even thinner still without having tried at all. Back then, I would have been triumphant. Now, I am only perplexed. Where did so much of me go, so effortlessly?

I used to be able to encircle the top of my right arm with my left hand, fingers touching. Every day, ten times a day, I'd check to be sure I was still able to do this, pushing up my sleeves, no matter how many sleeves I had layered on to insulate my showing bones. And today? I am only perplexed as to why I thought it mattered. I am only ashamed of all the knowledge and ideas which passed me by while I was busy obsessing about circumferences; about a body I never even liked in the first place.

The chemical blue sky which blazed a backdrop to my hedgehog prevails for the rest of the week. The temperatures tip over twenty-five degrees for what is the first time – and also surely the last – all summer. I lie on my back in the dying grass. We are both turning brown. From the sun room radio, volume turned up loud so that it reaches my wilderness, I hear a man say: '. . . clouds are the facial expressions of the atmosphere . . .'

I set out on foot for the shop. It's twenty-seven degrees, the radio says as I am leaving. The road up ahead is a mirage. I think I see a fallen bird. From a distance, it's hard to tell; maybe only a clump of tawny leaves in the ditch. But gradually, I am close enough to see that the clump is flailing, and closer still, that the clump is beady-eyed. I drop to my knees at the side of the road. I see that my clump is a small and beautiful and stupid bird – a sparrow – and that it has somehow managed to become fused to the melted tar of a freshly filled pothole.

I should know better than to help. I think of the whales, and of all the wounded creatures I tried to rescue in childhood. I can't remember a single one that survived.

There was a family of thrushes who nested in the dainty woodland, and every spring, our cats would upscuttle the nests, displace the hatchlings. How many times did I try to salvage the peeping babies before they had their bones crunched by cat jaws? I'd wrap them in my mother's linen napkins and feed them pureed worms through a surgical dropper. Once, I successfully nursed two thrush babies to a condition at which they might have been able to fly away, then I locked the cats into the house and left the birds in the woodshed with the doors opened wide. A few hours later, they were gone, and I was overjoyed. But before the end of the week I found a severed leg beneath the silver birch, some feathers caught in its lowest branches, fluttering, and the second thrush baby turned up a week later. It had fallen behind the woodpile and starved to death.

One-legged pigeons, bats with snapped or fractured wings, rabbits with myxomatosis. My sister and I grew up digging tiny graves. Dad had designated us a flower bed in which we were allowed to cultivate whatever we wished, but our plants were few and far between, wild or weed-smothered. Instead we used the flower bed for burying creatures, several deep, until we couldn't dig a new hole without unearthing a crushed matchbox coffin, a ghoulish hamster skull.

I try not to think about the countless lives I failed to save as I prise my sparrow from the pothole, cradle it in my T-shirt, carry it home to my grandmother's house.

Struggling bird clasped to stomach, I tip the gunge out of the basin, refill it with clean, warm water. On the back step, in the basin, in the water, in my hands, the sparrow's plumage soaks and shrivels to nothing, a ball of wriggling gristle.

'I can feel all your bones,' I whisper.

I don't understand why I remember how to distinguish the sex of a sparrow when I've forgotten so many other, more valuable things, and yet, I know from its dark nape that my bird is a male. My male's mouth and nose are bunged, the black glue is everywhere, encrusted with dirt and vegetation. I try for some time before I realise that tar does not come out of feathers, and remember, of course, I knew this all along. Everybody knows this.

I place him in the shade of the garden shed. My sparrow lies, exhausted. And I hope he will die soon.

I forget my trip to the shop, return to my wilderness, the shade of my grandmother's plum trees. But all afternoon, blaring above the words of my book, I can hear him beating his sopping wings, hammering the shrubbery down.

It's almost dark before I fill the basin again. This time the water is nearly scalding. This time I know it's useless; I do it anyway. I manage to clear enough mess from his beak to allow the sparrow to drink. He gulps and gulps, even though it's scalding, and suddenly he goes still, relaxes, floats on the surface without my support.

The state of his plumage is even worse. Coated with moss, with dust, with buttercups. Now my sparrow looks costumed, almost foolish.

In the kitchen, I find an old dishcloth. In the yard, I find a heavy, smooth stone. I place the cloth over my sparrow and wish he'll go quietly, but he doesn't. For a second before I weigh the stone down, my sparrow recognises that his light and air have run out, and he pushes against me with his last shred of useless strength, and eternity passes before the tiny bubbles rising to the surface from beneath fabric and rock and tar and feathers eventually stop.

When I unwrap him, my sparrow's beak is frozen open. Tongue extended, eyes vast with terror. I do not take a photograph. This is the rule, remember? I am not allowed to kill something and then steal its spirit as well. I only bury him in the compost heap. *Bird bones are fine as fingernails.* And back on the step, I sit with my arms folded around my knees and I cry indecently hard. I cry my throat raw and eyes puffed and head sore for a long, long time.

Have I cried out my deadness now?

I wake. And know. To get up is to be confronted by the continents of photographs on my grandmother's bedroom floor. Pawed and strewn, utterly muddled.

I think: Mum is going to fucking kill me.

But of course she won't. She'll only be angry and sad and disappointed, and this will be worse, and I don't know if I can stand it on top of every other time I've made her angry and sad and disappointed already. And so, I get up. I pad barefoot across the hall in only my vest. I fold my showing-bones into a crouch on the bottomless sea floor.

And begin, at last. To fix things.

*

The last photograph is easy; I know which box it belongs in as soon as I turn it over. My grandmother from the breast-bone up, a jaunty regimental hat pinned at an angle to her sensible hairdo.

Here is London at the start of the Second World War; the day she entered the Women's Royal Naval Service. She is nineteen and still smiles with her teeth showing. By the end of the war, most of the ones in the front rows had been knocked out: not by a bomb but a car accident – an ambulance which crashed into a crater. This is a fact that has proved helpful to me in the sorting of the muddled photographs. Some of those without a date scribbled on the back can be dated by whether or not my grandmother has opened her mouth to smile.

How beautiful she looks, but then everyone always says that about old photographs; it can't possibly be that people were uniformly better looking in the past, but that grainy monochrome is more generally flattering than crystalline technicolour, and because having your portrait taken was uncommon enough for people to bother dressing their best. Combing their hair just so, striking an elegant pose.

I place the photo in its place. I pause for a moment of silent appreciation: my grandmother's radiant yet under-celebrated life.

I crush the old duct tape into a fist and jot a note to myself to buy more. There's a dog-eared, mug-rimmed piece of paper on the kitchen countertop: my shopping list. Now it's both sides of a page torn from a sketchbook. I fold and pocket it. Now that I have fixed things, perhaps I ought to replenish.

The dusty shelves of the village shop will not do this time. I drive to Lisduff and park beside the supermarket, in the shade of the trolley depot. I flip down the sun shield to assess my face for public consumption. It must surely be a magnifying mirror; here's every pore and thread vein, every misdirected lash. I snap the mirror back into place and promise myself never to look in it again.

I refuse to take a trolley, even though I require a whole, torn-out sketchbook page's worth of groceries, both sides. Trolleys are for housewives and old women. The supermarket is so cold. I trudge the aisles until I am barely able to lift my basket. I drag it to a self-service checkout despite the fact I am significantly in excess of the ten-item limit. The robotic voice inside the machine grows angry. 'ITEM IN BAGGING AREA!' it scolds me, repeatedly, even when I have everything bagged and am trying to pay.

'But there's nothing there,' I say. I reason with it.

The attendant comes over and swipes her magic barcode.

'Do you want some free copybooks?' she asks.

I'd forgotten it's copybook time of year. The old summer's-end melancholy nips at my heels. There's no school to go back to; no detail of my life will change come the onset of September, yet still, I feel the old trepidation.

'No, thank you,' I say.

On the drive back along Lisduff's main street, I get stuck behind the London bus. I remember the year this route started: I was in my final term of secondary school. My well-behaved friends and I had been granted permission to go downtown during lunch breaks, and so for half an hour every weekday, we loitered between the park benches and the chip shop. Not drinking, not smoking, not even eating chips. And I'd see the bus pass and think how amazing it was that there existed a vehicle which travelled all the way from this middle-of-nowhere in the Irish countryside to the very heart of Western civilisation: Victoria Coach Station. I don't know whether, at the time, I realised it had started its route elsewhere and was only passing through Lisduff. Either way, in the torturous final term of school, the sight of the London bus was a great source of comfort. I took it as a sign that in spite of who and where I was, escape to an enormous metropolis overseas remained a possibility.

Works about Sailing Off, I test myself: Antti Laitinen, *Bark Boat*, 2010. The bark collected from the floor of a Finnish forest. The boat not a toy, but life-size. And then the artist climbed into the life-size bark boat, and sailed across the Baltic Sea. A childhood fantasy made true.

Since my twenty-first birthday present, since India, I haven't travelled anywhere at all. Every summer holiday from college, I worked in a poky off-licence on the main street of Lisduff, to save the money I needed for the college year to come, the art projects I had yet to realise, because I have always preferred the feeling of having a head start to the feeling of leisure.

Sometimes I'd consider putting money aside for a trip,

but then I'd glance at the chest X-ray on my bedroom wall and remember the swallows and their pock, the sound of enormous cymbals.

The off-licence job had slightly more credibility than being a shelf-stacker in the supermarket or a pan-scrubber in the chip shop, and it suited me nicely because it was evening work; my summer days remained free to read and make and draw.

The shop was rarely busy. The evening regulars were a handful of local alcoholics and Slavic labourers from the town's construction sites. They'd buy six-packs of Czech lager and pool their crumpled notes for the pricey Russian vodka my manager imported specially. The impoverished alcoholics would select plastic bottles of cider from the fridge, throw a pocketful of fluffy coins onto the counter. The better-off ones would ask for a naggin of something stronger from the high shelves behind me. A new one every night, as if, every night, they promised that naggin would be their last.

On a late drive back from work one night, on the long, quiet road between town and home, a car sped up behind my car and started to flash its headlamps. It was unmarked save for a portable squad light stuck to its tin roof above the driver's seat, like a jaunty cap. The road channelled a gap between two expanses of pine forest. The trees were tall and densely spaced, rising up slopes either side. No houses for a few miles in any direction. I couldn't see the shoulders and heads of the person or people in the car behind me. A cold clot of doubt rose in my chest. Don't stop, I thought, speed up. But my '89 Fiesta didn't have the poke to go faster than other cars even if I slammed my foot right to the floor. The year the Wall came down, I thought, and kept a steady pace.

Works about Slow Cars and the Wall, I test myself: Wolf Vostell, *Berlin Fever*, 1973. A motorised performance piece. Cars in groups of ten driving as slowly as cars can drive along the Wall's route for half an hour. A protest? The calmest protest.

I don't know whether or not I remember the night the Wall came down. I've seen it on television so many times over the years, it's impossible to know if any of the television memories are from 9 November. I was four years old; I wouldn't have understood anyway. I vaguely remember a stunned silence, my mum and dad and sister crowding around the black-and-white set, but this might have been a different occasion altogether; it might have been the episode of *Coronation Street* in which Brian Tilsley got stabbed, or the episode of *Glenroe* in which Miley and Fidelma tumbled in the hay. I can't remember.

After a while, the unmarked car ceased its flashing and doused every light at once. It would have vanished altogether if it wasn't for the short reach of my tail-lamps. But every now and again it would drop further back into the dark and I only knew it was still there from the glister of moonlight on metal.

By that stage I was about to reach a crossroads where there are two pubs and a petrol station, houses and street lamps. Just before I got there, the unmarked car switched its lights back on, performed a precarious U-turn in the narrow road, and raced away in the opposite direction.

My parents were in bed by the time I got home. The next morning, I didn't mention the ghost car; I still hadn't decided whether or not it was remarkable. Then, roughly two weeks later, I received a text message: a garda alert forwarded by my sister. In abbreviations, it described how a barmaid driving home from work alone and late at night had been pulled over by an unmarked car bearing a portable squad light, skull-dragged into the road by two men and attacked, brutally. And I felt a surprising equanimity at hearing this; I felt strangely as if I'd passed a test and was thus inoculated from such forms of harm from then on.

In the end I told only Jane about the car that followed me, and for a couple of years afterwards, we collected similar stories: of the cyclist who narrowly escaped having her throat slit by a length of fishing line pulled taut across the width of a street, of the driver whose credit cards were robbed after he had been forced to brake for an empty pram shoved into the road in front of him.

'Remember the golden rule?' Jane would say. 'Always hit the baby.'

The sun is low; the moon out early. As my Fiesta chugs up turbine hill, it holds position in my windscreen. An air-freshener without a string. On either side, there's a pleasing phosphorescent tinge to the valley, the view. It's windless, as if the weather has switched off the turbine and switched on a light beneath the rind of the landscape which makes all the vistas seem cleared, sharpened. Why is it that even inhabited places appear still from far away? As if distance is somehow capable of stalling everything. From turbine hill, the view of mountains comes and goes. And I have always admired this about the view: its unreliability.

When I was a child, August was always the ruined part of my holidays. I knew it by the stack of free copybooks at the end of each supermarket checkout, by the shoe shop's window full of patent leather, by the newsagent's cornucopia of trigonometry sets and novelty rulers. They'd fill me with a feeling somewhere between real-sick and the sick I faked to convince the teacher to phone my mum, to ask her to come and bring me home, so it could be the two of us again, for just a while.

There was only one place in Lisduff where you could buy our specific school uniform. A children's clothes shop attached to an undertaker's and run by the undertaker's wife; as if being fitted for new shirts and skirts wasn't morbid enough already. I couldn't have felt more wretched if I was being measured for a coffin.

There is a strange pool of water beneath the breadboard this morning, as though the kitchen worktop has sprung an upside-down leak. It reminds me that my grandmother's bungalow has a fate independent of mine, outside the limits of my control.

Please don't break, I whisper. Standing in the middle of the kitchen, addressing no appliance in particular. The tap drips, the fridge shivers. Now all is silent again.

A project for this morning: I strip the sheets, pillows and duvet from the single bed in the road-facing spare room. Yank off the mattress, haul the naked frame towards the door, flip it onto its side but the front end hits the hall wall and the rear end hits the wardrobe before it's even halfway out. I push it back into place and haul the mattress into my grandmother's bedroom instead. Now I position it where her bed was, on the patch where the dog used to lie. I dress it in its clothes again.

This bungalow has always seemed to me to have an awful lot of bedrooms for a single storey. Since I came to stay I've slept in all of them. This is partly so that I'll never need to wash any sheets, but also because I haven't been able to choose, until this morning.

Works about Rooms, I test myself: Gregor Schneider, *Dead House u r*. Since 1985, the German artist has been subtly contravening the infrastructure of his three-storey house in Rheydt. He has built replica rooms inside rooms, blocked entrances, bored hollows, manipulated lighting, replastered walls, over and over, so that certain spaces progressively shrink. Schneider's house has become so renowned that gallerists arrange for entire rooms to be transported to galleries across the world. Taken down, brick by brick. Built back up again, elsewhere.

*

I feel a little new now; I go out and travel a comprehensive circuit of the garden. Skirting the hedges, hopping the shrubs, reaching out to the dead flower-heads, crumbling them between my thumb and forefinger. Past the green-house, the compost heap, the plum trees. My wilderness is disappearing into ordinary grass again. I don't see a single rabbit; black, brown or Snowball.

My circuit returns me to the bench, the bike shed, the basin in which the mouse drowned herself and I drowned the sparrow. I smell my fingers. They are vile, worse than earwax, and it takes me a moment to remember why. The flowers, of course. This bitter smell is pollen vomit. And I realise what I've just done is a kindness, a scattering of seeds. Dissemination, germination.

There's a splotch of light on the wall of my grandmother's bedroom. This isn't unusual. I like to sleep, or not sleep, with the real and changing light, like a bird. And so the curtains are always open, my walls vulnerable to reflections. What is strange about this particular splotch is that it forms such an even shape, a tidy oval. What is strange is that I cannot figure out exactly where it's coming from; what it's being cast by.

There are no street lamps. This window doesn't face the dark stalk and shining eyeholes of the turbine, but the valley instead. And this bungalow stands alone on its hill, too high up and far away from other houses to be impinged upon by their artificial light. It might be the moon, but the moon doesn't make shapes; it makes whole rooms glow ethereal white, and even if it did, it wouldn't be an oval, only either crescent or round. And besides, it isn't a clear night, it's bumper-to-bumper night clouds.

My unfathomable light isn't coming from the sky. It can't possibly be.

Today, I leave my bike behind and walk. I crave firmament beneath me. A steadier pace. A lower, slower view.

My eyes prickle from the early cold, crying without my consent. Beneath an almighty horse chestnut at the roadside, a fresh fall of conkers. Their shells are rich red-brown, covered with fingerprint-fine swirls. Most have been popped by passing wheels and lie spewing their milky innards, a miniature battlefield of detonated tree bombs. I feel like I should photograph them.

I can't believe how many blackberries there are on the bushes and what a waste this surely represents. An old lady couldn't possibly pick all of these for jams and pies; a bird couldn't possibly eat them. I suppose they drop and rot and the seeds go back into the mud, that nature needs them for next year. In order that, next year, they can be too many all over again, to drop and rot and reseed for the year after.

Back in the kitchen, I see there's a leaf stuck to my sneaker. Small, yellow, sycamore, like the one which obsessed Littlefoot in *The Land Before Time*. The leaf of the last growing tree which kept the herbivorous dinosaurs alive. Perfectly centred on my toe, as if it was the only visible part of an invisible pattern.

Works about Lower, Slower Views, I test myself: Richard Long, *A Line Made by Walking*, 1967. A short, straight track worn by footsteps back and forth through an expanse of grass. Long doesn't like to interfere with the landscapes through which he walks, but sometimes he builds sculptures from materials supplied by chance. Then he leaves them behind to fall apart. He specialises in barely-there art. Pieces which take up as little space in the world as possible. And which do as little damage.

Now when I wake up, at least once every night, I check for my unfathomable light. My eyes move irresistibly to the place where it sits on the wall, level with the bookshelves, just below the hook from which a picture frame has been removed. I try to unfathom it.

Does the light go away when I draw the curtains? I'm not sure that I am brave enough to try.

Mum comes on Sunday with a boot-load of beige things.

'Annika phoned,' she says, 'there are some viewings coming up.'

I'd forgotten all about the FOR SALE sign in the rose bed. Now my mother rattles through my grandmother's rooms. She doesn't comment on the empty bed frame in one and the dressed mattress in another; she doesn't ask me why, nor tell me to put it back the way it was. The only comment she passes is that it smells damp.

I've noticed this too. The longer I'm here, the stronger the stench of abandonment grows. I am supposed to be keeping this bungalow alive; instead things break, things fall away, dampness sets in.

'Do you want me to put the heat on?' I say. 'Light scented candles, bake bread, brew coffee?'

'Whatever suits,' Mum says. We both know only the coffee suits, that I brew it anyway, that now I can use the damp smell and the viewings as an excuse to drink more coffee.

She takes the boxes away. I help her carry them to the car.

I shuffle from room to room, encountering lilies, lamp-shades, cushion covers. And everything clean, and the alien smell of cleanness.

I find that my mother has hoovered up the fallen flies from the sun room.

But nobody comes to view my grandmother's bungalow until the old lilies and new flies have all died. As I chuck the whole lot in my grandmother's bin, I'm confronted by what an awful lot of sardines I've eaten this summer. I'm not so fond of the taste; I eat them because I want to believe that consuming the skin and bones of a smaller creature must surely be a fast track to nourishing my own skin and bones.

This makes me remember my fingernails. I am at the sun room table absently clipping them with a penknife scissors when I hear the gate-screech and tyre-crunch of gravel. A first car, a second.

I slip out and down the garden. I can't hide inside; what if they want to open every wardrobe, check under every bed? But perhaps they'll also want to root through every shrub, circumnavigate every tree. So I keep going, summit the compost heap, sink onto my haunches at the edge of the cattle field, in the gap between my grandmother's hedge and the farmer's electric fence. Only now I notice I'm still holding the penknife. And so I crouch in the dirt grasping a tiny weapon.

The calves are way off on the other side of the field. Only one appears to have spotted me. He raises his head and stares. Above the tall trees in the distance, a crow, a crow, a crow. My mother says that all the birds and fish amass at this time of year. They remember they need each other and team up again, to leave. As soon as I think of this, the erratic bird-scarer sounds and the sky stuffs up, a frantically pixelating blackness.

Works about Blackness, I test myself: Kasimir Malevich, *Black Square*. Only there isn't just the one Black Square; the artist painted four between 1915 and the 1930s. And not one of them is properly, purely black any more. Now each is covered with craquelure: a zillion fine splinters in the old, spoiled paint. There is an original canvas, but when the conservation experts X-rayed it, a composition of brightly coloured shapes were revealed beneath the black.

How strange to think it possible that this pre-eminent symbol of nihilism can be scraped back to pattern and hue.

I'm too far from the house to hear voices. Maybe if it wasn't for the turbine, the swishing leaves, the cawing of the swarming crows. I wish I'd thought to grab my book before I fled. Instead I watch the calf who watches me; I watch the sky. I see how some birds fly so easily, glide and swoop, while others stutter, stagger. I see that there are different styles of flying, and all different characters of crow.

I remember, one morning when I was a teenager, my mother in her coat and boots, coming in from an early walk.

'All the different leaves make different noises in the wind!' she said as soon as she saw me. 'According to their size and shape and density. Have you ever noticed that?'

Back then, I hadn't, nor did I care. But in the years since, I've grown to appreciate my mother's remarkably perspicacious mind, and how this kind of remarkable perspicacity is impossible to learn. I've grown to believe that it's my mother who is the artist, and not me.

'You have to stand still and listen carefully,' she said, '. . . but once you hear it for the first time, it's easy to keep hearing. It's really quite wonderful . . .'

After a while, I raise my eyes above the parapet of the compost heap to spy through the branches and rotting fruit of the plum trees. I see no sign of life at first. I am about to give up and go back to the bungalow when they begin to appear in the sun room. Annika, I presume, is the one who comes first, clutching a clipboard. The people who follow – the people interested in buying my grandmother's bungalow – are a couple about my age, probably newly-weds. I watch them surveying, judging. The woman swings her ponytail as she nods; the man leans a hand on the back of my chair, stiffly. How like creatures-from-another-planet they are. Their easy-mindedness, their sense of priority. I wonder have they noticed my fingernail clippings scattered across the tabletop, the slivers of grime beneath.

Annika slides the door and they begin stepping out onto the lawn. I duck, turn my back. Now the calf who was

staring is ambling up the field towards me, the others following uncertainly behind.

I hear the lilt of human voices coming closer, but not so
close as to distinguish words. The viewers don't linger in
my grandmother's garden. They mustn't even venture as far
as the dog grave, perhaps having already made up their
minds.

By the time I hear the door-slam and tyre-crunch and
gate-screech again, only in reverse, the calves have me
pinned against the hedge. I can't understand why they
aren't being shocked back by the fence. Instead they stretch
their ringworm-riddled snouts to nuzzle me and I shimmy
and clamber myself to freedom.

My mother brings new health foods and replenishes the
lilies, tidies up where my tidying up has fallen short.

'Any offers?' I ask.

She shakes her head and we chant off the reasons why
my grandmother's bungalow will not sell. She is sitting on
the living room sofa and I am sitting on the hearthrug. She
has lit the fire I never bother lighting, to placate the damp.
Its profuse and uncomplicated warmth placates me too. I
watch its grate-sized theatre. Lights up, lights down. Dancing, collapsing. Now I watch my mother as she speaks and
remember when I was a child, how she used to tuck me
into bed at night – and if for some reason she didn't – the
bedclothes would not feel the same. They would feel
somehow less tucked, less secure, and I would not be able
to go to sleep. And then when I was a teenager, every morning before school, how I stood at the breakfast table and

filled a bowl with Raisin Bran, drowned the flakes in milk, carried my breakfast bowl upstairs to my bedroom. Then I tipped the cereal into a plastic bag hidden underneath my bed and poured the milk out my skylight and into the roof gutter. I'd accumulate Raisin Bran until my parents went to the cinema at the weekend, my sister to the pub, then I'd cart the bag downstairs and burn it in the fireplace.

How many times did I lie? I didn't care. I lied and lied.

Now, by the fire, I watch her speaking and remember, at last, to ask my mother what she does on all the summer days she isn't working.

And after she has left, I cook a gigantic dinner with all the things I like which she has brought me, and swallow every speck, and lick the plate. Now I eat one of the wheat-free, sugar-free, dairy-free biscuits she has baked, and another. I eat the dried blueberries, the cashew nuts, even the chocolate. I eat until I can't eat any more, as an apology to my mother.

A lightning storm. In the morning, when lightning, when storms, shouldn't be. I am out and walking. I miss the first flash and only know it happened when I hear the thunder clapping. I'm glad to be walking and not on my bicycle because it is metal, but then I remember the wheels and wonder if I wouldn't be better off mounted on rubber strips after all, whether the battered soles of my sneakers will be enough to save me.

A colossal flash, away over the fields, through the curtains of rain. My instinct is to take shelter under a clump of trees, even though, of course, I know this is idiotic, that what I'm actually supposed to do is lie flat in a wide open space. I stop at the nearest gate and check for cows. I climb the steel rungs as swiftly as possible and squelch across the spontaneously waterlogged grass, into the middle of the field. I check again, this time for cowpats. Clear.

I lie down and think about how this whole long, strange summer ought to end in a substantial event. But, probably, won't. For the first time, I acknowledge the possibility that nothing will die, or change, or even happen.

Works about Lightning, I test myself: Walter De Maria, *The Lightning Field*. An expansive plateau, Catron County, New Mexico. Standing seven thousand two hundred feet above sea level, there are four hundred stainless-steel poles with pointed tips set into the earth at varying heights, designed to survive the severest storm-force winds. They were erected in 1977, but they're still up and out there, still catching bolts.

I wonder what it would feel like to go on a pilgrimage; to try and catch a thunderstorm, to witness a pointed pole struck.

I make another trip to the supermarket, and this time, I don't feel the cold.

Standing in front of the bakery counter, I am studying a triangular bread-roll with sesame and sunflower seeds on top, grains of millet like bright pollen specks. Yes, these are the ones I like; the abstract expressionism of bread. I am not wheat-intolerant; I never was. And I like my salt sea, my pepper black and coarse, my honey pale and set, my lentils green and whole – I cannot understand why anyone ever thought that splitting every individual one might make them more marketable.

I am becoming weighed down again, so I decide to road-test a shopping trolley. I climb onto the axle and roll gently down the frozen vegetable aisle, picking up speed at the toiletries, swerving recklessly around the cleaning products. Now I understand: shopping trolleys are roller skates for housewives and old women.

At the fish counter, I find Rudolf Schwarzkogler. A photograph he composed of a man with the head of a goofy, gruesome, buck-toothed fish positioned over his penis. I stand facing the neatly trimmed fillets. Smoked kippers, seafood sausages, salmon darnes. And I think about a dead German's penis, and I feel a little bit like myself again.

I look up the Schwarzkogler photograph and an *Encyclopedia of Ocean Animals* so I can try to match fish faces. Eventually I decide it is an Atlantic seawolf. They have six fish-fangs and antifreeze flows through their fish-blood. In spite of being considerably large, the Atlantic seawolf is almost exactly identical in appearance to a tiny, pool-dwelling species called a blenny.

New viewers come. An older couple, middle aged. This time, I have no compulsion to jump the compost heap. I answer the door, introduce myself, apologise for the mess. Now I leave every room as they enter, trying, as I scuttle, not to think about how these might be the people who will eventually expel me from turbine hill and pillage all the places where my grandmother is still to be found.

But no, I have to stop this.

Grandchildren have no right to claim ownership of the death of a grandparent. Children share ownership of the death of their parents; husbands and wives own alone the death of their wives and husbands. But my grandmother's death? I am not allowed it.

If I can cook and shop again, if I can drive a trolley, then why wouldn't I also be able to use the washing machine?

I examine it. I find the buttons and dials are perfectly self-explanatory. I don't have any powder or tablets but I'm sure washing-up liquid will suffice. The machine does its thing for half an hour, runs through its full vocabulary of annoying noises. The clothes come out smelling like a wetter version of how they smelled when they went in. A sock has mysteriously vanished, leaving the sock's mate alone.

I ball up my lonesome sock, stick it back in my drawer of slightly bigger balls of sock.

And there it lies in wait, for me to lose a leg.

A cat which screams in the night. A humanlike bawling. Or at least, I hope it's a cat.

In a science laboratory, on the radio, somewhere in America, they are torturing fruit flies to study insomnia.

The common fruit fly, apparently, has the same kind of sleep pattern as a human, and so suffers similar symptoms when deprived of sleep. The producer intercuts the item with the sound of all the sleepless fruit flies. Batting against the walls of their bell jar, zizzing in despair.

I wake in the night to the scream of the human cat; I remain awake, like a fruit fly. By the light of the screen of my phone, I find my glass of water. The phone light, as well as the unfathomable one, catch in the water in my glass, hold there as if floating. Now I drink the lights, and lie back down again. It takes a moment before my screen returns to blackness, but the one on the wall doesn't.

If anything, I think, it is intensifying.

10

BADGER

I haven't opened the door of my grandmother's shed since the day I claimed her bicycle. I imagine other items of clutter have subsided into the bicycle-shaped space it left; I don't suppose it would open again even if I did try. Instead I keep it in the passage which runs between the shed wall and the garden hedge. I lean it against the bricks beneath the roof's overhang, sheltered. This is my small act of benevolence towards her bicycle.

Although I never see spiders, every morning the hedge is decked with webs. When I walk down the passage, I feel their silk stretch and snap against my face, and I know I am the first to pass this way.

I've never seen the mist lie as low as it does this morning. It has beheaded the bungalow, pruned the trees to shrubs, felled the turbine to a stump. If it was winter mist, it would be grey, but because it's summer mist, it's electric white. And from every direction, a cacophony of rustling; the sound of leaves and stalks and blades and petals sighing beneath the moisture's slow-building pressure. In the passage between the shed wall and the hedge, for the first time I see the threads I've only ever felt before. Each beaded by glinting alabaster, necklaces delicately strung.

At the bottom of the hill, I push down my feet to halt my freewheel. Heels skid against the chippings, vision blurred by the moisture on my eyelashes. And on my bare arms, a new alabaster bead clinging to each fine hair. There's no hint of breeze to propel the droplets. The mist is inert; I am the only detail which moves. Thrusting myself onwards through the decollated, albino world. Allowing it to bind me in necklaces, delicately, delicately.

Works about Whiteness, I test myself: Wolfgang Laib's 'milk-stones'. Each one a rectangle of marble with a shallow depression sanded into its surface and refilled with milk, so as to appear solid again. White and whole.

A brown moth is scurrying across the armchair cushion, an appendage almost as big as himself stuck to his rear end. He is dragging it, bumpty bump, across the uneven landscape of embroidered cotton, an image of a golden Labrador and a marmalade cat sitting up straight on a patio amongst flowerpots. They sit together so tranquilly, the fur of their shoulders brushing. They appear in cotton and thread as compatriots, even though everybody knows that cats and dogs fight like cats and dogs. And so, this is a visionary cushion, prophesying a future in which it is possible to cast off historic differences and coexist, harmoniously.

I pluck away the moth's moth-sized appendage. I see it is a vessel – a hollow cocoon – and I recognise it from a cluster stuck to the roof of the corridor beside the hot press. There's also a single one inside my red sneaker, another clinging to the kitchen tea towel, another again lodged into the fibres of my grandmother's bedroom carpet.

In the corridor I use a sweeping brush to knock a few cocoons down into my open palm. I select the largest and squeeze. It makes a quiet cracking sound and the crushed head of a grub erupts, followed by a blob of snot-coloured goo. I drop it and dust my hands off and examine the wall-hanging where the moths have chosen to pupate. Monochrome brown with a pattern of horizontal stripes, depicting nothing. The wool must be real because I can see the holes where the moths have chewed it. Some of the stripes have been eaten away entirely, leaving the weaver's guide-threads exposed, strained, textile tendons.

Works about Whiteness, again: Ian Burn, *Xerox Book*, 1968. The artist photocopied a blank sheet of paper, then he photocopied the photocopy, then he photocopied that photo-copy, and so on. He kept going for a hundred copies and bound the hundred pages into a book; the last page a hun-dred times less white than the first.

*

Today, on the phone, my mother tells me about some special spray I can buy to exterminate the moths. She tells me about how, once I've bought the right special spray, I will need to apply it in a well-ventilated area, then repeat the application every two hours for twelve hours.

My mother and I both know I will not do this.

'If the hanging is still here,' I say, 'then nobody wanted it anyway.'

This house is a depository for things whose fate is yet to be decided.

In the corridor, I stare at the hanging's desecrated stripes. I lift it down from its hook and carry it into the garden and peg it to the washing line. Perhaps I should beat it, like a rug, thrash the moths away. I fetch the kitchen broom, raise it up. But how can I hurt the hanging even more, after it has already suffered so much? It looks drastically worse out here in the brightness, sun bleeding through its abrasions. I lower my broom and go back inside. I sweep the pupae down from the corridor wall into the pan, and flick them away into the grass.

Stamp, stamp, stamp.

But they are too small and the soles of my sneakers are too creviced, and it soon rains. The moths flee back inside again. Finding their former pasture has mysteriously disappeared, they spread out around the bungalow, tasting new wools.

Works about Whiteness, there are so many. An early piece by Tom Friedman which came about while the artist was a student in the University of Illinois. The piece was Friedman's

studio. At a loss to think of anything to present for an obligatory project, he removed all the items from his work space,
boarded up the windows and painted everywhere brilliant
white. The walls, the ceiling, the cupboards, the floor, the
boards that boarded the windows. It's such a perfect work;
the one which every former art student is still wishing they'd
thought of. It captures, so concisely, the despair of trying to
think something which has never been thought before – to
make something which has never been made before – and
repeatedly drawing a blank.

Friedman was the one who realised: all he had to do was
make the blank his artwork.

On my first day of art school, after the mandatory orienta-
tions were over and done with, I fell in with a crowd of my
classmates and all together we trooped to the park and
lounged on a patch of grass by a pond in the last rays of
September sunshine passing between us an enormous bong
which appeared as if from nowhere. I'd only once smoked
hash before; at a rock festival in the UK with my sister and
her then-boyfriend. Because I am bad at inhaling, I only
managed to become very partially stoned. I lay in the grass
outside our dome tent and looked down across the sloping
field which had been transformed into a campsite at all the
other dome tents in every garish colour, and I remember
remembering the pool of featherweight plastic balls at the
fun park where we had been brought on trips as children
and how this made me want to push off down the slide and
thrust myself feet first into the ball pool which was not a
ball pool, of course, but a campsite. By the pond in the park

on my first day of college, scarcely nineteen, I inhaled as much smoke as I possibly could and still felt exhilarated as opposed to stoned; buzzed up by the knowledge that none of my family knew where I was, who I was with nor when I'd be home again. I didn't even know exactly who I was with or when I'd be home again or where home really was any more.

Every day is going to be like this, I thought, and then corrected myself.

Every day is going to feel like this.

Works about Comradeship, I test myself: Roman Ondák, *Good Feelings in Good Times*, 2003. Outside the Kölnischer Kunstverein in Cologne, the artist organised a queue. At the front stood people who understood that the queue was a sham, who were in on the sham queue. But soon, they were joined by other people, by a small crowd willing to queue without knowing what they were queueing for, who trusted absolutely in the uncontextualised conviction of total strangers, or perhaps, who simply craved the solidarity of temporarily standing in close proximity to other humans.

I never returned to the park with those classmates again. Within a couple of weeks we weren't particularly friendly any more. Sometimes, on a Sunday, I visited the pond alone with a plastic bag of stale bread. I'd sit at the same spot on the grass where I'd sat that day with the others and throw the stiff, torn slices clean over the tall necks of the swans to the herring gulls bobbing in the deeper water beyond, loitering for leftovers.

I felt sorry for the scraggy seabirds; everybody always wanted to feed the swans.

Today, I hear an item on the radio about feeding bread to birds; a warning not to do so because it swells inside their digestive systems, bungs up their bellies with damp dough. The bird nutritionist suggests the outer leaves of cabbages and broccoli stalks instead, shredded and diced.

I picture myself beside the duck pond. Squatting on a patch of shitty lawn by an expanse of murky water. Insidiously, obliviously, hurting the birds I believed I was helping.

A nature documentary about our longest, fattest river, and all the paddling, scuttling, fluttering creatures whose lives are determined by its ebb and flow. They are burrowing in its mudbanks and building caskets out of shale. They are wading in its still pools with their harpoon beaks poised for attack.

The presenter is a man with a musical voice. He speaks to the camera as if he is singing to the animals. He is camping at the edge of a fallow field in the floodplain. It's dark but for the light cast by his fire. 'Can you hear the corncrake?' he whispers.

There's a gentle whirr of crickets, but over the whirr the bird call is clear. It comes in twos and has a buzzing quality; the sound of the arrival of a text message, a second in quick succession.

The presenter explains how the corncrake we can hear is a male who has flown all the way from Africa, looking for a mate. He stays up very late, listening. 'I guarantee that when I get up in the morning,' he says as he zippers his tent for the night, 'the corncrake will still be calling.' They are almost extinct, he explains. Because of the intensity of modern farming practices. Because at the same time of year the female lays her eggs, the farmer cuts his hay and the nests are destroyed. The male is calling, the presenter says, because he can't see through the long grass; because he doesn't know that there aren't any females left to hear.

When I was in college, I never thought of myself as being friendless. I got along fine with my classmates, chattering away with whoever happened to drop in and out of the communal sculpture studio where I spent the entire day, a full twelve hours from nine to nine. But I always arrived and left on my own; I never went out to parties and pubs and clubs at the weekends.

My bedroom in the rented house I shared for most of these years overlooked a fire station. From my window I could see across the wall and into the yard behind the building where the fire engines parked when not in use, which seemed to be practically all of the time. I don't remember a single fire, though in three years there must have been at least one. Instead I remember a long, low net stretched across the open expanse of concrete, and how, at all hours of the day and night, the firemen would play tennis.

I never went downstairs to join my housemates around the television. I cooked dinner later than everyone else and carried the plate up to my bedroom. I knew they must have thought me aloof, or a little bit eccentric, or maybe even unkind, but I didn't care. Once the kitchen door swung shut behind me, I was alone, and so everything was okay.

In my room, night in night out, I watched the firemen play tennis beneath floodlights.

After college, I started working in the gallery and found myself surrounded by a whole new set of people who had not yet grown accustomed to my antisocial tendencies, who had not yet learned to expect me to say no, and stopped asking. I was invited to go drinking and dancing again, and so, I tried.

Works about Discomfort, I test myself: Tehching Hsieh, *One Year Performance*, 1980–81. From 7 p.m. on 11 April 1980 to 6 p.m. on 11 April 1981, Hsieh punched a time clock on the hour, every hour. At the end of the performance, Hsieh had 366 clock-cards, plus one photograph for every punch, and had not slept for more than sixty minutes straight in an entire year.

I think I know what discomfort is? I don't.

The last time I went out at night in the city was almost a year ago. It began with anxiety, then I was pleasantly pissed for a couple of hours, and finally, around the point at which people started taking to the dance floor, I sobered and saddened and the old chant returned: *I want to go home.*

I was talking to an up-and-coming artist, a brilliant and sharp man I knew vaguely from exhibition openings. He was chattering away about the Viennese Actionists, telling me how he believed there was real depth and empathy in their barbaric work. It should have been a fascinating subject, but was, instead, curiously boring.

This is something I was beginning to notice about every brilliant and sharp person I'd met while working in the gallery: there always came a point in the conversation at which something about them dulled and blunted, at which they became no more or less fascinating, really, than Jess or Jink or Jane or Dad; than my grandmother had been, and my mother is. It was during this particular conversation that I started to understand that everybody's pursuits are essentially useless, and that what I was trying to do with my life was probably perfectly useless too.

There's a dead cat in the ditch this morning, clean but undoubtedly dead. Couched by brambles as if blown up and back a couple of feet by the bumper. I wonder is it the same one who bawls?

I read in the weekend newspaper that swallows and swifts and sand martins all fly at different levels of the sky. They eat the same insects, catch them by the same means, but they never have to compete for food because they have divvied up the atmosphere, agreed without need of negotiation, born knowing this ineffable rule. The swallows fly lowest, the swifts highest, the sand martins in-between. Nature's air traffic control.

I had forgotten about the missing aeroplane, the inadequacy of human air traffic control. But this weekend, in the newspaper, it says that a section of wing has washed up on an island in the Indian Ocean, that the section appears to be from the same model of aeroplane as the missing one.

They've found it, I think. How disappointing.

This morning, when I go to fetch my bicycle, in the passage-way formed by the shed wall and the hedge, I notice that the night webs have been broken. First I don't feel them against my face; now I see the loose strands waving in the impercep-tible breeze. I stand and stare. Did the spiders forget to repair the ones I broke yesterday? But they never forget. Or has someone passed through here before me this morning?

I've been preoccupied with the moths. Forgetting to worry about the noises I hear in the night – the ones I tell myself are pipes creaking, hunting cats, branches tapping window-panes, calves in the field next door – but, maybe, aren't.

I don't take out my bicycle. I go back inside to my grand-mother's bedroom and lie down on the bottomless carpet with my camera still in one hand. I switch it on and scroll through the photos I haven't downloaded yet. Fox, frog, hare, hedgehog, all of the killed creatures. Toppling from the sky to land at my feet.

Where are they now? If they fall in the road, the traffic breaks them down, and if they fall in the ditch, the elements; and, in both cases, their fellow creatures. The carrion crows and rats, even when it is a carrion crow or a rat. After I find them for the first time, I never notice them again.

How magnanimous of my killed creatures, to simply disappear.

*

On the day my grandmother died, the undertakers took her away almost immediately. As swiftly and efficiently as the County Council men cleared the fallen tree. Flesh and wood were all gone by the time I'd finished work and driven back from Dublin. Only flesh came back again, to be laid out on the bed in her Sunday best. In the corridor, my mother asked me if I wanted to go in.

This bungalow, which has become so familiar to me as an empty place, was, on that day, crowded with people. Family, as well as neighbours she'd thought hadn't liked her, and friends she didn't know she had.

'No!' I said. 'I mean, I'd rather not. If that's okay?'

And my mother, who always understands and, even when she doesn't, forgives me and pretends to, said of course it was okay and could I please slice and plate up some of the fruitcakes instead?

Now I see the timber-screw-box atop her chest of drawers where I placed it. I pick it up. The grain of the lid traces a pattern of concentric circles, and there's a tiny triangle at the heart of the smallest circle, an eye. I gaze into the eye for a while. I find the box is small enough to close my whole fist around.

No one asked, seventeen years earlier, on the day of our grandfather's removal, whether Jane or I wanted to go up to the coffin and see him laid out. I suppose it had been agreed that we were too young, too easily perturbed. Instead I stood outside the funeral home holding my father's hand. The queue of passing people, the sizzle of their whispers, the reassuring smell of his cigarette smoke.

I didn't really know my grandfather; I wasn't really upset. For the six years our lives overlapped – the first of mine and final of his – I didn't see him very often, and in the years since, I've managed to mislay all but a single memory: this one from the day of his removal, when I slipped my hand free of my father's and peeped through the doorway of the visitation room. I recognised my mother's feet resting between the timber legs of a chair in a row of chairs, of feet. But my mother did not see me; every time a person stepped away, a new person took their place in front of her, and then I saw the coffin. A long, dark, wood box with its satin-lined lid lifted. The polished toes of my grandfather's funeral shoes poking out one end, and the pale tip of his aquiline nose poking out the other.

My grandfather was a basking shark out at sea. With only his dorsal and tail fins exposed, the rest sequestered beneath the black surface. The entire central stretch of his corpse was obscured, but what I saw was still enough to wipe out every memory I had of it as a living body. And so I was afraid, on the day my grandmother died too, that if I went into her bedroom it would wipe out my memories all over again. It would blanch her essence from the shoehorn, the kneeler, the compost heap, the panda-bear-shaped pencil sharpener.

I could not bear to witness – to remember – my grandmother as a body, but not a being.

Works about Being, again, about Body, again, I test myself: Marina Abramović, *Rhythm 0*, 1974. Performance in a Neapolitan gallery. The artist set out a table, and on the table, a collection of objects. Items like soap and lipstick, bread and honey, a scalpel and a nail gun. Then she invited the audience to use them on her body however they wished, and stood. Motionless, compliant. As she was unclothed, caressed, clouted, cut. What was the artist trying, without speaking, to say? *You can do what you want to my body; my body is not me.*

I open my eyes to my grandmother's bedroom carpet. Something cracked and woke me, as if the bungalow is a forest and someone has just snapped a twig beneath their foot.

It was bright when I lay down here but now outside it's dark; and dark – at this time of year – means late. I can't believe I slept undisturbed for an entire day, but this must be the case; I can't argue with darkness. I consider the last moments at which I was awake – the morning and the only thing that happened in the morning – the thing that sent me here. I remember the webs, and how they were broken.

I lie on the carpet and listen to the creaking pipes and branches tapping, calves rustling, twigs cracking, cats. I listen and listen and cannot be sure what any of the noises are any more.

I start to think it's unusually dark, darker even than it would be in the dead of night. I check for my unfathomable light. It's gone. I had believed it was intensifying. Instead, it's disappeared.

But it can't be. I get up, and move towards the switch by the door. My legs are watery, my head weighted down towards my watery legs, my eyes gunged with sleep. For no reason at all, a second before I reach the switch, I turn around.

And see. The reflection first. A white face in the window. Not mine. And in the corner of my grandmother's bedroom, facing away from the light switch and towards the turbine, across the valley. A grey head. A hunched and bony back.

I am out the front door within seconds. It slams shut, locks me out. I am lucky I left the car keys in the ignition; this small mercy of my carelessness. I don't untie the dog string; I wrench it loose. Its frayed pieces disintegrate, finally, in my hands and fall to the gravel and my tyres gnash over them as I drive away.

As fast as the throttle can carry me, and the car's rusted steel, its dust-steeped upholstery. Through the no man's land of countryside by night, the blacked-out trees and fields and hedges. Only the lighted houses remaining, the lemon blush of their inhabited windows.

Works about Inhabitation, I test myself, for calm and for focus, to find a bolthole for my galloping mind: Rachel Whiteread, *Place (Village)*, 2006–08. Tens of old doll's houses atop gentle, geometric hills against the gallery wall, stacked up from unostentatious boxes. And the houses rigged with miniature electric bulbs, and the gallery blinds drawn, its bigger bulbs doused. How many thousands of times have I ignored a scene like this in real life? Because, sometimes, replicas are more persuasive than what they replicate. Because, all of the time, art is the absolute.

In Lisduff, I park in a concrete yard down an alleyway off the main street, a spot where I'd sometimes leave the car when I used to work in the off-licence. Now I stare at this grey place in the grey light. Why did I come here? I thought I was heading for the famine hospital. If I'd driven there instead, as I should, I'd be in my child-bed now, beneath the roof window and the painted-over stars and the chest X-ray. I'd be safe and warm, in the foothills of sleep. How easy and rational that would have been.

And yet, when I wake up tomorrow morning, the embarrassment would be waiting for me. Crouched beneath the lumpish armchair, poised to throw itself under my wheels. And I would have to put on my clothes and shoes and the forsaken version of myself I helplessly revert to in the presence of my parents, and descend their staircase to face the torrid, sentimental fuss of the night before, the morning-after realisation that I'm too old to run home, that I have failed utterly at adult life, at independence.

Seven years, and I never once successfully used a washing machine.

If I'd driven there instead, all this would have ended as it began.

So I drove here. I stay here. This concrete yard, these concrete walls. A boarded-up window, an abandoned shopping trolley. In the grey moonlight.

I check, and check again, and check afresh, that all the buttons in the car are pushed down. I push them again anyway, just in case it's possible they can go further. I can't check if the boot is locked unless I get out. I know it is, still I cannot stop myself from imagining I hear its click and creak, see its reflection lifting into the rear-view mirror followed by the reflection of the face which lifted it, and the face's feet climbing over the back seat, and the face's hands reaching for my throat.

So I step outside and check the boot. It's locked. Of course it's locked.

I scoot back into the driver's seat, push down the driver's button. It takes less than ten seconds for the voice to return. *Check it again!* the voice hisses at me through the dark. *Check it again! Check it again!*

In the car, I close my eyes and see Jink.

I had been nosey about his life. I had wanted to touch it. But I should have been kind. I should have sat down with the old man and listened. I think about all the lonely people out there, alone. I think about what a prodigious crowd they'd make if only they got together, if only they knew each other.

I realise I am not kind.

Works about Comradeship, I think of another one: Francis Alÿs, *Patriotic Tales*, 1997. A camera set up above a large stone plaza somewhere in Mexico City, an oblique aerial view, a film. The artist walking a perfect circle inside the plaza and a sheep following him, unerringly. With every circuit, a new sheep appears, joins the cavalcade, follows. A new sheep, a new sheep, a new sheep. Until the circle has closed itself.

How many hours does it take to train an animal to do that? Or maybe they don't need to be trained at all, just like the humans don't.

*

I can't force my brain to sleep, but manage to keep my eyes closed until it is light again. The supermarket opens at seven. I don't know why I know this because I've never been in any supermarket earlier than nine. But perhaps we are programmed to know the supermarket opening hours without ever having to consult one another, like the swallows and swifts and sand martins.

My camera and the timber-screw-box are the only things I carried with me from my grandmother's bungalow. This was not something I thought about; they just happened to still be in my hands. Now they are on the passenger seat, looking on. I transfer them to the pockets of my cardigan. By the luck of my carelessness: my bank card is in the glove compartment. Maybe this is a sign; maybe some incomprehensible force is subtly endorsing what I am about to do.

I go first to the cashpoint. I collect no receipt. I roam the aisles with a basket dangling from my forearm like a tiny cable car. I've never seen the place so deserted, a scene from after the Apocalypse. But I must resist this impulse to lose control; I must pace calmly from aisle to aisle and try to picture what I might have brought with me had I not fled; had I known before fleeing where I was going to go.

After I've paid and before I leave, I visit the supermarket toilet, peel the annoying circle of foil from inside the toothpaste cap. Crack open the packet of my new toothbrush and christen it with froth and spit.

I go back to the car but don't get in. I only check for the final time that all the buttons are lowered, the doors locked.

Now I carry my plastic bag of belongings to the bus stop, stand by the red pole, and wait.

A man in the seat next to me. The laces of his sneakers are very loose. He doesn't look out the window or listen to headphones or read the newspaper lying folded in his lap. How curious that he chose to buy that tabloid, to carry it with him, and yet now he can't summon the will to unfold it, to pick a page, to read. He sleeps a little, checks his phone. I can't see what he's looking at, only the thumbprints on his screen, like contours on a map.

Almost everybody on the bus is only staring. Are they thinking about the thing they are staring at? Making sky studies, crowd studies, ditch studies. Are they thinking about something else entirely? Or somehow managing not to think at all?

Maybe everybody on the bus is meditating.

Rain scratches the glass.

A smudged-sky morning, the terminus of summer. Weather to match my feelings, as I always expected it to.

There's a fragrance of deep-fat fryer on the bus as though everybody's just got chips even though we haven't stopped for over an hour. According to my ticket, the ferry sails from Dublin port late this evening, and so there must be more stops to make, for more passengers, for real chips. There's the sound of a baby crying even though I can't see any babies. And out the bus window, here is my dead world come true, my whole dead world in motion. Mud lawns and milk parlours, caliginous fog obscuring a relief which

might or might not rise into a mountain. Abandoned building sites, boarded-up houses in fenced-off estates, the rusted
chutes and silos of a seed-processing factory, the base of a
stolen pump outside a derelict petrol station, and a lorry
stacked with telegraph poles, a portable forest. Another
lorry, this one decked with empty cars, and all the moving
cars, full and half full, and all the driving zombies with their
laptops and toddlers and uncompromising expressions fixed
across steering wheels and through shatterproof glass,
acknowledging only road and speed and time and progress.

On the bus, I am meditating too, against my will. I don't
have a book and I don't have my MP3 player. I try to remember the tracks saved inside it and sing them to myself; I
realise I know all the words to 'Zimbabwe' by Bob Marley
and the Wailers and no other song. I remember that
'Zimbabwe' is my favourite song and I have never admitted
this to anyone. I search the lyrics for something arousing,
but there's only rather a lot of impassioned stuff about
emancipation. And I realise it's the melody which moves
me; my weakness for 'Zimbabwe' has nothing whatsoever
to do with the words.

You can't dance to paintings. This is something Ben said,
during one of our White Cube conversations, back when I
was still wrong about him. He said it even though, at the
time, he was desperately trying to be a painter. He said it
because it was true and not because it was something either
of us wanted to hear.

*

The bus driver plays the radio. On the talking station, they are discussing how new pieces of the missing aeroplane are being found every day. Thrown by the sea to the shore, beaching like pilot whales. The wife of a man who went down with the flight tells the story of how their little boy begged his father not to leave on the morning it crashed, to stay behind and play with him instead. His Lego on the living room rug. Hundreds and hundreds of tiny, indented blocks. While other little boys carry home the beached pieces of the missing aeroplane and stick them to their bedroom walls between the posters of football players and Luke Skywalker.

I lean my head against the window. I bump-bump-bump and try to, but do not, sleep.

The road ahead is lined with strange structures. Some of them are definitely public sculptures, but with others, I'm not so sure. A billboard displaying torn and stapled paper fragments: art? Concrete steps up a grassy verge leading to nowhere: art?

I think: art is everywhere. I think: art is every inexplicable thing.

It was March. It was March and I was so bored to death of being alone in my bedsit. The winter, at last, was beginning to wane. Sometimes there were sunny spells and I'd take my book to the park. In my coat and scarf I'd sit on a wooden bench and drink the cold sun, the wind turning my pages for me.

The park was perfectly square with wrought-iron railings and ornate Victorian street lamps which didn't actually work. There were tall, brick-faced houses on every side. Stone steps rose to the front doors, which were painted brilliant yellow and red and green. I never knew for sure whether the park was meant solely for the residents of those houses. There weren't any signs to indicate it was private and nobody ever asked me to leave, but the time I spent there was always shadowed by doubt, by the wavering suspicion that I was trespassing.

It was the day before I lay down on my carpet and couldn't get up again until I knew my mother was coming.

I bought a hot chocolate from the Italian deli which I passed on the short walk between my bedsit and the park. It came with a paper case of chocolate buttons balanced on the lid. They'd melted into warm, brown goo before I reached my bench. I sat down, licked chocolate from paper, opened my book. Every other person was only passing through. With shoulder bags, briefcases or apartment-sized, hypoallergenic dogs – dogs who believed that nature was that square of lawn, that freedom was the five metres afforded by their extendable leash.

I remember the book I was reading. *Hour of the Star* by Clarice Lispector. I remember because there were so many things in *Hour of the Star* with which I found kinship that I'd brought along a stub of pencil in case I urgently needed to underline. With my hot chocolate, my open book, my pencil stub, the bench was a delicate accommodation of elements, small plates spinning on tall sticks, and so I was especially reluctant to move when an old man sat down heavily beside me.

Moving away is my instinctive reaction. I would never impose myself on a stranger's bench, and if I were to find every single one in the whole square park occupied, I'd sit on the ground rather than share. But on this occasion, I remained as I was. Because of the balance, but also because I felt sorry for the man, who was certainly lonely; why else would he choose the park's only already-occupied bench? And sure enough, within the space of seconds, he asked me what I was reading.

I answered, then closed Clarice, placed her aside. I decided I would stay and sup to the bottom of my chocolate, to talk to him for just a while. I could tell he didn't really care about books, so I steered us towards topics we were likely to have in common. The locality and its 'gentrification' – which he had observed and I had arrived with; the rain. We pointed out signs of spring to one another. The leaves returning to the plane trees, the crocus buds up but yet to open. Was I curious about his life; did I want to touch it? Or was I being, uncharacteristically, kind? I can't remember. We talked about what sort of summer might be in store, what sort of summers had gone before. And as soon as there was nothing left to coax through the sippy-cup lid of my cardboard cup, I gathered my elements, made my excuses, and left.

It wasn't until I was again alone, walking the short distance home, that I realised I had told this strange, large man where I lived, or at least the street name and that it was a bedsit, surely enough to find me, if he wanted to find me. I realised I'd told him that I was single, that I lived alone.

Was I supposed to be afraid? I did not even know whether or not I was supposed to be afraid.

I didn't go directly home. I walked instead to the DVD store and stood paralysed in the Documentaries aisle, combing back through the conversation in my mind for traces of menace, of indecency. Eventually I returned to my bedsit, and sat by the window, and twitched the net curtain like an old woman.

It was what made me feel so suddenly and inexplicably bad; the source from which the huge and crushing sorrow rose. Not the penguin in *Encounters at the End of the World*, the DVD I watched that evening, which struck the bottom of the deposit box with a hollow, rebarbative clonk when I returned it the following day. I have only wanted to believe it was the deranged penguin because this is a better reason for being inconsolable, a so-much-more interesting and complicated and quixotic thing to be disturbed by than the banal reality. Than attack, rape, murder. I have only wanted to believe it was the deranged penguin so I can consequently believe it is possible for me to be driven mad by concern for some creature other than myself.

I pull the bus curtain, and find it is huge, and so, I wrap myself up, cover my shoulders, neck, face. Like a child in a ghost costume at Halloween. Even though there is a NO SMOKING sticker right beside it on the glass, it smells like cigarette smoke, like my dad leaning against the kitchen sink way back when I was still slightly afraid of him. Now I wonder what happened to that man from the bench in the perfectly square park in March. Did he ever seek out the street where I used to live, and hide in the suburban shrubbery, and watch to see which door I would emerge from?

Of course he didn't. Of course he was only as I first thought. Lonely, harmless, bored. He forgot me as surely as I cleared the park gates, as pacifically as I ought to have forgotten him.

The bus driver pulls into a lay-by and we pile out and queue for the toilets, for coffee, for chips.

The sun setting. Rush-hour traffic thundering along the motorway, as if there might be a hurricane or typhoon or rogue wave closing in behind. I linger at the edge of the car park, waiting for the almighty wind or water to appear. And here is a badger curled on the hard shoulder. Of course. I put down my paper bag and cup. I take out my camera and lie in the road.

Black blood bubbles elegantly from its nostrils; it must be only newly dead. Cars pass so fast, their wind blows my eyelashes back to the sockets. It causes the badger's dense, monochrome fur to divide and swirl. It is of such great size and heft that it must have felt, to the driver who hit it, like knocking down a small child.

It is so utterly the end of summer. Back down the motorway in the direction from which I have travelled, there is a small tree standing solo on the horizon, and it waves its branches weakly against the whited-out sky.

The badger is magnificent, and so I lie beside it, cheek against tarmac, the smell of oil and dust and beast. I take picture after picture. A final showdown of concern for a creature other than myself. Until the bus driver sticks his head out the window to shout at me.

I am holding everybody up.

On the night boat, I find a quietish spot in the corner of the bar. I buy a pot of tea and scrunch myself into a seat beside my plastic bag. With my sneakers kicked off, I see my socks are from two different pairs. Though they are both black, the left is more vibrant than the right, its cotton-enriched polyester distinctly thicker. The engine starts to shudder, somewhere deep below the night-boat bar, a gurgling of mechanical guts. There is an enormous TV mounted on the wall, visible even from my quietish corner, though there is no sound; the jukebox drowns it out. The presenters on the 24-hour news channel mouth along, defectively, to classic pop tracks from the eighties.

Out the windows on the opposite side of the bar, open

sea has appeared. Out mine but behind me, Dublin thins to a stripe of lights laid along the shoreline, a queue with no particular destination.

I think: goodbye city-which-broke-me, bungalow-scarred-midlands, car-abandoned-in-alleyway.

Goodbye turbine hill.

At home to the sea. Even though the sea is not my home, and never has been.

Mum. I write inside my phone with only my thumb. *Don't freak out but I'm on a boat. I just can't open my eyes tomorrow morning to that same patch of ceiling I open my eyes to every morning. I promise I'll let you know, every day I'm alive, that I'm alive. I know it's stupid to say please don't worry about me, but please don't worry about me. Please worry about you. Please don't worry at all. Please stop all the worrying and just enjoy the slow stars, the leaf noises.*

When I was small, I became paranoid that my mother would die. That was the defining fixation, the source of every fixation to come. It made me perform all kinds of odd little actions, surreptitiously, over and over. I believed they were in exchange for keeping the person I loved most in the world alive. But I didn't believe, not really. I was just, as with the cat, too frightened to put it to the test.

Why don't I tell her about what happened in the bedroom in the dark? About the webs? Why do I blame the ceiling? The ceilings of my grandmother's bungalow have never really offended me. Even though, now I come to think of it, they are all white. Every carpet is green; every wall is pastel; every ceiling is a blank.

I didn't tell my mother about what happened because I already know it's nonsense, that nothing happened at all. The spiders only forgot to repair the strands I broke the morning before, and there was no Jink. The Jink I thought I saw was my unfathomable light, my unfathomable light was my grandmother, and she showed herself, at last, in order that I could leave.

I press send. How can there possibly be a phone signal out at sea? But it seems to go, so I write another.

Mum, I write. *What was the tree again? The morning Grannie died?*

It's late now, she is asleep. But the second message sends too. Her phone network is sympathetic, and I know my mother will be the same.

In the bar, people are beginning to lower their voices, to roll jumpers into makeshift pillows, to hoist their feet up. The excitement of sailing has worn off. The overpriced meals eaten, the cardboard coffee cups drained to gritty slosh, the pint glasses left standing empty but for a petticoat of froth. The lights go low, the passengers nod off.

The 24-hour news keeps playing, as does the jukebox. The screen shows a toy train on a toy railway track. Puffing toy steam. Rushing, rushing. But the landscape it rushes through is life-sized; the tracks it rushes along stretch for human miles and human miles. I can't figure it out and the TV is too far away for me to read the scrolling text which might explain it.

I give up on sleep, gather my plastic bag, get up from my seat to search for a deck.

*

Out in the air, pressing my cheek to the railings, there is a perfect path of brightness from the precise point where I am standing directly to the moon across the empty water. A moon blue as the sea, the night sky blue as a wet rook. I tilt my head down to the spume, hold my breath and wait for something terrific to surface. A tail fin, a mermaid, a Portuguese man-of-war. I watch so hard for so long, until my vision begins to disseminate, until, from foam and blue and will alone, I might see anything at all – anything I want to see.

I remember the timber-screw-box in my pocket. I lift it out and gift it to the spume. Plop. A blob of paint from the mouth of the tube. Splash. A tiny concentration of colour blown apart, of grey. My grandmother.

Works about the Marvellous, I test myself: Bas Jan Ader, his final artwork.

In 1975, Jan Ader cast off from the harbour at Cape Cod, Massachusetts. His intention was to sail single-handedly across the Atlantic in a yacht smaller than any other ever to have crossed it before, as a work of performance art. After three weeks, radio contact broke off. After ten months, his wrecked boat was spotted drifting approximately one hundred and fifty miles off the south-west coast of Ireland, and hauled to land by a Spanish trawler. The artist's body was never found.

Some of the people close to Jan Ader insisted that it was a tragic accident, that he had always intended to reach Europe, to return home. Others said it was unquestionably suicide.

Bas Jan Ader didn't do happy endings.
The artist's title for this work: *In Search of the Miraculous*.

My phone springs. Even though my mother is surely asleep.
Oh Frankie, she says. *I think it was an oak*.

Back in the bar, I find my seat still empty, and am finally beginning to fall asleep when I see, on the 24-hour news channel, through my half-closed lids, tribesmen. Naked but for painted faces, armed but with their spears lowered. They are walking out of the rainforest. I jump up and my bag thumps to the ground. I hurry closer to the screen, in order to make out the scrolling text. These men are from the last 'uncontacted' tribe, it says. The same tribe photographed trying to attack a low-flying aircraft which crossed the Amazon earlier this year.

I remember.

The tribespeople are sick and hungry, the scrolling text says, slowly dying. In the undergrowth behind them, a path has been channelled by their emergence, a line made by walking.

Out of the rainforest. Ambling in faulty time to, mouthing imperfectly along with 'Blue Monday' by New Order. Waddling, stumbling, waddling.

Casting off the uncontainable vastness, stepping into the known world.

Works about Trees, I test myself, the final test, I promise. Joseph Beuys, *7000 Oaks*. The first planted in Kassel in 1982. The mission to plant seven thousand, each coupled with a basalt standing stone, four foot high. A symbolic beginning, predetermined to continue through time, across continents. And so it did, does. Italy, America, England, Ireland, Norway, Australia. After Beuys had stopped planting them for himself, after he died.

The oaks which grow. The stones which don't.

Art, and sadness, which last forever.

AUTHOR'S NOTE

In these pages, many works of visual art from many different artists and eras have been named and outlined. I want to make clear that these are described as the narrator remembers and perceives them; they are interpreted according to Frankie. I urge readers to seek out, perceive and interpret these artworks for themselves.

LIST OF ARTWORKS

1 ROBIN

Bas Jan Ader, *Fall I, Los Angeles*, 1970.

Bernard Moitessier, 1925–1994.

Yves Klein, *Leap into the Void*, 1960.

Erik Wesselo, *Düffels Möll*, 1997.

On Kawara, the *Today* series, ongoing from the 1960s through
    to 2013.

  the *I Am Still Alive* series, ongoing throughout the 1960s
    and 70s.

Mona Hatoum, *Entrails Carpet*, 1995.

Helen Phillips, *Moon*, 1960.

Guido van der Werve, *Running to Rachmaninoff*, annual performance which began in 2010.

2 RABBIT
Tracey Emin, *My Bed*, 1998.
Felix Gonzalez-Torres, *Untitled*, 1991.
Cai Guo-Qiang, *Project for Extraterrestrials*, series throughout 1990s.

3 RAT
Anya Gallaccio, *preserve 'beauty'*, 1991–2003.
Mona Hatoum, *Recollection*, 1995.
L. S. Lowry, *The Irwell at Salford*, 1947.
Cornelia Parker, *Cold Dark Matter: An Exploded View*, 1991.
Cory Arcangel, *Drei Klavierstücke, op. 11*. 2009.
Bas Jan Ader, *Fall II, Amsterdam*, 1970.
Marco Evaristti, *Helena*, 2000.
Jan Dibbets, *Robin Redbreast's Territory Sculpture*, 1969.
Vincent van Gogh, *Wheatfield with Crows*, 1890.

4 MOUSE
Vito Acconci, *Step Piece*, 1970.
The Leeds 13, *Going Places*, 1998.
René Magritte, *The Treachery of Images*, 1929.
William Anastasi, *Constellation Drawings*, a series from the 1960s.
Allora & Calzadilla, *Half Mast / Full Mast*, 2010.
Gillian Wearing, *10–16*, 1997.
Tehching Hsieh, *One Year Performance,* 1978–79.
Hermann Nitsch, *Orgien Mysterien Theater*, a series of performances and 'actions' beginning 1962.
Sir John Everett Millais, *Ophelia*, 1851–52.

5 R O O K

Stanley Brouwn, *This way brouwn*, 1960–64.

Vito Acconci, *Following Piece*, 1969.

6 F O X

On Kawara, *I Got Up*, 1968–79.

Xu Zhen, *In Just a Blink of an Eye*, 2005–07.

Tim Hawkinson, *Bird*, 1997.

Mary Kelly, *Post-Partum Document*, 1973–79.

Lin Yilin, *Safely Maneuvering across Lin He Road*, 1995.

Peter Friedl, *The Zoo Story*, 2007.

Rudolf Schwarzkogler, 1940–1969.

Atsuko Tanaka, *Electric Dress*, 1956.

Felix Gonzalez-Torres, *"Untitled" (Toronto)*, 1992.

7 F R O G

Ger van Elk, *The Flattening of the Brook's Surface*, 1972.

William Anastasi, *Free Will*, 1968.

Christian Marclay, *The Clock*, 2010.

Jennifer Dalton, *What Does an Artist Look Like? (Every Photograph of an Artist to Appear in The New Yorker, 1999–2001)*, 2002.

Gillian Wearing, *Signs that Say What You Want Them to Say and Not Signs that Say What Someone Else Wants You to Say*, 1992–93.

Wolfgang Laib, *Pollen From Pine*, 1992.

Martin Creed, *Work No. 227: The lights going on and off*, 2000.

Jo Spence and Terry Dennett, *Final Project (What 1991 felt like . . . (most of the time))*, 1991–92.

8 H A R E

Urs Fischer, *You*, 2007.

Henrik Plenge Jakobsen, *Everything Is Wrong*, 1996.

James Lee Byars, *This is a Call from the Ghost of James Lee Byars*, 1969.

Robert Morris, *Untitled (Passageway)*, 1961.

9 HEDGEHOG

Adam Chodzko, *God Look-Alike Contest*, 1992–93.

Giuseppe Penone, *To Unroll One's Skin*, 1970.

Joseph Grigely, b.1956.

Piero Manzoni, *Artist's Breath*, 1960.

Conrad Shawcross, *The Limit of Everything*, 2010.

Antti Laitinen, *Bark Boat*, 2010.

Wolf Vostell, *Berlin Fever*, 1973.

Gregor Schneider, *Dead House u r*, a project beginning 1985.

Richard Long, *A Line Made by Walking*, 1967.

Kasimir Malevich, *Black Square,* a series beginning 1915.

Walter De Maria, *The Lightning Field*, 1977.

Rudolf Schwarzkogler & Ludwig Hoffenreich, *Aktion, No. 42*, 1965.

10 BADGER

Wolfgang Laib, *Milkstones*, a series beginning 1975.

Ian Burn, *Xerox Book*, 1968.

Tom Friedman, his studio in graduate school, 1989.

Roman Ondák, *Good Feelings in Good Times*, 2003.

Tehching Hsieh, *One Year Performance*, 1980–81.

Marina Abramović, *Rhythm 0*, 1974.

Rachel Whiteread, *Place (Village)*, 2006–08.

Francis Alÿs, *Patriotic Tales*, 1997.

Bas Jan Ader, *In Search of the Miraculous*, 1975.

Joseph Beuys, *7000 Oaks*, a project beginning 1982.

ACKNOWLEDGEMENTS

My thanks to Lucy, Jason, Lisa, Sarah, Helen, Jenna and everyone who worked with them on this book. My thanks to John and Virginia Stamler, for their Iowan cabin, and the Lannan foundation, for the continuing adventure. My thanks to friends, both human and animal, and to family, both here and gone.